For my husband, your c~~onstant love and belief in me,~~
made me remember that I can do anything.

For my girls, may your dreams be big and wonderful.

*For my mam, you told me I had to write this eleven
years ago – here it is.*

Dear Lottie

Dear Lottie

Mel Higgins

Introduction

<u>2020</u>

Rain splattered off the great glass windows of the beach house sat on the Cornwall coast. Despite the sound of impact, its resident, an elderly woman, did not hear it. She sat still in the sunroom —although no sun had been witnessed for some time — in her favourite chair, facing the empty one that had not been filled by its owner for nearly two years. Her white hair was tied in a tight bun and her cold hands clutched tightly around an open book; a battered suitcase filled with worn journals sat at her feet. Her eyes were closed, making her look as though she was in a deep sleep, the very last observations she made were the words written on the yellow pages.

My Dear Lottie,

May your life be filled with happiness, love, and no regrets. Do not reach for the clouds, reach for the stars.

Forever yours, H x

Dear Lottie

Mel Higgins

1950s

Dear Lottie

Chapter One

<u>28th July 1952</u>

We are here! I woke up this morning in a big, double, four-poster bed with satin bed sheets smelling of my nana's new perfume — Youth Dew by Estee Lauder — it smells gorgeous, and she let me have a little behind my ears; she has lots of pretty bottles on her dressing table. My nana's bedroom is every girl's dream. Her wardrobe is full of hats, gloves, fur coats, shoes, boots, and dresses in every colour. Her jewellery collection is worth more than my entire street back home, probably. Even at the grand age of sixty she still gets up each morning and carefully applies her make-up to perfection. She is beautiful, my nan. I always stay in her bedroom when I stay even though I have a bedroom of my very own up on the third-floor next door to Cathleen's.

We left Durham yesterday morning, me and Cathleen got an early train from Newcastle to London as it is a long journey and honestly Cathleen is such a bore to spend time with on a long journey.

"Do you want to play I-spy?"

"No, Charlotte, that game is for babies."

Sixteen-year-olds think they are so grown up, I'm ten and even I know I-spy is not a baby game but the ultimate travelling pastime.

"Should we spend some of our money on treats when the trolley comes?"

"No, Charlotte, Da gave us that money for some dinner otherwise we will be starving by the time we get to Nana's."

"Let's see how many things we can spot beginning with the letter T."

"No, I'm reading."

So, I spent the journey looking out the window in my own little world, thinking up stories and watching the towns turn into villages, that turned into fields and meadows. I did not mind too much really, I found it rather peaceful. Cathleen never used to mind I-spy but maybe sixteen-year-olds, that are courting choir boys, do not play those games anymore.

When we finally reached our stop at Kings Cross, Nana Florence and Uncle Albert met us at the platform. Nana Florence held me so tightly in a big hug; she wore a beautiful long pastel blue dress along with a big summer hat that tilted to the right, decorated with white carnations and blue ribbon. Her hands were creeping behind a pair of white laced gloves — she looked like a movie star standing on the platform and my uncle looked like her bodyguard in his expensive looking suit and shiny cufflinks. My Uncle Albert has a new thick moustache above his lip that goes up his nose when he talks. He always dresses smartly; I have never seen him in anything but a suit in all my life.

Uncle Albert ruffled the top of my hair. "Good to see you, kiddo, how was the journey?"

I looked over to Cathleen who was in Nana's arms. "Long and quiet."

He laughed even though what I said was not funny at all, then took my suitcase. "Well, you're here now and my mother has a lot planned for your stay this summer, and William will be with us next week. We have all been looking forward to your visit." He grabbed hold of Cathleen's case as she and Nana approached us. Eagerly we made our exit from the station, I linked my arm through Nana's pulling myself as close as possible.

"Auntie Emily has cleaned your bedrooms ready for you both, you have fresh sheets and I believe she has even put a bouquet of flowers in each of your rooms. She wanted it to be perfect for you girls," Uncle Albert said as he walked ahead with Cathleen by his side.

Cathleen made some comment back, probably telling him how nice that was of Auntie Emily I imagine; I find it hard to believe that Witchy Emily would ever do something sweet for us out of the goodness of her own heart. I looked up at Nana and she smiled at my puzzled face and tapped her nose. I giggled; she need not say anymore — Auntie Emily had done the kind gesture because Nana told her to.

He may not be a real bodyguard, but Uncle Albert was certainly our chauffeur for the day. His black, ever so shiny, Jaguar Mark V stood proudly in the car park, I only know the name of it because my dad thinks it's a snob's car and moaned about it for ages when my uncle got one. I have to admit though, it felt really good getting inside it.

Whenever I come to London, I feel like I've stepped into another world. Gone are the Durham lanes of my street, the mines, and the endless fields between each small town; now

I'm met with big, tall buildings, busy roads, so much noise, not a field in sight, and so many people rushing about. I don't think my mam would like me saying this, but I sometimes feel like I've come from rags to riches.

My Uncle Albert, who believes he is funny, was telling the worst jokes on the way to the house, we couldn't help but laugh because they were that bad! He is quite tall my uncle, his top half larger than his bottom half. He used to play a lot of rugby when he went to school, he and my mam went to a private school not far from Nana's house. I have walked past it many times; it is quite big and beautiful really. My cousin, William, goes to a much bigger school in Kent, a boarding school, he only comes home in the holidays. Could you imagine having to sleep at school?

When we arrived at the house Auntie Emily came to greet us at the door, you could have mistaken her for a twig, she's so skinny and tall; her face hard despite her smile, and as always, she was dressed like she was off to have dinner with the Queen. I've heard my mam complain to Nana before that all my auntie ever does is go shopping with her posh friends and have afternoon tea — oh, speaking of afternoon tea that is where my nana is taking me and Cathleen today, at The Ritz! The Ritz! Honestly, why my mam chose to live in our house in Durham with my dad confuses me — we could have all lived on the top floor here. We are buying new dresses for the occasion as well. We always get new dresses every summer. My mam then puts them away and they become our dresses for Church, Easter, and Christmas. I wish I could wear them every day, they are so much prettier, softer, and cleaner than Cathleen's stinky hand-me-downs.

I betta go, Nana is calling for me, see ya!

Chapter Two

7th August 1952

Our William has been home for almost a week, and I have hardly seen him. His tutor arrives at nine am on the dot each morning every Monday to Wednesday and doesn't leave until four-thirty pm. On the days he is free, his mam is dragging him to tea with her friends — to show him off more like — or taking him to get his new uniform measured, and to art galleries and other la-di-da places.

Sometimes when me, Cathleen and Nana are piled in bed having chats about the past, he lingers at the door until Nana invites him in to join us. He is incredibly quiet our William, but has a truly kind face. Even though he is a year older than me I feel the need to take him under my wing. All this schoolwork must not be fun, his mam also insists he wear a blazer suit whenever his tutor comes round as well. My nana gets ever so angry when his tutor comes to the house and William greets him dressed to the nines. She had a row with Uncle Albert only last night about allowing William to run around the garden in a pair of shorts, or sit in front of the TV, or better still come out with us for the day. From what I gathered from the row, men may be the head of the family but not in his, Auntie Emily is the top boss! My nana said Uncle Albert has no backbone. When William's tutor left this evening, I lingered behind the dining room door listening to their farewell.

14

"I will see you next week, William. I recommend in the meantime to perhaps read a little, do a little research even."

"Yes, sir. Thank you."

"Good day William."

"The same to you, sir."

Then I heard the door close and nothing else but silence. I peeped through the same gap I had kept open to listen and saw William standing by the door, his hand still on the handle and his head rested upon it. I opened the door further and stepped into the entrance hall. I didn't want to give William a fright, so I quietly called his name. He quickly turned to me and looked nervous, like I had caught him doing something wrong.

"Would you like to go for a walk?" I asked.

William stood still, he didn't say a word, he looked up at the staircase and then back at me. "I would love to go for a walk, Charlotte."

"Come on then let's go now before your mam comes."

We had only got to the courtyard gate when there she was, on our bloody heels, the witch! "Where do you think you are going William?" she asked, a hand on his arm.

"I was going to go for a walk with Charlotte, Mother."

"I'm afraid not, come on get upstairs I want to see what work you have done today then we are meeting your father at the hotel."

The hotel was where my uncle worked, and it was owned by none other than my nan. Her father bought it for her when she came to London from New York to make a fresh start after losing her husband in the Great War.

"All my work is on the table; you can have a look. I will just have a quick walk around the park and be back in time to meet up with father, I promise."

"William, I sa-"

"Let him go Emily, the boy needs a bit of fresh air after being cooped up all day," my nana said from behind her, she and Cathleen had been preparing tea together, so she must have heard, and my lovely nana just couldn't help herself. That's why I love her.

"Please, Mother," William pleaded.

A couple walked by our gate and smiled at us politely, Auntie Emily let go of William's arm and smiled back at them. "Good evening," she said to them.

"Good evening,' they choroused back.

"Ok, you can go for a walk, but I want you back in one hour and not a minute more, do you hear me William Anderson?"

With that me and William ran out of the courtyard before she could change her mind. Oh, I would have loved to have been a fly on the wall back at the house once we left. Me and William walked to St. James's Park which was a ten-minute walk from the house, with forty minutes to spare we walked around the lake before sitting under a big tree. It was so quiet, just a few dog walkers and couples taking a walk. William sat quietly picking the grass beside me.

"Do you like having a tutor, William?" I asked him.

"No, not really."

"So why don't you tell ya mam, if she knew you weren't happy maybe she would let you have a break in the holidays."

"I don't think it would matter to be honest, Charlotte. My mother said I have a big future ahead of me and work is what is going to get me there."

"That can't be true. I'm sure other things matter too."

"Not to my mother."

"Even so, you should still have time to have fun with your friends and to play."

William began to dig a hole in the mud with a stone he had found by the tree. "My only friends are from school; I don't have any friends at home. It's just me, my parents and grandmother."

"Well, you have me and Cathleen too, even if the sun does shine out of her backside."

William laughed. "I do like it when you both come, even if I don't get to see you that much."

"You know you don't have to be shy with us, we are your cousins. You can come and join us whenever you like. Nana said she is going to buy her own television for her living room, won't that be fun. Two televisions you would have." William smiled. "Do you like your school?" I asked him, interested to know more about his boarding school.

"It's ok, I suppose, the lessons are interesting, the teachers are good."

"Do you have your own bedroom there?"

"No, I sleep in a dorm with three other boys, Michael, Fredrick, and Timothy. They are my best friends." His voice seemed to chirp up at the mention of his friends. "Do you like your school?" he asked me.

"No, not really. The food at dinner time is horrible, it looks like what I imagine they give to prisoners." William laughed at that. "And the head teacher could break your arm with a tap of his finger."

"No," a shocked William said.

"I swear it and my teacher, Mr. Evans, talks so loudly you would think he was talking to a hundred kids. There is only twenty-three of us."

"Twenty-three! My goodness, there are only nine children in my class."

"Nine! God, that's a small class. Do the girls wear suits as well?"

"We don't have any girls in our school. I go to an all-boys school."

"No girls, I would love for my school to be just girls. That way I would never have to spend another day in the company of Henry Hollister. He is the most awful boy I have ever met."

We chatted more about school, he has a French chef, and they go on trips to Italy and camp out at the lake district. I am lucky to get a trip to Long Sands Beach in Tynemouth. Then we walked slowly back to the house.

"Why are you meeting Uncle Albert at the hotel?"

"I don't know, probably another dinner party. We always have them; my father and his pals meet up with their families at the hotel. We don't have a table big enough at the house you see, we normally have two big tables. One for the adults and one for the children."

"Is it fun?" I asked.

"It's ok."

I love going to The American Eagle Hotel. It is so big and has huge chandeliers and floor to ceiling mirrors everywhere. Before we go home Nana always books us a table for a farewell meal there. Behind the reception desk are lots of photos of the family. My favourite one is of my mam, she looks about Cathleen's age in the picture, at a charity ball my nana held, and she looks so beautiful. Her smile is that big that you can see dimples in her cheeks and her eyes are creased at the corners. She has her hair curled remarkably high just below her ears and her dress my nana said was gold silk.

When we reached the house Auntie Emily was waiting at the door. "Finally, your clothes for this evening are on your bed, please get dressed as quickly as you can. The car will be arriving to pick us up in fifteen minutes." William ran into the house as quickly as possible; I forgot how nice it was to spend time with my cousin.

<u>9th August 1952</u>

Hello! What a great few days I have had. Yesterday morning, while me and Nana were chatting in bed, Cathleen popped her head in asking if we would like anything from the shops while she was popping out (to the post office). Me and Nana glanced at each other and giggled, making Cathleen giggle too.

"Why are you laughing? I am just updating Rupert on what I have been up to, I received a very lovely letter yesterday so it's only fair to write back."

"Of course, darling, I am glad he is keeping in touch with you, some men are not so keen on writing. He is a keeper."

Cathleen's face beamed. "I think so too, oh you have dropped something on the floor." Cathleen picked up a piece of folded paper from the doorway. "It's for you Charlotte."

"For me?" I was so puzzled, she handed it over and in a neat scroll was the word *Charlotte* I opened it to read a note in equally neat handwriting and read it aloud:

"Dear Charlotte, I wanted to thank you for a lovely time at the park. Would you be free for another walk tomorrow afternoon? William."

"He must have slid it under last night," Nana Florence said, taking the note and reading it again. "That poor boy, he just wants some normality, someone to play with, to have a break from all this schooling."

Cathleen said that I should write back, and she will slide it under his door on her way upstairs to get her letter for Rupert. So, I quickly scribbled that I would love to and that I was free all day.

"Oh, and I would like a chocolate bar," I shouted to Cathleen on her way out.

"I beg your pardon." She looked at me puzzled.

"From the shop. I would like a chocolate bar."

"Oh yeah, I forgot, right see ya both later."

Sending a note back to William was only the first step, his mam was the second. Me and Nana were sat in their living room watching the television and we could hear William's pleading. He had no tutor today, so I didn't see the problem. My nana said the witch (she actually used the word witch) likes him to study and do homework on his days off. It wasn't until dinner time that William found me, armed with a metal tinned lunch box.

"I'm free Charlotte, let's go!" We quickly legged it out the door and ran all the way to the park in case Auntie Emily changed her mind. We had to sit at the nearest bench to catch our breaths.

"What's in the box?" I asked him.

"Sandwiches, egg, and cress. I made us both one, and some biscuits."

He opened his box and put it in between us, we tucked in and fed the ducks in the lake our crusts. "You shouldn't actually feed ducks bread," William told me.

"Why?"

"It's not good for them; you should feed them seeds."

"But everyone feeds them bread."

"I know," William said, throwing another bit in.

"They love it!" I told him as we ate our biscuits while walking around the lake.

"Do you go to the park with your friends back home?" William asked.

"Not that much, me and my friends, Molly and Carol, play in the lane normally."

"Is that far?" William asked me.

I couldn't help but laugh. "No, it's just behind my house, it's the gap between my side of the street and the street opposite us, we play at the front of the street too. There is normally quite a lot of us from school. We play knocky nine doors, although not for a while now, last time we played that Mr Brooke from number thirty-three chased us down the street with a bread knife. It was scary, we were too fast though, so he took one of his slippers off and threw it at a boy called Jeremy." William laughed spitting out a little bit of biscuit crumbs.

"What else do you do?" he asked.

"We go on bike rides, play hide and seek, kick the can is normally a favourite."

"What is that?"

"What is that? You're joking. Have you never played kick the can before?"

He shook his head.

"Wow! Well, it's best if you have a big group of you playing. Someone will be on and has to count to twenty. The rest of us will then hide. The person on must find us. If you get caught, then you are out and have to sit on the curb. If you're still hiding, if you are brave enough then you can come out of your hiding place and kick the can that has been left at the starting point and if you are not seen, then you are the winner."

"Sounds fun."

"I can't believe you haven't played it before; you will have to play it with your friends when you get back to school. I would show you now, but it doesn't work with just two." I looked around the park, there were a few children, but they were all dressed as smartly as William, walking with their parents. "I don't think we will find anyone here who would know how to play. If we leave the park and go and find a lane, I'm sure there will be loads of kids, it would be so much fun."

William looked at me horrified. "No Charlotte, I think we should stay here, if my mother found out we left the area she would be furious. She would never let me out again."

"Okay, that's fine. You play it at school, yeah?"

"Yeah, I will. The boys will enjoy that, I think."

"What do you play at school?" I asked him.

"Not much — football, rugby, cricket, chess, card games."

"Sounds spiffing, darling," I replied. William nudged me causing me to drop my last biscuit.

"Not everyone is posh and rich at my school you know; my friend Michael isn't. He is from a deprived area in the East End. He is incredibly clever, his headmaster from his primary school fought hard to get him a place at my school. After a lengthy battle he got transferred and his parents don't have to pay a penny, not even for his uniform. He keeps his old clothes under his bed though and always changes into them when we go home on leave. He said if he turned up in his school uniform the kids in his street would beat him up or call him names. He doesn't go out much when he goes home, his old friends don't want to hang out with him anymore."

"That's sad, so does he stay in all summer?"

"His big brother and his father work on the docks, they get him to help out. Keeps him busy and they say they don't want him to forget his roots."

"Are they happy about his transfer?"

"Oh yes, I've read some of the letters they send him, they are enormously proud of him. His mother calls him her little Einstein. I don't think he is very keen on the nickname to be honest. He invited me to come and stay with him during the Easter holidays, but my mother wouldn't allow it. She said, *You don't know what you will catch*," he said mimicking her voice. "I wish you could meet him; he is great fun. He reminds me of you. He will know what kick the can is, won't he?"

"Yeah, he probably will."

Me and William walked around the lake one more time before leaving the park to have a wander. I hadn't been anywhere but the park without Nana before. I felt very grown-up walking around London with no grown-up. One day I will know this place like the back of my hand. It will be home. We walked by Buckingham Palace — it was very crowded by the gates — we squeezed past some people speaking a funny language. They didn't look too pleased.

"Lo siento," William said to them. They tutted and walked away.

"What did you say?"

"I said sorry. They were Spanish."

"You can speak Spanish?"

"Si querida prima puedo," William said with a smile, as I nudged him.

"What does that mean?"

"It means, 'yes dear cousin, I can.' Look the flag is up, that means the Queen is home."

"Wouldn't it be amazing to be the Queen...or the King. To be the ruler and live in a big palace."

"I think it would be rather lonely. You wouldn't be able to do what you like, go where you like or even dress how you like. You would have to work in a big house on your own while everyone goes off and does their own thing. I think the Queen has a lonely job."

"I bet she has lots of televisions though, and dresses and jewels, her book collection must be massive! I bet she has every Charles Dickens ever made."

"I bet she does, but things don't make you happy, Charlotte. Come on, I have some money from Father, let's go to the shop."

The sun was beginning to go down when we returned to the house, again Auntie Emily was stood by the entrance, this time her face looked like thunder.

"Where on earth have you been, young man?" I was surprised when she hit William across his head. "I have been worried sick! One hour we agreed, just one hour at the park. That was five hours ago! Your father and Cathleen have been looking everywhere for you both."

"We lost track of time, Mother," William cried at her, while ducking from her continued strikes to the head.

"Five minutes is losing track of time; five hours is deliberately not coming back."

Auntie Emily was still hitting William, I wanted to do something, but I was frightened I would make things worse for him. "I was just having so much fun with Charlotte."

"Anything could have happened to you," she said, ready to strike again, thankfully Uncle Albert came in and grabbed her hand.

"I think that is enough, the boy has learnt his lesson, Emily. Go upstairs to your room William, I will speak to you later," Uncle Albert demanded.

William sulked off only to pause on the bottom of the staircase and faced his parents. "I knew I was late; I knew I was more than an hour, but I didn't want to come home. I didn't want to come back to my room and study. I wanted to stay outside, I wanted to stay with Charlotte. I was having fun; this house is not fun. This house is horrible, and I hate it!"

Auntie Emily gave what I thought was an overly dramatic cry.

"To your room boy," Uncle Albert repeated.

The hallway felt awkward and silent as the three of us stood watching him go upstairs, the only sounds were the small sobs coming from Auntie Emily. Suddenly I felt two hands grip onto my shoulders I looked down and saw Cathleen's hands. Never before had I been so glad to have her near me. I was afraid of what was going to happen to me, were Uncle Albert and Auntie Emily going to punish me next?

"Cathleen, would you be so kind as to go down to the kitchen and make your aunt a chamomile tea," Uncle Albert kindly asked Cathleen. I could feel her hands grip my shoulders tighter, I didn't want her to leave me.

"Of course, Uncle."

She grabbed my hand and pulled me with her, but Uncle Albert stepped forward and calmly said, "please could you stay here Charlotte, I would like to speak to you if that is ok." I looked back at Cathleen, whose face looked worried despite nodding her head. "Thank you. Emily dear, why don't you go and lay down, I will be up soon I will send Cathleen up with the tea. I shan't be long."

The witch silently left the entrance hall and made her way upstairs, leaving just me and Uncle Albert. Nana Florence had gone out for the evening, and I so wished she would come back.

"Why don't we sit in the living room," he smiled at me and held Nana's living room door open for me. I made my way to the smallest chair by the fire that way we would have to sit separately, I may have a quicker chance to run or duck if he went for me there. "How was your day?" He asked me.

"It was lovely, Uncle Albert. We went to the park, then we went for a walk around London, not too far."

"You go anywhere nice?"

"We just went to the Palace and walked around Westminster."

He nodded and looked at me, almost sad. "Is the Queen home?"

"Yes, she is, the flag was up."

"William seems to have enjoyed your company today, how did he seem to you, do you think he was happy?"

"Very happy, we talked about school and our friends, he even taught me some Spanish."

Uncle Albert smiled. "He did, oh that's good." There was a moment of silence and Uncle Albert looked deep in thought. "I don't want you to think that we are keeping William from spending time with you at all, Charlotte darling, if anything I think you are a world of good for him. It's good for him to have another child to play with, and of course you're family which is important. Your Aunt Emily is just very, erm, very, what's the word…protective, yes, very protective of William. We waited a long time to have a child, it wasn't easy for your aunt. There was a lot of heartache before William came to live with us." He paused again making it very awkward for me. I didn't know what to do apart from nod at him silently. "He was just two when we adopted him, and he never left your aunt's side until the day he went off to school. She hated sending him off to boarding school, that was my idea; I wanted the best possible education for him, and I thought some space between a boy and his mother would be healthy. Emily just wanted to keep him home with her, she even suggested home schooling him. She almost drove to Kent herself during his first term to bring him home, but I managed to talk her out of it. He came home so excited to see her, he followed her around everywhere. Within his first year he was speaking foreign languages and was a fountain of knowledge. Despite this Emily still tried to persuade me to keep him here in London, she felt like she was missing out on his life. It took a long time for Emily to realise that school was paramount for William's future. The world was going to be his oyster."

"Uncle, if Auntie Emily was so upset about missing time with William, then why does she make him do more work when he comes home, why does she not spend more time doing fun things with him?" I bravely asked him.

"That is a good question and one I know irritates the life out of your grandmother. Your aunt feels like she has sacrificed so much that she fears that it was all for nothing if she doesn't continue his studies in the summer. At the end of his school days, she wants to see results, she wants to see that it was all worth it." He shifted in his seat and leaned forward so he was closer to me. "Please do not judge Emily too harshly, she does everything from the heart. Now that William is getting older, she has noticed that he does not rush through the door with open arms for his mother, ready to please her every need and stick to her hip anymore, he is a young boy after all. He wants adventure and to be with his friends and I feel she is struggling with that."

"I see," I replied, just to say something.

"But William was happy today, did he say anything about his mother, me perhaps, anything that is upsetting him at all?"

"No Uncle, the only time he mentioned Auntie Emily was when he told me he wished not to go too far as she would not be pleased."

"That is wise of him…hmm. As William did not do much schoolwork today, his mother will no doubt want him to catch up tomorrow. If he does as she asks, how does a trip to the cinema tomorrow evening sound? I heard the film *The Crimson Pirate* is out now, yourself, William, and Cathleen may enjoy it. I will drop you off and pick you up and, of course, you will need money for treats."

"That would be great Uncle Albert!"

He chuckled. "Let me have a word with Emily first but I'm sure it will be fine." He smiled, and I swear he did the Florence nose tap, which made me giggle. "Right, young lady, you best be off to bed, I'm sure your grandmother won't be long, but you know what she is like after one too many Gin and Tonics, thinks she is twenty again."

"Good night, Uncle." He stood up as I did, and I was not sure whether to just leave right away or to leave with a kind gesture. So, I went in for a hug, I may have made the wrong choice as he was taken by surprise, but he squeezed me back and tapped my head.

"Uncle Albert, William is very lucky to have a dad like you."

"Why thank you, Charlotte." He paused and then squeezed me again, this time a little tighter. "Your father loves you; you know. You might not think it at times but his family… your mother is all he has in the world. He needs you all. The war…the war changed a lot of things."

"It changed my dad, didn't it?"

"Sadly, yes it did," he said with a nod.

"Did you see much of my dad before the war?" I asked. I am always interested in my family's past.

"Oh, I knew your father very well; three weeks of every summer he would come down with your mother and little Cathleen, they even came down in the Easter. Your dad was a proud man, he would come in his best suit and respected our way of doing things around the house, although he did say no servants on the guest floor, it was too much, I think. I remember I took him to the hotel for a poker night, I leant him one of my suits and he was a good sport, such a laugh he was. He managed to put on a Southern accent for half the night until the drinks started to hit him, and the Geordie came out." He sat down again. "He got me back, your father did. He had me down the East End in a little crowded pub in matching outfits and flat caps. At first, I was right out of my comfort zone, I must admit. However, Frank led the way and I have to say it was one of the best nights out I have ever had. Cannot say the ladies of the house were pleased when we arrived home, we walked it from the East End. Looking back, I don't know how we made it, we could hardly walk, and we woke everyone up." He laughed thinking of the old memory. "He was a gentleman in every way, and he would do anything for your mother and Cathleen. He was so proud of his family, there was always

31

so much laughter and Cathleen was always on his knee. He was a better father than I was, I saw him change her nappy!" Uncle Albert then looked at me seriously, making me feel a little uncomfortable. "You know he always spoke of a brother or sister for Cathleen, he would always say one day there will be more children and if he was lucky enough to get another beautiful little girl, he would name her Charlotte."

"He did?"

"Yes, he did, I remember him saying it as if it was only yesterday. Try not to be too harsh on him darling, your father has seen things that are unthinkable. He must live with those thoughts every day. Although I do not see Frank much anymore, he is a friend I once loved; I respect him highly and will always care about him. I only wish I had been able to join him, but a medical problem stopped me so I stayed behind and helped at the hotel, which was used as a hospital, but hey it is late, you really should be off to bed now. I will see you tomorrow."

Uncle Albert did not get up this time, so I wished him goodnight and left. I was surprised to see Cathleen on the other side of the door, she looked like she had been crying. I said nothing to her but gave her a hug as we parted, going separate ways to our beds.

Chapter Three

12th August 1952

Over dinner Cathleen was all smiles and giddy talking about Rupert this and Rupert that, she had received not one but two letters from him this morning — what a girl! However, this led me to start a conversation about our mam and dad.

"How did our ma and da meet, Nana?" I asked her curiously; I never ask my mam and dad questions about the old days in case it sparks any pain from the days before the war.

"Your parents, oh their love story is quite something and if your mother had been born to another it may not have gone so smoothly." She stopped to sip some tea from a floral China cup and continued. "As you know up until the war we had maids, butlers, and chefs back at the house; we had help since the day I moved in, my father insisted on it and to be honest after losing my husband and bringing up two small children in a new country I was more than happy for the help. I appreciated every one of them and never saw them as my servants, but as members of my household. Some of the maids were my own age and sitting alone in the evenings in a big house was lonely at times once the children went up to bed; I preferred to sit downstairs to eat, where the atmosphere was lively and I would make sure that we all ate the same meal together. Your mother and uncle grew up around our staff, as any child would around extended family. I was ever so sad to see them go after the war; I still write to some of them now. Anyhow back to your parents."

Nana took another sip of her drink with a sad look on her face, remembering the days before the war. A lot of adults do it, the war really changed a lot for people.

"Our chef, Maggie, had a niece who lived in Durham who was looking for work and asked me if I would possibly hire her as her assistant which I was more than happy to do, Maggie had been with us since the very beginning, she was like a grandmother to the children and a great friend to me. Maggie's niece was a pleasant girl and was around the same age as your mother; oh, they did get on well. Just before Christmas Maggie invited her nephew down so he could surprise his sister. Your father arrived at our house on the front doorstep with a bouquet of flowers and a tin of biscuits and was met with a frustrated butler ushering him away and to come around to the back door. Your father was mortified until your mother stepped in telling him that it was fine, and she would show him down to his family. My goodness I had never seen the look that your mother had on her face ever, before then — it was a look of pure love."

"Aww," Cathleen said, looking all in love herself as if she was picturing her and the choir boy.

"It was love at first sight with the two of them, the three of them were together all day every day. I had given your Auntie Joy some time off over the period of your father's visit; and love blossomed, I saw it and your

Uncle Albert did too."

"How did you know?" Cathleen asked.

"I'm guessing Mam didn't stop talking about how great Dad was all the bleeding time and her face became as red as a tomato at the very mention of his name," I could not help myself from saying. Cathleen shot me a look that could kill, and Nana continued (I swear I heard her chuckle a little — she knew what I meant).

"When asked about her day with Joy and Frank, she had such enthusiasm in her story and a twinkle in her eye, that told us all we needed to know. I liked what I had seen of Frank, as did your uncle who was very protective of his younger sister. When Frank returned to Durham he and your mother wrote back and forth for many weeks before a letter arrived one day addressed to me — asking for permission to marry your mother. I always remember his loving words about her, he was clearly as besotted as she was. Me and your uncle liked his mannerisms and how happy he was making your mother. His family had been friends with our own for many years, so it was an honour to join the two families together, and he fulfilled his promise in making your mother a happy wife." That was debatable now, I thought — what about having a happy family, a happy daughter? I did not ask those questions though and kept them to myself.

"Why did they move to Durham? Why didn't they live with you like Uncle Albert does?" I asked, wondering why William lives a life so different to my own, one that could have so easily been mine.

"Your father is an enormously proud man; he inherited his parents' home at the age of eighteen and dreamt of raising his own family there. He didn't disrespect our ways, but it was clear that a life here was not one he wanted. All he needed was your mother and himself in their little house near the mine that he worked in, earning an honest wage."

"I've never heard of an Auntie Joy before, Nana," Cathleen said, neither had I come to think of it. Nana looked at us both sadly and a little annoyed.

"Neither of you? My goodness as much as I love your parents sometimes, I do think I would take immense pleasure in strangling them both as well. Your Aunt Joy was rather lonely when your mother left home, and it didn't take long for her to strike a new friendship with your Uncle Albert in fact." Me and Cathleen looked at one another wondering where the story would lead.

"It took a while after constantly trying to get one another's attention with a joke or a reason to be near each other before he asked her to join him at the park on her day off. Then that was it, I suppose, from then on they saw each other more and more and became remarkably close. She was a gentle kind soul and your Uncle Albert doted on her. Many people thought us strange, mixing classes together, but love is love and I would never deny any of my children the chance to be with who they truly wanted no matter what their status in society."

"What happened to Auntie Joy? Why have we never

seen her before? Why did she not stay with Uncle Albert?" Cathleen asked, and I was just as eager to know.

"Oh, Darlings, she did stay with your Uncle Albert; they had a beautiful wedding over at the hotel, they were just wonderful together. Sadly, however when she was in the family way, she…" Nana choked a little. "She and their dear little daughter died during the birth. It shocked us all to the core. We all lost a bright star in our lives that day. Your Uncle Albert was utterly devastated, as were your parents."

"So why has everyone forgot about her?" I asked.

"I doubt anyone has forgot my dear, she will still be here," she tapped her chest and smiled. "Your parents deal with things like grief in their own way and if not mentioning Joy is how they cope then that is their choice, it doesn't mean they have forgotten her at all."

"And Uncle Albert?" asked Cathleen.

"Next time you visit the hotel have a good look at the photos on the family wall. You will find her there where she has always been, your uncle is not one for emotions most of the time, but I've caught his glances towards it over the years and it has never changed. She is very much still a part of him."

This Auntie Joy was someone completely new to me and Cathleen, it was like we had resurrected her in some form by speaking about her for the first time. We never really see Dad's other sister, Alice, who lives in Northumberland and there are no photos of Auntie Joy at home. It's as if she never existed. I wondered about her

last night, as well as today. I want to know all there was
to know about her. How different it may have been if she
had lived and was with us today, I believe the house
would have been filled with cousins, ones that didn't
have to go to boarding school all the time. I think she
would have been very kind, the type of auntie that treated
you like one of her own children.

"Nana?"

"Yes, dear." We had just gone to bed and a question
came to mind.

"Does Auntie Emily know about Auntie Joy?" I asked
her.

Nana put her fingers to her lips and quietly said, "yes,
she does but she does not like to speak of her. Emily has
known your Uncle Albert all her life, her father managed the
hotel for me, and she went to school with your mother. She
had always been in love with Albert and was very envious
of Joy. When Joy died, she was very quick to be a shoulder
to cry on. A little too quick for my liking, however even in
death Emily was highly jealous especially when your uncle
took over a year to propose and she did not bare him a child.
If she'd had it her way that picture at the hotel of our Joy
would have been long gone. Thankfully, your Uncle Albert
refused to take it down."

"The witch has controlled him ever since though."

"Your uncle has a firmer grip than you think, he just
takes his sweet time figuring out how to deal with certain
situations and chooses his battles carefully."

"Hmm, I think I would have really liked Auntie Joy."

"Oh, you would have dear; she was a sweet, sweet girl."

18th August 1952

"You're going to have a brother or sister!" Mam told us full of joy as we arrived back home from London. My heart was still with my nana, but one day I would never have to leave her again. Once I finish school, I am going to live with her and be an author.

Me and Cathleen were taken aback, but as it sunk in, I realised that this was something special. I would no longer be the youngest, Cathleen will have another sibling to boss around and this baby might grow up to really like me. The biggest thing about this news was it was already bringing our family closer together. For the rest of the night, we all chatted about baby names and stories of when we were little. Apparently when I was born Cathleen cried for days because she didn't want a sister to share Mam and Dad with, which explains a lot! I still can't believe this — not only am I going to be a big sister, but Dad ran out last night to grab us fish and chips from down the road to celebrate. Gladly no one saw the tear that left my eye, dripping onto my salt and vinegar chips. Before the war, Mam and Cathleen would meet up with Dad every Friday once he finished his shift for a chippy tea. A tradition that ceased when the war broke.

Yesterday evening will stay with me forever, our home felt loving and warm. Looking in you wouldn't have known that the Germans had taken away the souls of my family. You would think they had given them back, even if they were only borrowed for a short while. Me and Cathleen couldn't stop smiling. As I drifted off to sleep one thing really stuck with me from what my dad had said, "I remember around late December time one night, Charlotte, I was in a trench head to toe in mud, cold to my bones and I looked up at the stars and I prayed. I prayed that ya mam would safely bring you into this world and that you would be healthy and strong like our Cathleen was. I wanted to be here so much for all of you, it angered me that I could not be, but nothing made me prouder than ya mam's letter telling me I was a Da again to another little lassie."

Maybe, just maybe my dad does love me.

Chapter Four

<u>22nd June 1957</u>

What a day, a long day may I add. The long-awaited event
of the century took place, at last, when Cathleen walked
down the aisle to Rupert this morning. I have to say it
wasn't as awful as I expected. I imagined it would be quite
a bore — a long church ceremony, lots of old folk
drumming on about how beautiful the bride looked, toasts
after toasts wishing the couple well, however it was quite a
lovely day I must say. Cathleen hasn't stopped talking about
the big day ever since Rupert got down on one knee on New
Year's Eve last year…on my fifteenth birthday, of course.

With Cathleen becoming a married woman, last night
was the last time she and I shared our bed in our little room.
As much as I have always complained about having to share
everything with Cath, it will be strange tonight when I sleep
here alone for the first time. I have only ever slept with
either my sister or my nana. I think Cathleen was thinking
the same last night when we jumped into bed.

We must have been in bed for a good twenty minutes
before she nudged me. "Charlotte are you asleep?" she
whispered.

I was wide awake.

"No," I replied, sitting up against my pillow beside her.
We both sat in silence looking around the room before
staring at each other.

"Are you nervous about tomorrow?" I asked her.

"A little," she began to fiddle with the ribbon on her nightgown, "but I'm excited as well. I've dreamt of this day with Rupert for a long time. I can't actually believe it's really happening, tomorrow."

"You're going to look lovely Cath."

"Mrs Rogers did do a fantastic job of altering the dress, you would never think it was over twenty years old."

When it came to the wedding dress, Cathleen knew she would be presented with Mam's dress. As Mam and Dad brought it down from the attic and unwrapped the tissue paper protecting it from decades spent in the cream box, they looked delighted. Mam held the dress up and they both looked at Cathleen waiting for her response. She exchanged looks with me and then gave a very over the top, "it's perfect!" I know she didn't mean it; it's not that Mam's dress is awful because it isn't and back when she married Dad the dress was bought from a little London boutique and cost more than Mam and Dad could ever afford for a new dress for Cath. It was just a bit…old.

"We will get Mrs Roger's to give it a good clean of course," Mam informed Cathleen.

Mrs Rogers ended up giving it more than a clean. With Mam's permission Cathleen asked if the dress could be altered a little to bring it to the fifties but keeping the classic look it had back in the thirties. Mrs Rogers is everyone's go-to lady when a stain on a favourite blouse won't come out or when they want to keep a favourite outfit that is getting too small. She really did a wonderful job, she brought the floor length dress higher up, just below Cathleen's knees, and shortened the full lace sleeves to her elbows, with a few extra layers of material sewn underneath the skirt. Cathleen now looks every inch the bride of today, with the beauty and details of Mam's original dress still present.

"You're right, Mrs Roger's really has worked her magic on it. It's going to be strange not returning here tomorrow, you will have this bed all to yourself."

"I will be able to starfish in it, and I won't have to listen to your snoring anymore."

"I do not snore!" Cathleen nudged me. "Do I really snore?" She looked suddenly worried.

"Ha, no you don't," I put her out of her misery, even though I have heard her occasionally. However, the last thing she needed is to worry about snoring when she had to share a bed with a man for the first time.

"Are you nervous about tomorrow, tomorrow night I mean?"

Cathleen looked embarrassed, returning her fingers to the night gown ribbon. "A little, but Mam had a chat with me this morning about it all and what I should expect from it. Rupert is a gentleman; I know I will be well cared for."

I may only be fifteen, but I know what happens in a marital bed, I've read about it in books, heard about it from friends, and Carol is always sneaking her Mam's magazines which are full of information. If I were Cathleen, I would be frightened. I don't know how anyone could love a boy that much to want to do the things married couples do. I have no interest in boys, Molly has a new boyfriend almost every week and they are always sneaking around kissing, and one even groped her boob!

"I am sure Choir Boy will be good to you," I smiled up at her, she hates it when I call him that however tonight she ignored the name calling and rested her head on my shoulder.

"Are you going to be ok, Charlotte? Once I am gone."

"I'll be fine, it will only be for a little while and then I will be moving to London."

"Finally, eh, I hope life hasn't been so terrible here in Durham for you, you have always been desperate to run off to Nana's."

"No, it's not been terrible, life is just… better down in London. There are more opportunities for me there. You have your life mapped out here, you have your receptionist job at the hospital, you're getting married, moving to your new flat in Newcastle, you're happy here. I want to write and have a different life to what you have chosen, and even Mam. Not that it's the wrong way of life, it's just not what I want."

"Wait till you meet someone you really like Charlotte; you may think differently."

"But I want to be a writer."

Cathleen laughed making me feel slightly foolish. "That you may, do you think every writer is a lonely person living in their nana's big house. They have lives as well, you know, families of their own, other commitments."

"I guess so, I just don't want any distractions, that's

all."

"You're a girl on a mission, that's what you are Charlotte Ridley." Cathleen looked around the room.

"You will still visit when you move to London, won't you?"

"Of course, I will come every summer for three weeks." She smiled at me and for the first time I felt sad at the sudden thought that this was it.

Looking back, without realising, Cathleen had always tried to be there for me or teach me some sort of lesson. I always saw her as the one getting me into trouble or sticking her nose in where it didn't belong; now I see she just cared about me. She knew in her heart that our parents were not who they once were, and I never got to experience the love she once had before the war, which in a way must be so much harder to deal with. Cath was always making sure my hairstyles were on trend or that I wasn't getting up to mischief. In reality she was just a kid herself, she shouldn't have cared for such things, but she did. As we have both grown older, we have become closer in the last few years, and I find that now she is married — probably toasting to her new life with Rupert right now in Newcastle — I'm saddened that our childhood together is now over.

After finally catching some sleep, the day of the wedding arrived. We were woken by the loud knocking of Mam at the door.

"Cathleen, you better get up or you're going to be late for your own wedding!"

I looked over at Cathleen whose eyes were wide open, and I threw the covers over our heads, and she squealed so loud with excitement. "Oh, my goodness. I'm getting married. Ahhhh!"

The ceremony was held at our local church, of course, St. Mary's, the place where Cath and Rupert met years ago as choir singers and where they are now exchanging vows. She looked every inch the blushing bride in her dress, with little white heels. She bought me a matching pair. I watched on from her left, clutching onto her bouquet of primroses, as she married Rupert. I could see everyone from my view, they all shared the same beaming smiles, and some sniffles of happy tears from Mam and Nana. Everyone was wearing their best dresses and sharpest suits. I myself felt like a princess in my bridesmaid dress, a lilac ruched chiffon gown that shimmered in the light to a shade of blue. It was by far the prettiest thing I had ever worn in my life.

The reception party was held back at our house, what a squash and a squeeze that was; I don't think Dad thought that one through when he put the offer out there. We had guests from Rupert's side along with Cathleen's friends, Nan, Uncle Albert, Auntie Emily, and William. Mr Flint arrived at the reception in a suit that dated back to the twenties I believe but compared to his usual gardening attire he certainly looked dapper and was met with approval by Nana Florence. Mr Flint and Nana have met on several occasions now, both were rather eager to meet the other. I have been helping Mr Flint for five years around the house and his allotment, he is a lonely soul. At first, I detested the idea to help when Cathleen organised it, bribing me with pocket money in exchange. They got on like a house on fire the moment we all met in the allotment over a flask of tea and Victoria Sponge. I believe they even exchange letters, both widowed so early in their lives yet neither of them found love again, a friendship however has truly blossomed between the two. Of course, the Hollister's were also invited — not a single event in our family can pass without our next-door neighbours joining us. They are as good as family Mam always says. Walter and Betty are the kindest people you could ever meet but their sons, Joe, and Henry, have been the biggest tyrants of my life, especially Henry.

"Charlotte, you coming out back here?" Joe was heading out the back door with Henry with a look of mischief on his face. "You can bring the geek with you." He was referring to William who I was catching up with in the kitchen.

"He is not a geek; he is cleverer than you will ever be!" I shouted, only making the two of them laugh.

"It's ok Charlotte," William said in the smallest voice. The Hollister's obviously made him feel uncomfortable.

"Come on Charlotte!" Henry shouted, before slamming the door behind him.

No good comes from the two of them but I was curious to what they were up to and with the speeches, enough dancing with old relatives, and cake all out of the way, boredom was creeping up on me, no offense meant to William, who was telling me about the tennis player Lew

Hoad.

"Come on William, let's go outside," I dragged him by the arm before his reluctant face could argue. The back gate was ajar where the boys had swiftly shut it behind them. We sneaked out making sure it was closed properly. Sat against the back yard wall was Joe and Henry swapping a wine bottle between them.

"Want some?" Joe asked with cheeky glee in his face.

Joe was almost the legal age to drink now whereas the rest of us were far from it. I had never tasted alcohol before and from the look on William's face neither had he. I sat beside Henry and patted the empty space beside me for William.

"I don't know, Charlotte. I think I will go back into the party," William had one hand on the gate ready to escape.

"What a wuss," Henry laughed handing me the bottle.

I looked at William and then back at the shiny green bottle and took my first swig of wine. The taste was awful and stayed in my mouth long after the liquid had gone down my throat.

"It gets better after a few more sips," Joe said, taking the wine from me for his next drink. By then William had quietly taken a place beside me.

"I don't like this," he whispered. "What if someone sees us. My mother will go crazy."

"It will be fine. It's just a little bit, they've already started it. Just try it once, show them that you're not a wuss."

Henry passed me the bottle and I took another

unsatisfied sip before handing it over to a nervous William. He held the bottle to his nose and sniffed it with a face of disgust.

"Just drink it!" Joe called out from the top end of our row.

William took the bottle to his lips and took a mouthful, just as the gate swung open causing him to dribble some down his chin from the fright. Out came Nana Florence and Mr Flint in fits of laughter until they met the four of us out on the lane. Nana took one long look at a guilty William and a nervous me. Joe and Henry had huge smirks on their faces.

"Good evening, Florence," Joe laughed.

William put the wine bottle slowly down to the side of him, rather too late but worth a shot.

"William, Lottie." She looked at each of us sternly, this was it, we were done for. I have never been on the wrong side of Nana before, and I wasn't looking forward to it. My dad will give me such a hiding. I will be grounded for life, I'm sure of it. Cathleen will moan that I've ruined her big day and Mam, well, she will give me the silent treatment and the look of disappointment for weeks. To my utter surprise Nana along with Mr Flint burst out laughing. The four of us exchanged puzzled looks. William's face still showed an element of fear, not yet believing that he was not in the deepest trouble of his life yet.

"If you're going to sneak away with a bottle of wine, don't sit outside the house. Come on you lot wise up, do you want to get caught?" Nana smirked.

"The house on the end of the lane is empty, old Mrs Pritchard moved out yesterday," Mr Flint pointed to the bottom of the lane. "Go and get ya self in her back yard away from this lot."

The four of us slowly stood up. "So…we're not in trouble, grandmother?" William cautiously asked.

"Not from us Will, however if any of your parents come out here and find you all sat here up to no good, I can't say it will be good for you. Now go, you silly lot."

"You're the best Nan," I ran over and squeezed her tight.

"You are pretty great Florence," Joe said genuinely, quite marvelled by my nana.

"I just re…" She stopped to cough. "I just remember wha…" she stopped a second time to cough clutching tightly to my body that was still wrapped round her. Ever since the London smog in 1952 Nana has had a chesty cough and loses her breath but she always perks up. "My bloody chest."

"Do you want some wine, Grandmother," William handed out the bottle to Nana.

"Oh no, darling, you keep it. What I was trying to say is that I remember what it is like to be young and curious. Off you go then."

"Come on guys," Henry took the bottle from William and led the way. William followed the Hollister's like a lost sheep.

"What are you two up to?" I asked Nana.

"Me and Rufus are just going for a little walk, it's

beginning to get a little rowdy in there. We won't be long," she hooked an arm around Mr Flint's and smiled at me. "Have fun now Lottie, but be careful, and look out for William I think he is a little out of his depth here."

"I will, enjoy your walk."

The night had started to appear, and the cool evening didn't bother us when it arrived as we were warm in the back yard of the empty house with wine in our bellies. When the bottle was long empty, we sat in a circle laughing and talking nonsense. My head felt light, and the company of the Hollister boys seemed too good to be true, normally they tease me. William told us mischievous tales of his days at boarding school while Joe, who had friends the other side of Durham, had a collection of drunken tales already much to Henry's disbelief.

"When have you ever gone dancing?" He questioned his older brother.

"All the time."

"With girls?"

"Yes, with girls."

"Real girls?"

"Yes, real girls."

"Nah, don't believe ya."

We all jumped as the gate flung open, Mr Flint poked his head in to tell us that Cathleen and Rupert were saying their goodbyes. The night was dark now and the stars were shining ever so brightly above us as we headed back. The music from the house was still blaring and the place was very much still cheery and alive. No one had even noticed our disappearance, even Dad was drinking with a smile on his face, and a tear in his eyes as he held Cathleen with her suitcases at her feet. Mam was in floods of tears; Betty Hollister held her close telling her that Cathleen was a married woman now and off to start her new adventure. As the house filtered to the front, I wasn't able to reach Cathleen to say my own goodbye, she was waving to the crowd as Rupert opened his car door for her to slide in slowly keeping her dress tight against her body, as not to jam it in the door. I managed to see it all on my tip toes. Rupert put her cases on the back seats and waved goodbye to us all. The crowd outside of our little Durham terraced house cheered and whistled as the engine started, and with a rattle of the cans on string attached to the back of their Ford Consul, the car drove away taking my sister with it. I felt like the drink's magic had dissolved as I watched the car disappear, everyone returning to the house leaving only me and William outside. My eyes filled with tears, and I suddenly felt alone.

"Don't cry Charlotte, Cathleen is happy," He put a protective arm around me and squeezed me tight. "Anyways, it won't be long until you are packing your own case to come and live with us."

This cheered me up. "That is true. I'm just being silly."

"Come on, let's go in. Link my arm will you Charlotte, I fear I may fall without support. The wine is making me rather wobbly on the feet."

This made me giggle as we joined the rest of the party.

Joe and Henry were nowhere to be seen for the rest of the night; the natural order of our relationship will commence no doubt by morning, leaving our little wedding party a one-off event. Nana Florence and my brother, Peter, were snuggled on the chair out for the count and the guests carried on partying well into the night.

Chapter Five

26th June 1957

I had my shift at the library today, it was far too hot and stuffy. It was my first shift since Cathleen's wedding. We have already seen her twice; she can't stay away from home. She and Rupert are off to Bournemouth today for a week's honeymoon. She seemed very grown up, chatting around the dining table with her rings sparkling as she held her cup of tea, chatting about the flat and a couch she spotted in Newcastle that she *has to have*. It was as though she had gone from household member to guest overnight and by the looks of it, she doesn't mind one bit.

Today's shift went slow, and it was all down to the envelope sat at the bottom of my cardigan pocket. I got a letter addressed from London this morning and I was hoping it was going to bring me the news that I long to hear. I have sent my short stories for children to seven publishers now and all have replied with a simple no. This one felt different though it was too small and thin to have my story returned to me. I waited until I was home before I opened it carefully and with a heart ready to burst out of my chest, I took a deep breath and read out the letter.

Dear Miss Ridley,

Thank you for sending us your collection of children's stories and showing interest in our publishing house. My colleagues and I sieved through your work and cannot disagree that they show arduous work and a vivid imagination. However, we do prefer our authors to have more advanced writing skills which normally come from those who have had further studies once leaving compulsory education. As this is not the current situation in your case, we are going to have to decline your book today.

We wish you luck for the future and please do not hesitate to get back in touch with other work once you have more knowledge and experience. If you would like us to return your draft, please write back to us along with 2d for the postage stamp.

Best regards, Theodora Foreman
Normandy House Publishing

In all honesty, I want to give up!

15th July 1957

To my Darling Lottie,

I am sadly writing to you to ask you to please postpone your move to London. I know you are desperate for your long-awaited adventure here, but I would kindly ask you to hold out for a week or so. I am not feeling too great at the moment, the doctor has ordered me to stay in bed. What a fuss. Albert is running around trying to play nurse, I know his heart is in the right place, but he is getting on my wick! All I want right now is some peace and quiet and maybe a large G and T.

I am sorry to hear about Normandy House Publishers. Mr Flint is right; you are better off without them. I know it's hard being told no but do not give up on hope. I didn't want to tell you this yet, but I can't bear to hear you so down. I have a meeting arranged for you, for when you move down here. I will not say who with but let's just say it's a big deal sweetheart, I pulled some strings and I have to say I have every faith that this could be it for you. So, hold your head up high, the future is bright, and my goodness you are so young. You do make me proud. I will write again when I am feeling better.

Love, Nana Florence xxx

When I received this letter this morning, I looked at my suitcase by the door, it had been packed for the last week and a half. Next Wednesday I was meant to be moving, with Monday being my last shift at the library. I best ask Mrs Morgan if I can have a few more shifts. Honestly, it's just one thing after the other at the moment. On the flip side though, I wonder who my nana has arranged for me to have a meeting with. Maybe its Penguin or Ladybird or even Puffin. Hmm, Ladybird did return my book so maybe not them. For my nana to get involved though, and to say it's big, it's got to be a leading publisher, surely. She wouldn't give me false hope. I best practice my best meetings voice.

Chapter Six

27th July 1957

I can't quite believe what I am about to write in this journal, or if writing it is even appropriate. Yet something inside me wants to write it. Something tells me that I should write everything; I write about the great times and the upsetting times, so why not the terrible times.

Three days ago, I was babysitting Peter while my mam and dad had tea next door with the Hollisters, with Peter asleep after reading not one but three bedtime stories at his request, I had fallen asleep with my own book on the couch.

"Charlotte, wake up." My mam had shaken me awake. "Come on, off to bed. Henry needs the couch."

I sat up and slowly took in the people in the room. Mam was stood over me with puffy eyes and an arm around Henry whose eyes were equally puffy, if not more. They had been crying for sure.

"What's happened?" I dared to ask, sitting up making room for Henry to slump down beside me. Mam sniffed and walked over to the cupboard under the stairs. She pulled out a spare pillow and blanket that we normally keep ready for Nana.

"You will need these, Henry," she said leaving them on the arm of the chair, Henry didn't say anything or even acknowledge the kind gesture from my mam. He just stared into space in silence, his whole body looked frozen.

"What's happened?" I asked again directing my
question to Mam.

She tilted her head towards the kitchen, I looked at
Henry once more and realised she was suggesting we have
a private conversation. The kitchen was dark, only the dim
streetlight from outside making its way through the nets
sending a jolt of yellow light across the back wall of the
kitchen. Mam didn't turn the light on so I closed the door
behind me ensuring that Henry couldn't hear us and joined
her in the dark. Leaning against the sink where I could not
see her face Mam told me about the following through
silent tears that I know she was fighting. I could hear it in
her words and her breathing.

"Bettys had a heart attack. She was just in the kitchen
peeling potatoes and the next minute she just cried out and
collapsed," Mam took in a deep breath. "She's gone."

I stepped forward, closer to her. I know what Betty
meant to my mam. She had been her closest and only
friend. They had supported each other through the war and
after. They chatted to each other every day, did the food
shop together, brought up their children side by side, she
was a good, kind woman. I had always liked Betty, no one
on earth could not like her. I reached out my arm and
gently touched my mam's back and rubbed it while resting
my head on her arm. I wasn't sure what to say to her to be
honest. Sorry? It will be okay? I'm here if you need me.
Because are any of them honestly true statements. I'm
surprised she let me comfort her; I half thought, and
guiltily half hoped she would shrug me away, but she

59

allowed me.

"Where is Dad?" I quietly asked her.

"Out looking for Joe — he ran off."

"And Walter?"

"He is pretty much in the same state as Henry, I thought it would be best for them to stay here tonight but Walter insisted he would stay. I think he wants to be left alone. Least here I can keep an eye on Henry. He is bound to be in shock, today...today...he has lost his mam," she let out a cry and to my disbelief turned her head into my shoulder and hugged me tight and what came next made me cry too. "I love you, Charlotte. I really love you."

"I love you too, Mam. I really do."

It is true I do love my mam; we just haven't had an emotional relationship or a nurturing one like I have with Nana, or even Peter. She washes my clothes, my bedding, puts food on the table. She has kept me alive, but I wasn't always sure whether she did it because she had to rather than because she genuinely loved me. Our house had never been one filled with good night kisses and sweet gestures but tonight as her heart broke for Henry, who was now motherless in the other room, and her dear friend Betty taken too soon, it had made Mavis Ridley — my mam — realise how time is precious and it made us both realise that we will always love each other even if it is not shown. We stood like this for several minutes until she pulled away wiping her tears on her sleeve.

"Why don't you check on Henry and I will make us all a cup of tea."

I headed to the door and turned back to my mam, who had begun preparing the tea in the dark, knowing her way around the kitchen regardless of the lack of light. Back in the living room it was as though time had not moved. Henry was as still as the Monument statue in Newcastle. I approached the boy who had teased me countless times for as long as I could remember cautiously. Despite him not being in the mood for pranks I did not want to be too careless. I took the blanket from the side of sofa and slowly sat beside him laying the blanket across both our knees. For the first time in my life, I actually felt pity for Henry Hollister, here was the boy who had made me cry, poked fun of me, got me into trouble and made my school days tough, and all I really felt like doing now was putting an arm around him, to comfort him how I would Peter. His face was blotchy from the tears and his blue eyes held a rim of water ready for the next flood. I did not say anything I just stayed beside him, the event of the evening and late night was catching up on me and I felt my self-drifting off.

It was Dad who woke me next, I felt my arm shake but without being touched as I slowly became more awake, I realised that it was in fact Henry who Dad was waking, whose head was leaning against my shoulder.

"Come on, son." Henry sat up like someone had pressed on a button, as he took in his surroundings you could see the penny drop. The flash of the night before danced across his pale face. I saw it and Dad saw it too. "Let's get you home, your dad needs you, Henry," Dad helped him up and together they headed out the room. Dad turned back to me with a weak smile, and said, "go and get some more sleep upstairs, Pet. I won't be long."

I stretched out my arms and pulled off the blanket that had wrapped up me and Henry. I had no idea what the time was, the sun was trying to make its way into the day, but I do not think it was his time to shine just yet. The birds sang on the terrace roof like they did each morning as if the day were no different to any other. As I headed upstairs, I spotted three full mugs of cold tea on the table. I must have nodded off while mam was making them. Quietly, I tiptoed to my room and collapsed onto the bed without removing any clothing.

6th July 1957

Betty's funeral was as beautiful as a funeral could be. If that is the right word to describe it, how do you describe a funeral? The bright colours of the flowers showed us all how we were all lucky enough to know such a happy lovely person. Everyone wore black but a relative of the Hollister's passed each of us a bright flower to hold as we entered the church. The last time a lot of us were sat there was only last month for Cathleen and Rupert's wedding, a happy occasion, and even Betty herself stood in the pews in a lilac dress with a matching hat. It seems surreal that here we are again for such a different occasion, where Mam's tears now spilled with grief rather than joy, and Betty now lay in the mahogany box before us all instead of beside her family.

Henry and Walter were sat in front of us their faces as white as sheets and their shoulders often trembling. It took all my power not to reach a hand across to them to give them some sort of comfort, but men do not want a fuss when they are down and Henry, well, he is Henry, the Hollister boy, the tyrant of my life yet right then I wanted to hold his hand and tell him that everything was going to be ok even though I have no idea if it will. Since the night Betty passed away Joe has not been seen, causing Walter even more distress. My dad and many others have searched for the eighteen-year-old but with no luck.

The reception was held back at the Hollister's, Mam had made a small spread of cakes, sandwiches, and sausage rolls, Dad brought a collection of beer and wine which was used to make a toast to Betty. Walter sat himself on the floral chair by the fireside and never moved for the entire evening. Henry took himself away upstairs and was not seen until people started to make their last condolences before leaving. One woman, a friend of Betty's from school, broke down in tears as she said goodbye to Walter and told him to call her if he needed anything even just for a chat. Walter nodded and thanked the woman before her husband put a protective arm around her weeping body and guided her out.

"Is there many left?" Henry asked me from the staircase as I made my way through to the kitchen. His eyes, like they had been for the past week, were red and swollen. His face was pale, and he looked in desperate need of a good night's sleep.

"About seven or eight I would say, not including my

63

parents, Cathleen, and Rupert. Would you like anything? There is a couple of corned beef sandwiches left and a slice of Roly Poly."

"No thank you, I am not very hungry."

"Ok, well I will plate them up with some foil in case you fancy it later."

"That is very kind of you, Charlotte. I do not believe I have thanked you or your mam yet for all your help. You have both been brilliant to me and my dad."

"It's nothing, really, my mam wouldn't have it any other way and that is what neighbours are for."

"That is what friends are for you mean," he gave me a small smile and for the first time I realised I felt relaxed in his presence and not on edge waiting for him to throw a spider at me or stamp on my toes as he ran past. He looked so vulnerable and weak, I think I could outrun the boy and knock him down with one punch now. He had his mam's eyes I realised, bright blue like the sky on a warm cloudless day, they were beautiful yet had been wasted on a wart, but perhaps the wart could be changed for he seemed very innocent sat on the stairs looking straight at me suggesting that we were friends.

"Of course," I smiled back. "I best wrap the leftovers; I will leave them in the fridge for you."

For a funeral, people still seemed to have quite a big appetite as, apart from the food that I mentioned to Henry, there was only half a sausage roll left, not a drop of alcohol, and a pile of paper plates sat beside the over-filled bin. I squashed everything down to make room for more plates and headed out to the back yard to empty them into the large metal bin. As I opened the back door the gate swung shut fiercely leaving a bang as the catch hit the post. I quickly tried to see who it was but whomever it was, was gone in a flash. Perhaps someone thought they forgot something then realised they had it after all, perhaps an old friend had popped by but had not the courage to speak to Walter, or maybe it was a drunk person entering the wrong garden. Whoever it was had gone and I did not give them a second thought until this morning.

Walter and Henry told us last night that they were going back to work, they needed something to occupy their minds and Henry needed to continue his training as he, in Walter's words, *'Has a long life ahead of him and must learn a trade. There is no time like the present.'* Walter was a carpenter and had his own shop in Durham selling all sorts of furniture that he had made, he was quite well known, and many neighbours had purchased pieces from Walter.

There was not much to tidy at the Hollister's today, and I was pleased to see that the plated up corned beef sandwiches and cake had been eaten. I washed the endless cups of tea and binned the beer bottles, giving the kitchen a quick scrub before moving on to the living room, it was there that I was faced with none other than a sleeping Joe. He lay comfortable and relaxed across the couch on his back, his legs were crossed, one arm lay across his chest while the other lay across his face resting his hand on the arm of his chair where his head lay. His dark hair was overgrown and beginning to curl.

My heart began to race, and I saw red, grabbing the nearest cushion without thinking I hit it off his sleeping face repeatedly, I could not understand my deep anger but felt I had no control over it at all. I could hear Joe wake, he was shouting something at me, his arms flinging in the air, but I could not make out what he was saying above my own voice. "You horrible boy! You have no idea what you've put your family through!"

Joe managed to grab hold of the cushion and pulled it off me. Of course he did, he was much stronger than me, but my brain did not care for that, or had I planned what the result may be either. Joe stood up angrily in front of me, his face was so close to mine I could hear his rapid breathing. "What the fuck, Charlotte!"

I was frightened now but I could not show it and act the scared little girl I now felt inside, I had to act as though I did not feel intimidated by him at all.

"You heard me, you are a pig Joe Hollister, running off like that. Your dad needed you; Henry needed you, you abandoned them and caused nothing but more stress and worry on your dad. Every night someone round here has been looking for you. You're a selfish bastard!"

Joe grabbed my neck and pushed me back against the wall, causing my head to hit a picture frame of the Late King George. His grip hardened as the wall supported his push on my throat. "Tell me why I shouldn't squeeze the life out of you right now."

I could not speak, the grip was too tight, I could feel

my head heating up from the lack of oxygen. If he did kill me right now in his living room, then he was not going to do it with me squirming like a fish out of water. I used all my power to let out a small laugh which seemed to have humoured him for he lost his grip slightly and smiled allowing me to use my vocals. "You haven't got the balls."

It was Joe's turn to laugh, he let out a nasty chuckle with the grip on my neck still quite tight. "You have no idea what I am capable of Miss Ridley, however it's your lucky day."

Joe's hand let my neck free, he straightened out my hair softly and pulled my cardigan sleeve, which had fallen to my elbow, back up onto my shoulder. He never spoke but touched me ever so gently before letting out a sigh. He supported his body by leaning his left arm onto the wall I was eager to move from yet frozen to. His head fell low leaning his forehead against my own. Making me anxious to what his next step would be. Would he headbutt me? Change his mind and kill me right here in his dead mams pride and joy? It seemed like we were stood like this for ages and all I could hear was my own rapid breath and beating heart.

"I'm sorry, Charlotte. Please forgive me. I have been a selfish bastard you were right, but I had to get away, I had to. My mam she was...oh man," I jumped as Joe punched the wall inches from my face then turned his back on me, starting a pattern of pacing the room backwards and forwards from the fire to the sideboard on the wall opposite a shrine of happy family memories smiling into what was in this moment a dark empty shell. "My mam," he began again, "she was amazing, the Queen of this house, she would do anything for us, and I didn't treat her right. I was a little shit; I always have been, and Henry. I know we drove her nuts."

Joe sank into the sofa, his messy hair nested between his hands as he held his head in them, without his eyes on me I looked over to the front door, seven steps max and I could be out of there, yet I could not bring myself to move. I was rooted to the spot just like King George.

"We killed her, Charlotte." Joe began to sob alarming me with his words taking me away from my thoughts of escape. "We killed our mam, we drove her too far, we stressed her out, we killed her."

"No," I squeaked.

"We did, the night before Mam found cigarettes in my trousers that I forgot to take out and she flipped her lid, she said she was sick of us letting her down. She said we caused her nothing but trouble."

The pair of them were always up to no good, however no one could deny that Betty Hollister loved her children with every fibre of her being.

"You didn't kill your mam, Joe, and neither did Henry. It was a heart attack, and the doctors told your dad that sadly your Grandad died from a heart attack too. It's genetic."

Joe wiped his face on his sleeve before looking up at me, red rimmed and snotty. "I blamed myself, that is why I ran, I couldn't face it."

Now he was breaking. While everyone had been processing Betty's passing together, Joe had locked himself and his emotions away convincing himself that it was somehow all his fault and now I was witnessing the aftermath of it all as the *tough guy* broke down into tears. I slid slowly into the seat beside him and to my surprise he nestled into my arms. I embraced him like I would if Peter were upset, as he wept for what felt like an eternity.

"I'm sorry Charlotte," Joe's muffled voice said from within my arms. He lifted his heavy head and looked at me with so much sorrow.

"It's ok, you've had a lot to deal with. I shouldn't have woken you so aggressively."

"I deserved it, that's what made me angrier. It's true what they say, the truth hurts. Yet I should never have laid a hand on you. Not ever," I flinched as he grabbed the side of my face; he didn't hold it hard but tenderly.

He saw my reaction and looked hurt by it. "Sorry," I whispered.

"No, I am. Please forgive me. I've never done that before; I hope you believe that."

I nodded looking at him straight to try and make him see that I was not frightened by him. Joe smiled at me and placed my hair behind my ear.

"Has anyone ever told you how beautiful your eyes are?"

I instantly laughed and pulled myself away. I could feel my face start to reddening, but Joe pulled me back. "I mean it, I have to say Charlotte Ridley you have grown up to become quite the beautiful swan."

He traced my face with his finger, for some unknown reason my heart began to beat heavily as his body leaned in closer to mine. I thought he was going to kiss me, in fact I would bet my life on it, as he leant in, I saw him shut his eyes and I was going to let him! That is when we were interrupted or even saved perhaps.

The front door barged open quickly, "Charlotte, have you seen my-" it was Henry. He stopped in his tracks when he saw me and Joe on the sofa. His eyes widened. I blushed and felt somewhat embarrassed and annoyed with myself. I was going to let Joe kiss me after he had pinned me to his living room wall by the throat! Henry looked at me with a look I could only describe as deeply shocked with a hint of disgust. Joe retracted his last move and jumped to his feet.

"Hey, little brother."

Henry sprinted towards Joe, red faced and angry. "You Fucker!" he shouted before punching his brother. The impact was to his face, I gasped as Joe straightened his buckled body. As blood escaped his nose, Joe used his overworn t-shirt to clean it.

"Ok, I deserved that but you w-"

Henry threw a second punch, this time Joe staggered into the fire surround behind him knocking an ornament to the ground with a smash. This time Joe blew his bloody nose into the fire pit. Both Hollister brothers were angry now, and I could predict the next move just as I suspected they did, for without any more exchange of words, Joe punched Henry in the face making him lose his balance and stumble into the sideboard, that was it — they both lost it and fists were being thrown back and forth at such speed that I could no longer tell whose arm was whose. I screamed for them to stop for in the mix of hot sweaty flesh I could see flashes of red, of blood.

"STOP, YOU IDIOTS!"

My next plan was the most foolish yet, I used my own body to try and stop them. Me, skinny Charlotte Ridley, tried to stop two terribly angry boys. As imagined, it did not go well as a fist, of whose I do not know, caught my cheek with force. I did not feel the pain until the shock of the fist coming towards me had made impact with my face. Both Henry and Joe instantly stopped when I yelped, Walter had also joined the lovely scene in his front room.

"What the bloody hell is going on here?" he shouted.

The boys were panting covered in blood, I held my face in agony, frightened at the sudden ache in my tooth. Walter scanned the room, the knocked over picture frames on the sideboard, the smashed ornament, wonky King George, and especially at his oldest son, home at last.

"I think I am going to go now. Everything is tidy in the kitchen, Walter." I stepped past the boys; they were panting like dogs in need of water.

Henry grabbed my arm as I passed.

"Charlotte are…are…are you alright?"

"I am fine. I best be off."

"Something cold will help with the swelling love." Walter had the look of shame that Betty often had on his face as he looked at me. "I am so sorry."

"Don't be, honestly it was an accident. I will be fine," I gave him a small smile that caused me great pain, but I wanted to give Walter reassurance in some way to cushion the blow to the bigger picture of what had just happened.

My face has swelled like a balloon since. My Dad went ballistic! However, Mam managed to calm him down once I explained again what had happened, missing out the part about Joe threating to kill me and then almost kissing him on the sofa like a fool. I am so angry with myself, why on earth would I have allowed that pig of a boy kiss me, my first kiss should be special, not from an abusive neighbour. One small compliment and I had forgotten the minutes prior when I could barely breath, I would have acted like a tart to have kissed him, and the look on Henry's face told me that also. I feel so stupid, he looked so annoyed by the scene. I am going to stay away from those two. They have never brought anything good to my life, I've helped in a sad time but now I am going back to work, and a good distance can be made again. Back to normal.

Chapter Seven

12th July 1957

After my shift at the library, I headed to the allotment to catch up with Mr Flint. I love his garden this time of year — it feels like I am a world away. He has his vegetable patches in the middle, boxes of herbs and spices along the bottom wall and on either side, there is a ray of colour as his flowers are in full bloom, there are peach and pink roses, bright purple orchids, dahlias whose colours look like they are on fire, white lilies, and sunflowers. My favourite are the blush pink peonies I think a rose is overrated, for a peony to me is just as delicate and beautiful. Mr Flint's pride and joy are his Irises, for he planted them in honour of his late wife. The violet and yellow plants tell a thousand stories and I love hearing them in this little haven.

In the back shed Mr Flint has a little stove for making cups of teas, endless tools, and empty flowerpots. There is always compost everywhere but tucked in the back is two little deck chairs, cushions, and a picnic blanket for days like today.

I asked Mr Flint what he thought about my latest letter from Nana, asking me to postpone my move again. He simply shrugged his shoulder. "I think you should listen to her, be patient, stick with work and not worry."

"So, you don't think there is more to it?" I quizzed,
for I suspected that there was. I have my own bedroom
in London so I wouldn't disturb her rest and surely,
she would much rather that I be helping her rather than
Auntie Emily if she needed help. "For I do not see the
problem with me moving down now, she has a
meeting arranged for me and I won't be no bother, I
know my way around London like the back of my
hand. It isn't like I need her very much personally."

"Just be patient kid, she wants it to be perfect, the two of
you have planned this all your life. She wants to be there in
the moment with you." Mr Flint had a way of changing
things round and making things sound clear, he was a very
laid-back man who seemed as though everything bounced
off him.

"I am not as convinced as you, have you heard from
her?"

"Just a little," he was watering his orchids with his back
to me now.

"And she hasn't said anything more to you?"

"Nope, I know as much as you do."

"Fine, guess I best unpack at this rate."

14th July 1957

After work today I decided to pack a little picnic and
waited for Henry to return from work. Yes, Henry. I had
bumped into him yesterday after trying to distance myself

from him and his brother, who has been up to no good since his return home, the police are always bringing him back in a state and you can hear the arguments through the walls between the two. Yet when he perhaps needed someone to talk to, I was dismissive. I felt bad all day thinking of last night. Yes, he was unkind in the past, he has never been an angel, but I have to remember that the boy is in great pain right now which I could never compare to or pretend that I understand. His world as he knew it has crashed down on him, and his brother isn't making things any easier.

The Hollister tribe arrived home at five on the dot, all in matching emerald overalls covered in a day's work. Their green Morris Minor van parked up outside their home. I felt a little nervous sat on a wall opposite with my little hamper and pale yellow and white gingham dress. It had been Cathleen's, what a gem of a find it was in the wardrobe, for she had worn it just the once having decided that it was too revealing on the shoulders. I however thought it was a gorgeous dress for a warm summers day like today and had received a few compliments at work for it.

"Henry!" I nervously called. All three pairs of eyes darted across the road to me. Walter's were warm, Henry's were full of surprise, and Joe's were deep and concerning. I smiled and Henry walked across the road to me after a small exchange and giggle with Walter. A tease no doubt. He held his cap in his hands twisting and fiddling with it.

"Hey," he smiled. A smile that would do him no good,

for it was a charming sort of smile.

"Hey, I packed a picnic, thought we could take a walk to the allotment. It's quiet there, maybe it could be nice for you to get away for a few hours. If you would like to that is. You don't have to. It was just a thought."

Henry, still smiling broadly, looked at me and the small hamper. His hands relaxed a little. "A picnic sounds super. Would you like me to change out of my work clothes?"

"No, not at all, it's only the allotment. Nowhere fancy."

"Are you sure?" He patted down his overalls causing an escape of sawdust into the air. I couldn't help but giggle.

"You are fine, let's go," I grabbed a dusty arm and we walked to the allotment. I felt like a bright yellow angel coming to rescue Henry from his chaotic world. I wanted him to feel the escape and the allotment was the perfect setting.

"How was your day?" I began with the light general chat that everyone exchanges day to day.

"It was busy, we have been asked to build tables and chairs for a new nursery being opened in Chester-Le-Street."

"Oh, how sweet they must be so small. Is it just the three of you at the shop?"

"Yes, for now. One day Dad would like the company to expand, with a warehouse, making and delivering bespoke furniture all over the country. It is quite a squeeze in the shop, we often find on days like this, that we are extending to the back yard."

"A warehouse sounds exciting."

We left our street, passed the corner shop, and walked up a small row of yet more terraced houses.

"That one there belongs to Mr Flint," I pointed to the shabby looking house. The nets that hung on the window were yellow and the black paint on the front door had mostly scraped off. Henry raised an eyebrow.

"Gorgeous."

"Don't judge, I did that once. His home is nothing but shelter for him. A place to meet his essential needs it is not his castle or even a place he calls home."

"I've heard it is covered in cobwebs, and rats feed off his leftovers."

"That is not true. I clean that house each week to help the old man out and I can be sure of it that in all my years I have not seen any rats. When I first started to help Mr Flint, yes it was a mess, so awful I thought I would pass out from the smell, but it was mostly piles of clothes, cigarettes piled in the ashtray and plates in the sink. Chores he had neglected but not food."

"Hmm, I've also heard that he hates children and hasn't washed his hair since his wife died."

"You'll be surprised to know that one of the walls in Mr Flints living room is covered in coloured pictures and letters sent from his nephew's children. I myself have been visiting the man since I was a child and he is a great friend of mine, he is like family even. So, in answer to your rumours, he does not hate children and as for his hair I do not know nor care how often he washes it for he is a truly kind man who has his reasons for everything he does."

"His wife?" Henry questioned as we left the houses behind us walking along a small country lane behind the allotments.

"Yes, I believe so. She was very dear to him, so much so that he has remained alone his whole life with no interest in finding love with another woman."

"Apart from your nan," Henry commented cheekily. I gave him a little shove.

"There is nothing going on between my nana and Mr Flint, they have a friendship, it is companionship that they share with one another for my nana too did not remarry after my grandad died."

"That must be what they call true love."

"Yes, but also rather lonely do you not think?" I questioned.

"Hmm, probably but maybe once you fall in love for real then there's no point trying to fall in love again. What if you can't? I doubt my dad will. If he were lonely, I would understand but I don't think he will."

"What if he did fall in love again, do you think that would be possible?"

"Could he still love my mam?"

"Of course," I opened the gate to the allotments bringing us to a row of picket fences and small grey pallet fences around many sheds and small gardens. Some had chickens, some large vegetables that entered competitions, and some were a place to just plant and relax in.

"Then I guess it could be. I think each heart acts differently though, to each person's loss."

"I agree."

"Good evening Charlotte."

"Good evening Mrs Blake."

Mrs Blake had the greatest garden of all, it was a paradise of wildflowers and seasonal plants. She has four sunflowers that she planted at the bottom of her garden to stand for every child she lost in the war, out of her five strapping boys only one came back to her.

"Well, here we are," I put down my basket and tried to open the little white gate. "It's a little wonky and the latch has gone quite tight. Just give me a second." The lock needed small little wiggles to come undone and with a lift of the whole gate, which slanted to the floor, we were in. I let Henry in first, I had come by earlier and had set out a blanket on the small patch of grass outside of the shed with some cushions for us to sit on. In July, the allotment was at its most beautiful.

"What do you think?"

"It is definitely not what I imagined, I believed we would be sat on weeds and nettles."

"Harsh." I led him to the picnic area. "Now I don't have much, this was a last-minute decision, so it is just jam sandwiches, cheese and onion crisps and lemonade I'm afraid."

"Sounds perfect, better than chips from the chippy for

the fourth night in a row."

"Oh really, oh now I feel bad. I can get some food in for you all if you need me to. I am off work tomorrow. I am sure my mam won't mind cooking a pie or something as well."

"No, you have both done enough. My dad said you can't look after us forever."

"That is true, of course my mam would if given the choice."

"And you?" he asked me with his mouth full of jam and bread — the etiquette of a three-year-old.

"I will hopefully be on my way to London soon, to live with my nan. In fact, I should be there now, having meetings with publishers and getting settled, instead I'm still here in bloody Durham working in the library handling every other author's novel and looking after my little brother."

"Well, I'm glad you are not gone just yet. You have been a good friend…Oh God," with his next bite jam had squirted out onto Henry's white shirt sitting snug underneath his overalls. I couldn't help but giggle.

"Now I really do feel under dressed, I thought I was going to have a picnic in a jungle and instead I'm sat here in a scene from the secret garden with you over there looking so beautiful in that dress."

"Oh God, really?" I blushed pulling my dress down further passed by knees. "You and your brother are nothing but flirts."

Henry's smile quickly faded and he casually lay back

on his elbows. "What has Joe said to you?"

I felt as though I was about to cross a boundary that I shouldn't, although I had no loyalty to Joe it felt wrong to discuss with his brother what was exchanged. Henry saw this in my face and frowned.

"Come on, tell me."

"Nothing, there is nothing to tell. Lemonade?" I offered, in the hope of changing the subject from Joe.

"Yes please, why did you say we were both flirts then? Come on Charlotte, I won't tell him."

"It was nothing, not even flirty at all come to think of it, he just commented on my eyes."

"Your eyes?"

"Yes, my eyes, he said I have beautiful eyes."

"Hmm," Henry gulped down his lemonade and I felt a sudden change in my emotions, I felt dissatisfied with Henry's reply. I don't know what I wanted him to say but I would have liked more than *hmm*. "So, the old guy, Mr Flick?" Henry moved on.

"Flint."

"He doesn't mind us being here, does he?"

"Not at all, I know he keeps his spare key to the shed under the sunflowers; he lets me come and go as and when. It isn't very often that I do come alone though, I normally come to help Mr Flint out with his garden and give him a bit of company."

Henry smiled at me, that handsome smile that a Hollywood actor should own, not one that should be on the face of a scrawny teenage boy.

"What?" I asked.

"I don't know, you're just the neighbourhood angel, aren't you?"

"I only do what I can to help people who need it."

"Hmm."

There he goes again with the *hmm*. What does it even mean? I must have been frowning without realising, for he laughed at me.

"What?" I asked.

"You, what is that face for?"

"What face? I don't have any sort of face."

Henry laughed.

"What now?"

"Nothing, bit feisty aren't you, Miss Lottie."

It was strange hearing him call me Lottie, only Nana Florence calls me by that name. She has called me Lottie my entire life, it used to drive Mam crazy. She used to always correct Nana saying, *"her name is Charlotte, not Lottie. If I wanted her to be called Lottie, I would have named her that."* None the less, Nan never listened, and Mam has come to accept it, I personally do not mind it at all. It's a special nickname to me because of how much Nana means to me.

"I am not, would you like some more crisps?"

"I'm good thanks, watching my weight." He smiled at me, and I couldn't help but laugh.

"It's probably for the best, those nights of chippy teas are giving you a bit of a podge there Mr Hollister."

He looked down at his stomach, the boy was as slim as

a rake, but he prodded it anyway. "You may be right."

The rest of the evening went lovely. We stayed at the allotment until the sun began to fade away and the evening chill crept up on us giving me goosebumps. "We best start to head back."

"Do we have to?" Henry moaned, packing the lemonade bottle back into my basket.

"Come on, you." It felt good to stand up and have a stretch, we had been sat there easily for three hours. After a quick tidy and replacing the shed key safely back under the sunflowers, we walked back up the track home.

"Thank you, Charlotte," Henry almost whispered as we passed Mr Flint's house which was all dark but a flicker of dim light from a candle. We had been walking in silence since leaving the allotment. I smiled at Henry whole heartedly, he needn't explain his thanks, I have tried to help as much as I can. I couldn't help but feel for him. My right hand was then taken into Henry's, gently he chained our fingers together and held it all the way home. I never pulled away nor did I want to, for I found that I quite liked it. Neither of us spoke for the remaining part of our walk home. When we passed neighbours, Henry did not remove his hand or blush like I have seen some of the boys my friends have held hands with do. He held it all the way home rubbing his thumb back and forth on the skin of my hand. When we reached my front door, I feared that he may kiss me goodnight. I have heard that is what gentleman do when out walking hand in hand with a young girl. He looked at me and smiled, my hand still grasped in his. If my dad had witnessed this, I am sure he would have had a few words to say on the matter.

"Thank you, Lottie. Today was very kind of you. I must return the favour." Henry shuffled around on his feet, unable to keep still.

"There is no need, I invited you as a friend."

Henry looked up to me as I said the word friend. "I do not deserve that title or your kindness. I have been such a dick to you over the years." Henry pulled my hand up to his lips and tenderly kissed my hand. "I'm sorry," he whispered.

I didn't expect the reaction I felt, but my heart raced as I felt his lips, and my stomach flips every time I think back. "It's ok," was all I managed to whisper back before he let go of my hand and wished me goodnight. I remained outside for a few minutes before going into the house; I felt as though I had to compose myself. Henry Hollister's little peck on my hand had made me smile like a cheshire cat. Who would have thought? Most definitely not me.

16th July 1957

I feel like I am writing this as a new woman. Eek! Today was the most perfect day! As I left the house to drop Peter off at school Henry was leaving for work and gave me a grin when he spotted me before getting in the van. Remembering that mouth against my hand the night before gave me butterflies, and I felt like I couldn't stop smiling.

"Morning Charlotte," Mrs Blake called from behind her huge sunflowers.

"Morning, Mrs Blake," I called back, always happy to exchange pleasantries with the lovely lady.

As I approached Mr Flint's garden and was about to open the small wooden gate, he popped his head out of the shed and gave me a fright when he shouted, "stop!"

"What is it?" I asked startled, jumping away.

Mr Flint smiled. "Open it."

Puzzled I unlatched the gate and was surprised to find that it opened with great ease. "It's fixed, you finally fixed it."

"Not I," Mr Flint winked his eye at me.

"Then by who?" I asked curiously.

"That young fellow you have been hanging out with, the one who lost his mam.'

"Henry?"

"That's the one, came down early this morning with his little metal toolbox, asked me if I minded if he fixed it. Said he noticed it needed a mend. I of course happily obliged; the damn thing has been bugging me for years now."

"That was very kind of him."

"It certainly was, who would have thought only a few weeks ago he would have probably ripped it off its remaining hinges."

That is true, I thought, only a few weeks ago he would have probably been tormenting me. Something had changed.

Well obviously, it was Betty's passing that had changed, he now seems more kind-hearted and sincere. I believe his mam would be proud of the change in him, he always was a handful.

"Are you going to help me then Lass or are you going to stand there daydreaming about Master Hollister all day."

I gasped, embarrassed, as Mr Flint laughed.

We had a lovely day in the allotment, although by one o'clock it was far too hot to be outdoors, so we took refuge in the shed.

"Have you heard from your nan?" Mr Flint asked me from his spot in his favourite chair by the window overlooking his garden.

"No, I have not. I am beginning to think she has forgotten all about me," I replied sadly, pouring us both a cup of homemade lemonade that my mam kindly dropped off along with some fairy cakes.

"Don't be daft, she thinks the world of you, and you know that. She must just be very unwell that's all. You know she gets badly ill after that horrible smog."

"That's true but not normally for this long."

I sat back into my chair and took a big bite of my cake — I was famished. I quickly regretted my greedy bite though for I spotted Henry entering through the garden gate, I immediately sat up brushing away the crumbs from my pale blue skirt and wiped my mouth as well. I ate as quickly as I could trying to take away the bulge of cake in my cheeks before he knocked on the open door of the shed.

"Hey," he smiled.

"Hi Henry," I could hear Mr Flint chuckle from behind me, the menace.

"Just came to check that the gate was working ok," Henry said.

"The gate? Oh, yes, the gate is great. Thank you. That was very kind of you."

Henry smiled. "It was nothing."

I couldn't help but smile back, the heat had caused Henry to remove the top half of his overalls letting it hang over his hips. His white shirt was darkened with sweat.

"We finished early today; the shop was a sun trap. Thought I would pop by and see if you fancied going for an ice cream. That's if you aren't too busy, and you of course don't mind, Mr Flint."

"I don't mind at all, go and have fun," Mr Flint said with a grin, shooing us away with his hand.

"Are you sure?" I asked.

"Course, it's too hot to do anything here. I'm just going to sit here for a while with me thoughts. You two go off and get an ice cream."

"Ok, I will see you later Mr Flint."

"Bye, Mr Flint."

"See you later," he called back at us. As I looked back, he gave me a wink which made me giggle.

Henry looked at me and my heart began to beat quickly, and I felt myself blushing. It is silly. I have known this boy all my life, he has been my neighbour, he has been in every class I have been in all the way through school, he has been in the street as I played out as a kid, he is there every Sunday in church, so why now do I find myself heating up at the very sight of him?

As soon as we were out of sight from Mr Flint's garden, Henry chained his fingers around mine. We both walked silently, the sun beaming on our skin. Our hands didn't take long to start sweating but neither of us let go of the other. I kept thinking of things to say, a conversation to start, but my mind was blank, so I let the silence carry on until we reached Frosties, the local ice cream van parked up outside the school.

"What can I get you young love birds," the ice cream man asked. He was an old gentleman who has been driving the van for as long as I can remember.

"What would you like?" Henry asked. "It's on me."

"Just a ninety-nine please."

"Make that two, please," Henry took some money out of his work trousers to pay. I couldn't help but think how strange it was that a boy was buying me an ice cream. I looked around to see if anyone could see us, but most people were more than likely in their gardens or cooling off in the house in this temperature.

"Thank you," I said to Henry as he passed me my ninety-nine and we proceeded to walk, I wasn't sure where to; we just kept on walking, past the school, past the church, past the playground, past the lanes until I could walk no more.

"I'm too hot Henry, I need to sit down somewhere."

I could feel my skin burning and this time it was not from blushing but from the heat.

"Let's go over there?" Henry pointed to a tree perched perfectly in the middle of a green surrounded by some bungalows. "There is shade underneath."

He pulled me over to it, quickening our pace and my legs were thankful that I had let them stop as was my now very sweaty body. Henry sat close beside me, so close I could feel the hairs on his arm touch my skin. My eyes felt heavy, not realising how tired they were as they began to fight with me to stay open.

"Are you tired? You can rest your head on my shoulder if you like?" Henry suggested.

"I didn't realise how much the heat has taken it out on me."

"I don't mind if you take a nap, here rest your head on me."

After a small hesitation, I lay my head onto Henry's shoulder, I felt the arm beneath it move position and felt its new resting place on my back. I liked the feel of his touch I thought before my eyes won the battle and I fell asleep.

It was slightly cooler when I woke. Henry was asleep too, his head rested upon the bark of the tree, as I moved my stiff body upright away from him, he opened his eyes.

"Hey," he smiled.

"Hey," I replied.

"Want to head back?"

"Yes, I think we should."

Neither of us moved, in all honesty I didn't want to go,

I was fine where we were under the tree together. Just silently enjoying each other's company. We were both just looking at each other smiling, I was the first to break the stare and giggled, then looked away to hide my warm face. Henry pulled my face gently back round to face him. He looked at me more seriously and whispered, "Can I please kiss you, Lottie?"

I nodded without hesitation, without even a second thought, and very slowly and gently he leaned closer into my face and that is when he kissed me. Ha! I can't stop smiling and thinking about it. He pulled me up from the grass afterwards and walked me home. Just before we reached our street, he turned to me and moved my (sweaty) hair from my face like I've seen them do in the movies and leaned in to kiss me again. This time he had his hands clasped around my waist. He asked me if he could take me to the cinema in town tomorrow. Of course, I said yes.

Luckily, Mam agreed when I asked her. "You two have changed." she was darning Dad's sock and said it with a smirk as if she knew about the kiss and the hand holding.

As she never elaborated, I left her to go hide up in my room where I could daydream and smile about my day.

Ahh. Good night! I have a date!

Chapter Eight

24th July 1957

It's been a week now. A week since my heart stopped beating. Since my mind has become shadowed with darkness. Since I feel like I stopped breathing. I can't come to terms with it all. I am still in so much shock. From the minute I wake to the minute my mind finally allows me to escape reality and gives me hours of peaceful slumber, I am in so much sorrow and pain.

A week ago, my beloved Nana Florence — my best friend — left this world, leaving me behind. Now I feel like I am living life on my own for the first time. Even though she lived so far away I knew she was there, waiting for me, writing to me, being my biggest supporter. Now I feel so alone.

We arrived in London, closely followed by Cathleen and Rupert, to what felt like a different house. Normally I would arrive at the large house full of excitement, welcomed with love and warmth. This time, despite the bright day, the house felt cold and dark and the atmosphere was quiet, saddened, and hollow. Auntie Emily did her normal greet at the door, dressed in a dark long black dress, her acting skills were on full, she hugged each of us expressing her sorrow. She went on to say how hard the last month had been seeing Florence grow weaker. Apparently, you can nurse an elderly lady as she died and be full of grief, but still have the ability to fix your hair into perfect curls and paint your face full of makeup. I sensed my mam noticed this just as I did because her hug with Auntie Emily was stiff and quick.

"I really do not know where we are going to keep you all, I thought I would let you all decide for yourselves. We have of course the girls' rooms at the top. They each have double beds in..."

I left the family to organise rooms in the entrance hall and headed slowly to the room on the right of the corridor. My favourite room of all. My nan's room. I entered and closed the door quietly behind me. The window was open sending a breeze into the room, the nets flapped occasionally. Her bed with its pink silk sheets were perfectly made. Her room was as it always had been. It looked as though she had popped out to see a friend or gone for a gin or two. Her perfume sat in a silver dish on her dressing table, the last book she was reading sat on her bedside table, her slippers were sat by her bed on the rug waiting for cold feet to slip in. A sun hat sat on a chair in the corner. I lifted it up and put it on my knee as I sunk into the chair and just looked. Her room was where we exchanged stories and secrets. Where we read to one another. Where she held me in her arms after I had a nightmare or sang me to sleep as a small child. She always let me try on her clothes, her jewellery, and perfumes. She would sit by the mirror and perfect her face before we could ever leave the house.

Now it was silent with only the sound of people

occasionally walking past her windows. People whose lives were normal, getting on with their day-to-day things while within the walls beyond the house they passed, life had changed completely.

The days at my uncles were quiet, no one knew what to say or do. We were not the type of family to hold each other and cry openly, however the reddened eyes of most of us showed that behind our doors we were grieving privately. My appetite has gone completely I think in the last week I have eaten little more than a few pieces of toast and some fruit. No one cooked a full meal despite Auntie Emily telling us all that we should get some food even if we popped to the hotel and have it made for us. I don't quite think the life of grief was one for my auntie, the life of luxury was missed more than my nana. We all passed each other in the corridors a quick check of, "are you ok?" or a small smile was given. My mam and uncle planned the funeral together with the help of my dad. He had not left my mam's side for a moment.

We left as soon as the funeral ended. It all seems such an emotional blur. We began at a small church at the City of London Cemetery and Crematorium. I didn't believe it was grand enough for my nana. She would have much preferred somewhere like St. Paul's or Westminster Cathedral if it were possible. My mam said it was her wish to be laid to rest there as it was a peaceful place away from the hustle and bustle of the busy city allowing her to rest with the sounds of birds singing and trees swaying in the wind. It was peaceful but I know my nana, she won't be laying beneath the dirt listening to birds singing. She will be singing to her sweetheart and drinking gin and tonics in the clouds.

After the service we all gathered at the American Eagle Hotel for the wake. By this point I just wanted to get home where I could be alone in my own bed to gather my thoughts. I am glad that the wake was held at my nana's hotel though. That I know she would have definitely liked. The function was filled with people, many I did not recognise and some I had met over the years. My nana's good friend Dora was there with her fifth husband Harry. Both passed on their condolences and Dora squeezed my hand tightly with a teary-eyed face and a small smile that explained everything she wanted to express to me. On a side table was the biggest bunch of pink and white lilies sent from the ballet dancer Anton Dolin with a message of great sadness that he couldn't be there due to being on tour in Australia. I escaped from the large room where I had shared many meals growing up with Nana Florence. Many times, I had run through the hotel corridors exploring with Cathleen and William. Never had I sat here without her, and now in her place sat my parents, who had never travelled far from Durham since the end of the war.

Having gotten fed up with the sad speeches, old stories and songs that made you want to stick a knife in your heart, I wandered off to the reception area where the doors were tightly shut for the day and the reception desk stood empty. Behind the desk that had welcomed people from all parts of life over the years my nana had owned it — and will continue to in the future despite her absence — was a wall that had over the years become my favourite part of the hotel for it was filled of photos of everyone that was dear to my nana. There were pictures of her parents, her sister. Photos of her wedding day, baby pictures of my mam and Uncle Albert and professional photos of them as a family. My own parent's wedding pictures framed on the gold papered wall alongside pictures of me and Cathleen. Uncle Albert, Auntie Emily and William made an appearance also. The wall was full of smiles and captured memories that made up my family. There was one photo that stuck out that I had never really took in before, and that was the bronze framed photo of a young woman whose eyes I felt I had seen all my life but not from the woman's face, but my own. I knew right away that the woman was my Auntie Joy. She was beautiful. I traced the photo with my finger gently. *I had never gotten to meet you I thought to myself. I bet you would have been fantastic.* I know my nana had loved her very much. Joy had grown up as a Ridley just like me. She had been born and raised within the very walls that I had.

"That was taken here, on her twenty-first birthday."

I spun round and leaning across the reception desk was my Uncle Albert. "Your grandmother made such a fuss about making it special. We had just found out we were expecting, and everyone was so excited. That day, however, my mother wanted it all to be about Joy for it was her special day," he smiled at the memory.

"I wish I had got to meet her; she looks very kind." My eyes met with Joy's own dark eyes in the photo.

"She was extremely kind, and I know the pair of you would have got on like a house on fire. She enjoyed writing you know?"

"She did?" I gasped.

"Yes, she was always writing poems and wrote a few short stories in her little notebooks. She was very clever, my Joy."

My Joy. I sensed sadness and remembered my nana telling me that she believed my uncle to still be deeply in love with his first wife.

"Do you miss her?" I asked.

"Every day," he replied, "but life must go on. I know that she would have wanted me to continue living. Your Aunt Emily and William have helped heal many scars. No one could replace Joy; she will always have my heart but that doesn't mean that there isn't any room for anyone else. I know what my mother meant to you Charlotte and my God I know the next few days, weeks, months, maybe even years are not going to be pleasant, but you must know that even though your heart is filled with pain and anger and everything in between, it will get better."

My whole body sunk at my uncle's words. We had all for the past week wandered round the large house like strangers. No one dared speak of feelings. Out of everyone in my family there was something warm about my uncle that I liked. He always seemed for a man to have more feelings than most, he didn't always express them, as men do not. But he was always there with a cheery smile and an awful joke and every now and then a little love and care that for someone like me was appreciated and always went a long way. In all honesty I feel like I hate the world right now and everyone in it; it makes my insides curl, but my uncle's calm words sent my emotions, that I had spent all day suppressing, to the surface.

"How can it get better without her in it. This was meant to be our time."

"I know and believe me when I say it, she did too. She spent many of her last days worrying about you. She worried what you would do without her, how you would cope. She was angry with herself and her body for not being strong enough for you both to follow your plans. She loved you beyond words and dreams, and like Joy, I know she would want you to live your best life. It will not seem possible now but one day, Charlotte, you will be happy again and the pain will subside. You will not forget, and you will miss her some days more than others but what you feel right now, this raw unbearable feeling will pass given the right time and care."

I wiped a tear on the sleeve of my black cardigan.

"Why didn't she tell me, Uncle Albert? Why did she keep how serious her illness was from me?"

My uncle smiled. "Love. She knew you would drop everything and be on the next train to London. She didn't want you to see her grow weak. She wanted you to be a teenager enjoying summer with your friends and living with hope. She didn't want you nursing her and watching her disappear. It was important to her that you remembered her how she was and the times that you shared together. She did not want to burden you with her illness."

I nodded acknowledging his words, though I do not find that I sorely agree with them for I still would have preferred to have been by her side and gotten the chance to say goodbye to her. My uncle did a three-sixty look around the lobby before pulling a small black leather box out of the inside pocket of his blazer. He placed it on the desk and smiled at me. He nodded towards the box.

"For you," he spoke. I slowly approached the box and opened the leather lid. Perched carefully between the slit of the soft velvet cushion was a gold ring. There was a cluster of clear small diamonds around a ruby-coloured centre stone. "It was my mother's engagement ring which she then passed on to me for your Aunt Joy. I couldn't think of anyone I know who would take better care of this than you. I know you will cherish it."

The diamonds still shone projecting a rainbow light. It was beautiful, so much so that I was afraid to handle it. "It is yours, if you will have it," my uncle pressed on.

"Thank you," I managed to say, as I picked up the ring to fully admire it.

"It suits you." My uncle smiled as I placed it on my right index finger.

"I will take good care of it, I promise." I really meant

this. I felt like I had the hearts of two woman and the love of four on my finger. I felt honoured that my uncle trusted me to have such an heirloom as this.

"I know," he replied. "You will make her proud. I know you will."

"There you are, I've been looking everywhere for you." My Auntie Emily barged through the double doors to the lobby. Her long black gown only just making it through with her before the double doors slammed shut behind her. "People are wanting to leave Darling. We have to say goodbye to everyone and thank them for coming."

Emily hooked her arm around my uncle's and guided him through the doors, which once opened again brought in the noise of music and chatter, before slamming shut again leaving me in the still, quietness but not before I was given a wink from my uncle, which in return I gave an appreciative smile as I carefully placed the delicate ring back into its box.

This morning, Henry has called for me twice already. I had long forgotten about the Hollister boy and our kiss. I have no wish to see him right now. The only place I wish to see are the walls of my bedroom and the only thing I wish to feel is my bedsheets tightly wrapped around my skin and the escape that sleep brings.

29th July 1957

"You have a letter Pet," my dad called from the other side of my door this morning. "Could be good news, a publisher perhaps. Why don't you come downstairs and open it? Your mam has some tea brewing. Maybe you could have a piece of toast as well. You must be famished."

"Come on, Ottie!" Peter wailed. I could hear them both hovering on the landing for a little while. Every day my dad had tried to tempt me from my room.

"Mr Flint's asking after you. Why don't you go and see him this afternoon?"

"Henry is at the door again. Wants to know if you fancy a walk. Some fresh air will do you good."

"Molly and Carol want to know if ya fancy going dancing. I know I'm not a huge fan of those places, but it could be nice to spend some time with the girls. What do you think?"

"Cathleen is popping out with your mam, they are going to buy a few bits for the baby. Why don't you join them?" (Yes, Cathleen and choir boy are expecting, I forgot to mention it with all that has been going on. They have known some time but felt it inappropriate to spread their joy in a time of grief).

Overnight my dad had become this incredibly concerned man, it was as though my absence had made him realise my presence for the first time.

"We will try again later, son," I heard him say on the other side to Peter before heading downstairs. I haven't left my room since we returned from London. I don't want to see anyone. I do not want to do anything. I just want my nana so badly, and as selfish as it may sound, I am also grieving that because she has gone, I now have to stay here in Durham. I highly doubt the letter I have received is from a publisher if so, it would only be news telling me that I have been unsuccessful yet again.

Another dream popped!

1st August 1957

Well, my parents got their own way today! I was woken up very rudely by a cup of water to the face by my mam followed by Peter jumping on top of me shouting.

"Come downstairs!"

"I've had enough Charlotte; you're getting up and you're getting dressed!" my mam shouted, as she fought me my bedsheets. "These sheets need washing, you need washing. Look at the state of you. This is not healthy."

"Mam, get off! What are you doing! You can't make me get up. I don't want to!" I shouted trying to scramble bits of the duvet off her to cover my legs.

"No, no more hiding in this room. It stinks Charlotte. It needs air in it, it needs to be cleaned." With the duvet fight won by my mam I clung to the railings of my bed. This resulted in a dark look in my mam's face; one I had not expected.

"Do not make this hard, young lady. Get up and get washed! Put some bloody clothes on. Go and sit downstairs and get something proper down you and then I want you to see that poor boy next door who needs his friend and then you are going to see Mr Flint and see if he is okay. You are not the only person suffering. Now get up!"

"You seem to be doing okay, shopping trips with Cathleen and park trips with Peter. You wouldn't think your mam had just died!"

The blow to my face I probably deserved, but at the time I meant it and partially still do. Peter cried as he watched our mam slap my face and the shock of the impact made my eyes water, or was it the pain, I'm not too sure. My mam's eyes were both teary and angry now.

"I am trying to prevent my family from falling apart. I am trying to keep things normal for everybody's sake. That does not mean that I am not hurting, you selfish cow. Now I am only going to say this one more time. Get up now!" She grabbed Peter's hand and dragged him out my door, his concerned little face looking back at me as the door was slammed shut behind him, the duvet gone with them.

As soon as she was gone, I cried, I had never been hit by my mam before, my dad yes, teachers also, but never Mam. I reluctantly did as she asked. I probably had smelt, apart from trips to the toilet as infrequent as possible I hadn't taken care of personal hygiene, my teeth felt awful against my tongue. No doubt my breath was bad too. With a quick brush of my teeth and a face cloth to my face, I brushed the knots out of my hair and tied it up in a low ponytail. I grabbed the first outfit I could find, my orange tartan skirt with a white blouse before opening the window of my bedroom to let air in. It was the biggest effort I had made and a one that was more than enough.

Outside my window I saw Henry sat out in the yard, he was sat on the floor with his head between his knees. In his hands he was holding what looked like a photo. My heart sank as I watched him.

Ever since Joe had returned, Henry hated being at home. The arguments had continued between the three Hollisters and the police made their regular visits as well. Henry looked up to my window, I quickly noticed his red rimmed eyes before closing my net and taking a step away. Mam and Dad reckoned he needed me, but how can I help him now? How can I give him words of hope? How can I tell him that everything is going to be ok, when I don't even believe that for myself? I am no good for him now.

"Ottie," Peter crept into my bedroom. He looked nervous. "Mam said dinner is ready and that you have to have some."

I sighed and made my first steps downstairs. I don't know why I was surprised to find that everything was as it always had been. The same furniture, the same crockery, the same photos on the mantelpiece. Although it looked just as my house always had, it felt somewhat different or was it I who was somewhat different.

"Ah, Lass, come and get some beef pie down ya. It smells great, Mavis." Dad put his newspaper down as Mam laid the pie in the centre of our round mahogany table. We all sat round it like a big happy family, yet we were nothing but a fragile piece of China waiting to crack. Peter's innocence was nothing but annoying, Dad's protective care towards Mam and me felt peculiar and strained, and Mam's face was hard behind her smiles.

"Here's the letter that was sent to you, Pet." Dad handed me a small thin envelope as Mam cleared the table. "Could be good news," he said with a smile.

"Maybe, I will open it later." I stood up from my chair and all six eyes stopped and looked at me. "I am going out for a walk."

"Can I come?" Peter asked.

"Not today, Peter. Another day. I am just going to get some fresh air."

Mam hurried into the kitchen with her hands full of plates and Dad lit a cigarette. "Be back for tea."

"I will."

I was out the house like a flash and found as I felt the air hit my face that it washed over me like a blanket and felt like I had just taken my first breath. I had no plan of where I was going but found myself heading to the allotment. I felt like my feet were taking me there without my brain sending any signals. As though they just knew where they wanted to go themselves.

As I approached the familiar garden, I noticed two figures were attending to the vegetable patch. Mr Flint was hunched over, and beside him holding a spade was Henry.

What am I doing? I thought to myself. I didn't even want to be there. I wanted to be home in my room away from everything and everyone. I turned to head back home.

"Lottie!" Damn! Henry had spotted me. "Lottie, don't go!" Henry ran out of the garden, and I heard his steps quicken behind me as I quickened my pace. "Lottie! Please stop!" he shouted.

I looked over my shoulder and he began to run, my goodness did I run for it. I ran past a puzzled Mrs Blake, I ran down the narrow lane leading back to the houses. It wasn't until I had passed Mr Flint's house did Henry reach out and grab my arm having caught up.

"Just stop for God's sake, Lottie!" He was angry when he spun me round to look at him.

I hadn't felt his touch in a while, his warm hands sat on each of my shoulders. His blue eyes stared at me with a look of care and concern.

"Why are you avoiding me?" he asked.

"I'm not," I quickly replied. A lie of course.

"Yes, you are, every time I call round you won't see me, the other night you didn't want to talk either."

"You woke me up."

"You are avoiding me, and I don't know why. I know your upset, Lottie. What's happened is really shit I get it, but you don't have to hide away and cope on your own. There are people that care about you. I care."

"How is caring going to help anybody?" I could hear my voice get snappy and I sounded like a real bitch, but it was coming out like vomit. "No care in the world is going to make this go away."

To my alarm Henry laughed.

I pulled down his hands off my shoulders. "Why are you laughing?" I angrily asked him.

"You are making me laugh. *Nothing is going to make this go away*. You're right no care, nothing will bring Florence back, but it bloody helps."

"Well, I don't need help. Not from you, not from anyone."

"You don't mean that, Lottie."

"Stop calling me that! That is not your nickname to give me. That is hers. That is what she calls me. Not you!" Anger was building inside of me now and tears blurred my vision. "I'm going home, Henry."

"Lot- Charlotte." Henry jumped in front of me. His hands now reached for both of my own, despite wanting to run far away from him as fast as possible I allowed him to take them.

"I'm sorry for laughing, that was inconsiderate. I just... I just want to be there for you." He leaned his forehead against my own and wiped away my tears, my body was stiff under his fingers. He gripped my hands again tightly, keeping me with him. "I know your hurting, please let me be there for you, just like you were there for me," he said softly.

My anger subsided as he slowly drew me in closer to his body and embraced me with both arms, a tsunami of tears took over my body and I surrendered to him. My knees gave way and Henry caught me just as I collapsed to the floor. He slowly lowered me down to the ground and held me like a mother would hold a weeping child, or a grandmother would hold a weeping grandchild. I don't know how long Henry and I sat on the floor like that. My fingers were gripped onto his shirt and my tears had soaked his neck. As I wailed, Nana filled my head, her face, her laugh, her voice, her singing. Memories quickly flashed by like a broken film reel. She was gone I told myself. She was really gone.

"Henry." A voice I knew only too well quietly approached. "Bring the Lass inside. I'll put the kettle on."

Mr Flint's front room had truly been neglected since I had stopped coming round to clean. Letters lay unopened at the front door. The couch was filled with packets of seeds, newspapers, and empty cigarette packets. The table had many empty stained tea mugs desperate for a wash. Mr Flint as always was unaware of the untidiness and got on with what he said right away with putting the kettle on. I only hoped the mugs he was planning to use were not like the ones left on the table.

Henry made a space for us on the couch and lay what felt like a protective arm around me.

"I am sorry, Henry. You're right I have been avoiding you." I twined my fingers with his. "I knew you would be kind to me, and kindness feels hard to accept at the moment. I don't know why."

"It's fine. I get it." He kissed the top of my head unexpectedly. I thought about kissing him back, but the thought disappeared as Mr Flint slowly walked in with a plate of digestive biscuits.

Not once did Mr Flint ask me how I was, and I was grateful for it. He never mentioned my nana, who I know meant a great deal to him. He never offered me advice as people often tend to do when they have lost someone. He acted as though I had just popped round for tea and biscuits on a normal August afternoon. Therefore, I love him. He told me about how well the vegetables have turned out this year and how his tomatoes were the biggest yet. He told me how he was thinking about growing rhubarb and possibly even fruit. The longer I stayed the more normal it began to feel. It wasn't until I returned home this evening back to my room with its fresh clean sheets that I realised how much going out had helped. I had locked myself with my grief in a prison of my own bedroom without realising, now I had found a new escape. I had to get out.

Chapter Nine

7th September 1957

Ever since I was little, I knew what I wanted in life. I can't remember a time when I didn't know. I had it all mapped out, I was going to write. I was going to be a brilliant author and write children's books and they would be loved by children all over the world. I would move in with Nana when school was finished, and my bedroom would have my published books up on a shelf. In the day I would write and in the evenings me and Nana would go to the theatre in the West End and have tea at the Ritz. My life would be filled with the noise of the busy city, and I too would be just as busy with new friends who were other authors and famous poets. Every day would be exciting.

Now my life is in the same routine day after day. The letter sent to me was not from a publisher but from the library informing me that my job was still there for me once I was ready to return.

I no longer wish to be confined to my room. I am afraid that the demons in my head will trap me in with my own thoughts once more. Thoughts that frighten me, thoughts of the past, thoughts of the future and thoughts of what could have been. Instead, each day I get up and take Peter to school before heading to work at the library, I have taken on more shifts now that it is to be a more permanent job position. Then in the evenings I visit Mr

Flint with Henry or Henry and I go out for a walk until my curfew. The next day is the same routine, as is the day after that and the day after that. This is my life now. There are no fancy shows or the Ritz, there is no publishing deal. I am a librarian, one day I will be a wife — perhaps even Henry's — and then a mother and that will bring a new routine. A new cycle to my life.

I can't help but feel frightened by that.

1st December 1957

It's been a while I know; I just haven't wanted to write really. What do I write?

Peter was being picked on at school, so I had it out with the bully's mam. Mam was embarrassed and said I can't take Peter to school for a while now until everyone *forgets* about it.

I went to work at the library. We have new stock. My colleague, Evelyn, has a new boyfriend, Jim the builder.

Went to the allotments, a fox has been sniffing around or some other creature. Everyone's gardens keep getting eaten.

Henry and I went for a walk. It began to rain so we headed back home early. He leant me his jacket to put over my head. He is sweet.

There you go. My day and my life in a nutshell.

Goodbye.

4th December 1957

To my delight Carol popped by this evening. Once my mam was out of ear shot us girls got to chat.

"So, you and Hollister. How's it going?" Carol asked with a childish giggle.

"What do you mean?" I asked, suddenly feeling rather embarrassed.

"Oh, come on Charlotte, you are with him all the time. I hear you're like a married couple already. Tell me, is he a good kisser? Has he asked you to be his girlfriend yet?" Carol sat there, eyes wide open, waiting for my response.

I didn't quite know what to say. Me and Henry were not kissing like crazy lovers, like Molly does with every guy she gets with. We are taking it slow. He is a gentleman. He treats me with respect, he walks me home in the evenings and holds my hand when we go out for walks. He makes sure I'm warm when it's cold and he makes me laugh. When we do kiss though it's in private and its soft and gentle and I get butterflies every time. Just thinking about it made me want to leap off the sofa and go next door.

"So, tell me, is Hollister a good kisser?" Carol impatiently asked again.

"I have no complaints," I said giving her a coy look.

She gave a squeal. "Wow, you, and Hollister, who would have thought. So, my other question, are you his girlfriend then?"

This question stirred something inside me, for this topic has never come up before and it was not until that moment that I thought of it. Me and Henry first kissed back in July, that was 5 months ago. Should he have asked me by now? Should I ask him about it?

"We're just taking it slow," I responded.

"Oh well, least you have someone. Unlike me." I was pleased by her satisfied response even though I wasn't, and still am, not as satisfied with the whole boyfriend/girlfriend thing. "I tell you who is looking hot these days, Henry's brother!" Carol continued.

"Joe?"

"Yes! Oh, have you seen him in that leather jacket on his new motorcycle? Yum."

"Wow, Carol. Really, Joe? Believe me you do not want to go there. He is bad news."

Carol pretended to be in a daze humming, "Hmm."

I playfully hit her on the arm. "No, Carol. NO! NO! NO!"

Since our little episode when Joe returned home, I hadn't spoken to him at all. Henry and I avoided hanging out at the Hollister's when Joe was around, and he spent most of his evenings out.

"He is up to no good," Walter would sadly tell us as he sat up waiting for his oldest son to come home night after night. He always did return, sometimes in the morning, sometimes a day or two later or in the back of a police car. Although he made Walter angry, the man couldn't help but worry and get himself into a state each time Joe didn't make it back home. Henry suggested they changed the locks and see how Joe felt then, but Walter said he was worried how Joe would retaliate.

"There is a dance on at the community hall on Saturday. Molly and I are going. Please come along. We haven't done anything together for ages," Carol pleaded, giving me her best bottom lip pout. Dancing really was not my strong point.

"Oh, I don't know."

"Please, Charlotte. Henry can come along too. It starts at half six. Please come."

"I will think about it."

"Fantastic! Oh, it will be so much fun. Music, dancing, boys. Molly went to one last month and she said many of the people there were much older. You never know I may get to dance with an older man, Miss Ridley." She gave me a wink that made me laugh.

"You do know you sound extremely desperate, Carol," I admitted.

"Hey!" she said, hitting me. "We don't all have cute boyfriends you know. Right, I best be off. See you on Saturday."

"I haven't said I'm coming yet."

"You'll be there. Bye Mrs Ridley," she called out to my Mam.

"Bye Carol!" Mam shouted back from the kitchen.

Boyfriend. Was Henry my boyfriend?

8th December 1957

"Please come to the dance?" I asked for the hundredth time, furiously Henry's answer remained the same as it had all week. No. "Not even for me," I said trying to guilt trip him. "I'll be dressed up all pretty."

"You're already pretty."

"Oh, Henry, please come. I want to go with you."

"I'm sorry Lottie, but like I've said already the community hall dance is not for me. I don't need to go to the local hall to dance with my girl."

The words *my girl* gave my heart a little somersault. I hadn't yet asked Henry if I was his girlfriend, I hadn't found the moment or the courage to ask. I felt silly and felt that if I were his girlfriend then he would have told me so already.

"We never do anything exciting though," I winged tugging at his overalls. We were at Walter and Sons, and I had been begging Henry while he worked for ages now and was getting nowhere with it.

"We went to the cinema last night, was that not fun?" Henry asked giving me confused glances over a piece of wood he was sanding down. I felt bad but the truth was I wanted more than a trip to the cinema.

"Of course, it was lovely, but we've done that before. Dancing, however, we have not. I want to show you off to my friends, I want to have you twirl me across the dance floor."

Henry put down his tools and walked over to a

busy work bench and turned up the volume on a dusty radio. He began to tap his feet and swayed over to me slowly before grabbing hold of my waist, sawdust instantly stuck to my coat like a magnet.

"You wish to dance, Miss Lottie."

Henry waltzed me round the workshop. He is a fool. It wasn't long before the small workshop had us bumping into stools and tables and what not. Walter came out from the back and chuckled as he watched us trying to avoid everything in our way as he twirled me around the room in hysterics.

"So, you'll come?" I asked him again.

Henry stopped abruptly, "I really don't want to go."

"Fine, I won't go either," I said in a strop.

"No, that's not fair. You should go, it will be nice for you to have some fun with Carol and Molly. Have some *girl time*," he quoted.

"He's right, Charlotte. Go and let your hair down; be good to get away from this one." Walter pointed to his son.

"But not for too long," Henry smiled.

Half six on the dot me, Carol and Molly entered the community hall. I wore a white off the shoulder dress with a big puffy skirt and let my hair fall in curls. I borrowed some pink lip gloss from Molly and also wore some small kitten heels that she insisted would look good on me. I had to admit they did look cute; I however did not look so cute trying to walk in them.

"I bet Henry wishes he came now," Carol teased as we entered arm in arm. "He has no idea how good you look right now."

"Why didn't he want to come, Charlotte?" Molly asked.

"He had to do some overtime at work," I lied. I don't know why I lied but I didn't want to tell my friends that my maybe boyfriend refused to come even though I begged him to.

"Oh well, we don't need boyfriends tonight girls." Molly ran immediately to the dance floor and began to let out a jig. Carol and I sat ourselves down at a nearby empty table. We were not as confident as Molly was. We chatted amongst ourselves and tapped our feet to the beat of the music. Carol scanned the room on the hunt for *a man*.

"Oh my, Charlotte, look who Molly's dancing with now. Isn't that Joe?" Molly had her arms draped round Joe deep in conversation. He was head to toe in black from his shiny shoes to his leather jacket and his hair had enough lacquer in it to dish out to the whole of Durham. Molly looked over the moon as he guided her around the room easily bringing her body close to his. "I know you said he was bad news but come on you have to admit he is bloody gorgeous," Carol gushed.

"Carol! He's Henry's brother."

"And, you have eyes right. Oh, they're coming over." Carol quickly fixed up her hair and gazed at Joe Hollister in a way that made me feel sick.

"I need a drink," Molly gasped, heading over to the

drinks table.

Joe sat down behind me and moved his chair close to mine. I hadn't spoken to him since he was inches from my face seconds away from kissing him. I felt the hair on my skin prick up as he leaned in to speak to me in my ear.

"You look beautiful tonight. Just like a swan." I looked down at my white dress then looked forward again, watching the dance floor. "Molly said Henry was too busy to come out tonight. My brother is an idiot."

I spun round to face him. "Don't speak of Henry like that."

Joe laughed. "Woah, I'm sorry. I just meant he is an idiot to not accompany a pretty girl like you. If you were my girl, I wouldn't let you out my sight."

"Is that so?" I asked as he slumped back into his chair lighting a cigarette. He had a big smirk on his smug looking face.

"It is. What's the little weasel doing then?" Joe asked.

"Nothing, he's at home. He...he didn't want to come," I admitted, feeling gutted with the truth.

Joe shook his head. "You both serious then?"

"What do you mean?" I asked coyly.

"Are you together?"

"They are taking it slow; Henry hasn't asked her to be his girlfriend yet, but I think he will soon," Carol butted in from across the table, regrettably once I shot an evil glance at her.

Joe was smiling even more so now. "Wow, I'm surprised. You two have been hanging out for months

117

now. Like I said before he's an idiot. Maybe you need someone who knows your worth, someone who would snap you up in an instant."

I tutted and turned back around. "Want to dance Carol? We did after all come here for that."

"Yeah, course. See ya, Joe."

I grabbed Carol's hand and together we rocked the dance floor, shortly joined by Molly. The rock and roll music played song after song, and I worked up quite a sweat. In the corner of my eye, I could see Joe who was now stood at the back of the hall with his friends, staring at me. I pretended I did not notice that his eyes were piercing across the floor to meet me. Part of me felt uncomfortable and very conscious of every move I made. His look was almost intimidating, yet I found that I also rather enjoyed it. There was something about being watched by him that I secretly liked.

My white dress swished and lifted as I spun around and felt the music play. At seven-thirty a band performed and as they played Frankie Lymon's, '*Why do fools fall in love,*' Molly spun me round right into the arms of Joe. His hands gripped my waist tight, and I tried to pull away from him, but his grip was hard.

"Joe, let go of me," I said in almost a whisper.

Joe didn't let go of me, instead he just stared right at me. "Dance with me."

"No," I replied immediately.

"Yes, you must."

"Why must I?"

"Because I'm not leaving tonight until you do."

His grip on my waist slowly relaxed, his hands gently moving along the sides of my torso before stroking along my arms, until each of my hands were in his. I felt fixated to the spot, my heart raced as I felt his touch, it was exciting and wrong. His eyes never left mine. Joe spun me round and with a firm grip held on to my hands during the fast-paced songs and pulled me in close during the slow ones, close enough to smell his cologne, close enough to feel his breath on my neck, close enough to know that if Henry was to walk through the double doors of the hall right now that fists were sure to be flying once more. Maybe I hoped for Henry to come through the doors and see us, maybe then he would see how not only do I need care, but I also need a little excitement too, he should have been the one that I danced with tonight…all night. Maybe he would shout at his brother to get off his girlfriend and sweep me off my feet in front of everyone.

"Thank you and goodnight!" the band called out just before nine, the lights of the hall coming on; a sign that the night was over. I let go of Joe without a second glance and headed over to Molly and Carol who were retrieving their handbags.

"Let's go, now," I demanded, hoping to leave as fast as I could.

Molly laughed. "He lives next door to ya, Lass."

"All you did was dance with him, Charlotte it's hardly a crime, at a dance as well," Carol said looking at my

alarmed face. "Bloody hell man, come on then."
I clung to their arms linked in between them, they felt
like a security blanket to me. I dared to look back at
him, at Joe.

We sang songs that had played throughout the night and
for the first time in ages I felt genuinely happy, the night out
had been a great idea.

"Oh, I don't want the night to end yet," I moaned. "I'm
having so much fun."

"Well, if you don't want the night to end just yet, I
do know where an after party is being held," Molly
teased.

"What? Where?" I asked intrigued.

"Down by the abandoned farmhouse just outside the
village, they have parties there all the time."

"How do you know this?" Carol asked.

"I've been a few times with this guy I was dating. It is
pretty insane. We can go if you like."

"I think I'm good, my dad would kill me," Carol said.

"Charlotte?" Molly asked me. As I looked down the
street, I could see light in my front room window and knew
my own dad would go ballistic if I went out late, yet I
wanted to go. I wanted to do something insane.

"Mine would kill me too," I said with a sigh. "But I so
want to go."

Molly smiled. "Give me a second I have an idea."
Molly ran towards my house and knocked on the door.

"What is she doing?" I thought out loud.

Within seconds my dad was at the door and words were

exchanged, a glance towards me and Carol and then my dad closed the door again and Molly raced towards us beaming.

"And she shall go to the ball!"

"What did you just do?" I asked Molly.

"Asked your dad if you could stay over at mine for the night. You're welcome."

It was deceiving I know, but I was beyond excited at this point. It was around ten past nine and the night was still young. "Do you want us to do the same for you Carol?" I asked.

Carol looked the opposite to me right now and shook her head. "I'm happy to call it a night."

"Ok, well we will walk you home first," I told her, turning right on the corner we stood on, to walk towards Carol's place.

The farmhouse sat on the outskirts of our minor village, from the north you couldn't enter without passing the decaying walls of what was once a living home before the war brought bombs to its roof and left it to rot as no one had declared it theirs. Now it was left abandoned in the open, for young teenagers to meet up and let their hair down away from strict parents, away from boring day to day life and dead-end futures.

It was quite a big farmhouse and inside of the remains I was surprised to find fires burning for warmth in the December cold and tartan blankets scattered around the place. The open roof had surprised me, and it wasn't long before I felt the chill reach my shoulders.

"Molly!" a guy happily called from the corner of the room. "You haven't been round for a while. It's good to see you. Ben isn't here if that's what you were hoping for," the guy said, he had a bit of stubble and was wearing a blue checked shirt.

"Ben who?" Molly and the guy laughed. "No, I just came to have some fun with my girl, Charlotte. What do we have tonight?"

The guy smiled and guided us to a small wooden table at the back of what I believed may have been the kitchen of the old home. On the table lay bottles upon bottles of different alcoholic drinks in bottles of all shapes and sizes.

"Take your pick ladies. We have glasses over here. We have vodka, gin, wine, beer. Go for it, take what you like. By the way, welcome Charlotte, I hope you have a good night."

"Th-ank…thank you," I stumbled. "That's very kind."

The young guy saluted us like a solider would before going off to battle and left the room.

"Who the hell was that?" I asked Molly.

Molly chuckled. "Oh, that's Ed, he organises these parties. He's been arrested like five times for having illegal parties, yet he just keeps on planning them. He's lovely, honestly. Right, what would you like?"

My experience of alcohol didn't reach any further than a sneaky bottle of wine shared between four at Cathleen's wedding. However, it didn't take me long to figure out just what I wanted to taste first. "I'll have a gin please," I said reaching for an empty glass.

"Ok, one gin coming up. Oh, I do wish Carol had come with us. She is missing out," Molly said as she poured me and herself a glass of gin.

"I know, but you know what her dad is like." Carol's dad was a strict man. He had big ideas of how and what Carol should do with her life. Her freedom to do as she pleased, such as visiting friends and going to community parties, was limited to curfews. These curfews were to be met always, if she disobeyed, she would be punished. Unlike my dad, Carol's dad had been equally as strict before the War so we can't blame the Germans for that one. Molly passed me my drink and with a clink of our glasses we took a big gulp. The clear liquid felt like fire travelling down my throat.

"Jesus Christ!" I called out, looking round for a drink of water. "God Florence," I found myself saying. "Why the fuck was that your go to?"

Molly laughed her head off as I gathered myself together. "You'll get used to it. I promise."

The next few swigs were no better and may even have resulted in a few curse words towards my dear nan even though she had nothing to do with anything tonight. Even though the liquid burned my throat and chest, each sip seemed to get easier, as Molly had mentioned, and with the next glass in my hand, I could feel the effects. My head felt lighter as well as my body. I felt like if I stopped still long enough my soul would float away, separating me from my flesh and slowly sway through the clouds. I felt like all my thoughts and worries about Henry, Nana, my job, my future, and everything in between disappeared. I was just a young girl in a fire lit room full of amazing happy people, having a drink with my good friend and some new kind people, relaxed and eager to have some fun. People played music on guitars and others sang and danced. Drinks were flowing, cigarettes lit up in dark corners of the night and a tartan blanket warmed my shoulders in the chilly night. Molly introduced me to people she knew, and they immediately made me feel part of the party, taking my hand for dances, sharing new drinks with me, and together having a good laugh. I looked over to Molly who was deep in conversation with a red-haired girl and mouthed, "thank you." Molly understood perfectly and blew me a kiss.

The night had blown me away. I remember stumbling to the drinks table for another gin when there leaning across the table casually was Joe Hollister.

"Having fun?" he asked.

"Yes, yes I am," I said, as I poured myself a glass and spilling some onto the table in the process. "Oh shit," I said, giggling to myself.

Joe watched me and smiled. A cigarette in his hand. "You ran off from me tonight."

"I didn't," I responded, wiping up the spillage with the woolly blanket.

"I think you'll find you did," he smiled.

I laughed even though it wasn't funny. "Yeah, yeah I did run off from you."

"Why?" he asked.

"Because," I said, taking a swig of my gin.

"Because what?" he asked.

I laughed again and walked out the kitchen. I suddenly began to feel my chest becoming hot and uncomfortable and needed to feel some air. I left the farmhouse and took in the cold air of the night. Outside, I leant against a stone brick wall. My breath deepened to try and take over the pain that sat on my chest.

"Fuck!" I shouted out loud rubbing my chest.

"Charlotte, Charlotte are you ok?" Joe had followed me out.

"My chest, it feels tight," I breathed in and out heavily. Joe removed the gin from my hand and chucked it out onto the grass.

"I think you have heartburn."

"Heartburn?" I asked, puzzled I had never had heartburn before.

Joe held my shoulders and told me to breathe in and out slowly. "It will pass," he told me. "If not, I can get you some water. Milk is what you need really but there is fat chance of that being here. Even water may be out of our depth really. Just breathe."

I breathed, in and out, in and out. Slowly until the tight feeling in my chest began to subside.

"Better?" Joe asked.

I nodded. "Yeah, God that was painful," I grabbed my empty glass from the ground. "I best fill this up," I said cheerfully.

"Whoa, I don't think you should," Joe said, guarding the entrance back into the house.

"Joe, I want a drink, let me past."

"I think you've had enough."

His words immediately made me feel annoyed. "Well, you're not my parent and tonight I am going to do whatever I like." I tried to push past him, but his broad shoulders held me back. "Joe!" I shouted.

"Why do you want more?" he asked me. "Have you not had enough already? You've been here longer than me and I know I'm pissed."

"No, I have not," I said, stumbling on the spot.

"How do you feel?" Joe asked me.

I stared at him, I tried to give him a serious look, but it didn't last long for I began to laugh and leaned into him, wrapping my arms around his neck. "I feel alive!" I smiled. "I feel like I can do whatever I like. I feel like I can be whoever I like."

Joe held onto my waist to support my leaning body on his. I leaned my head against his foolishly yet at the same time I felt that it was what I wanted to do.

"Kiss me," I whispered.

I felt Joe's fingers search my body, his hands touched me everywhere, yet his lips never found mine. "Not here. Not like this," he whispered. "You don't really want to kiss me."

"Fine, I'll find someone else," I said walking away from him back to the house. Joe grabbed my arm and pulled me back towards him.

"Let's get out of here," he said smoothly. "There is somewhere I want to show you." He walked away and I found myself following him like a sheep might follow a sheepdog. I followed him away from the house to a small, cobbled area — there stood Joe's motorcycle, the body of it glistened in the moonlight. He sat himself down on the front seat and handed me his helmet.

Although I felt I was still a little stumbly on the feet, in that moment I felt like, for the first time, I had control of my body and my decisions.

"Take it," Joe pleaded. "Get on, believe me. You're gonna love it." I reluctantly put on the helmet and looked behind me towards the farmhouse. "We will come back, I promise," Joe insisted starting up the engine.

I must have been crazy drunk; I don't know, but I put the helmet on and jumped onto the back of Joe's bike. At first it felt nerve wracking and I clung onto him for dear life as he came out of the drive and onto the main road. It was late and we met no other vehicles on our journey; it was just Joe and I on the road. I found that I began to relax a little and surprisingly found I was actually enjoying the ride. I screamed loudly in delight into the darkened December night. I felt Joe's body ripple as he laughed before me. The chilly air was forced onto my face as was the small welcome of sleet. To protect my face, I buried it into Joe's back.

He drove until we reached a hill only about fifteen minutes away from the farmhouse and he parked at the foot of it. I placed the helmet onto the top end of his vehicle and took Joe's open hand. "Come," he instructed, and together we walked up the hill until we reached the very top, and there my breath was taken away. My hand was still in Joe's and below us was a sea of yellow lights.

"It's Durham," Joe said.

"It's beautiful," I replied. We sat down on the cold blades of grass and huddled close together.

"I come up here all the time, just to get away from everything," Joe explained playing with a blade of grass. "It's quiet up here, it allows me to think better."

I nodded in understanding as I looked out to the town centre where life was busy and thriving still, somewhere at least, even at the hour that we were sat there.

"I can't do what Henry does; I can't carry on with life as normal. I need something else, something extra," he continued. "I could be wrong, but I feel like you need that too. I saw you tonight, I feel like I could see that you too needed something more, something out of the ordinary."

I was taken back by Joe's assumptions. Joe leaned into my face that had been nestled close beside him and carefully stroked my cheek, wiping away a tear that I had not planned on releasing, yet it had.

"Tell me if I am wrong," he said in a whisper.

It took me what felt like a long moment, but in my state of mind it may easily have been a mere few seconds, before I grasped Joe's hands and tangled our fingers together, answering, "You're not wrong."

I met Joe's gaze, and this time I predicted what was going to happen next, or had I wished it, I am not a hundred percent sure but what I do remember is that Joe kissed me. This was no gentle kiss either. This was a passionate kiss, an urge even. Not just on his part either, for I felt the urge too. I wanted it just as much as he did. It all happened so fast, but I remember my tongue touching his, his lips touching mine. His hands reaching for my face, my hair, even as mine reached for his. Joe then grasped my back and lowered his body onto mine causing me to lay down onto the frozen grass beneath me.

Joe's heavy body was on top of me; I held him closer not wanting any gap between us at all. His lips covered my neck, my shoulders, and the small line where my dress sat on my chest in heavy kisses. Each one made my body ache for more. Each one sent an adrenaline rush through me that told me that I wanted Joe. As his lips met mine once again his hands reached for my neck delicately.

"God, I want you; I want you so bad," Joe whispered. I found that I was gasping for air. Gasping for air from the passion.

"I want you too," I replied.

So, he took me there and then on the small hill looking over the lights of Durham, and I let him, I wanted him to. I let Joe Hollister take me like a man takes a woman. How a husband may take his wife, and it was magical underneath the stars.

Small butterfly kisses woke me in the morning, and I found that I was wrapped heavily in blankets in a corner of Mr Flint's allotment shed with Joe

Hollister's mouth all over my skin. It took me a
moment to take everything in, the fact that I was laying
there with Joe and the events of the previous night
flashed in my mind like fragments of a smashed
mirror. So many emotions took hold of me, the first
and foremost was guilt. I had betrayed Henry, whether
he saw me as his girlfriend or not. Henry is so dear to
me, and I love being around him, I love how he takes
care of me. Then I felt excited and a little nervous,
would Joe want us to be intimate again, would he kiss
me like he did the night before, like I've never been
kissed before? Henry kisses me tenderly, each time
like he is frightened he will hurt me, with the softest
lips and a devoted manner; whereas Joe kisses me like
he is desperate to have me, like our lives depend on it.
Then lastly, I felt like I had been bashed across the
head with one of Mr Flint's large clay plant pots
stacked up beside me.

When we returned to the farmhouse last night the police
were getting everyone out so me and Joe escaped to the
allotment, a place of sanctuary to many.

"How do you feel?" Joe asked me in between the many
kisses across my bare shoulders.

"Like I've swallowed sand," I replied.

Joe stopped to laugh. "It's all part of the parcel I'm
afraid. You feel wild and free for the night and then you
feel like death the next day. As it's your first, you are
going to feel rough all day."

"Really? All day?" I already wanted the pain to go,

every movement felt as though I was going to throw up, as for my head... I felt like it was glued to the floor, it felt that heavy.

"We should get you home, you need your rest for tonight."

"Tonight?"

"I thought we could go out on the bike, there's a place in Chester-Le-Street I want to take you to."

"I don't think so Joe, what will I tell my parents? I can't lie again."

"Don't worry I will have you back by nine. I'll pick you up at five, that gives you plenty of time to sleep."

"Where are we going? What do I wear?"

"Where anything you like, you always look beautiful."

I felt myself blush at the compliment.

So here I am ready in Molly's heels, a knee length navy dress with a Peter Pan collar and buttons all the way down the front and a little bit of my mam's red lippy. She only ever wears it on special occasions so won't notice. With everyone out I am going to leave a note for Mam and Dad telling them I've popped out with Molly and Carol. Joe is meeting me on the corner of the street. Silly really, when we are neighbours, but I don't wish for Henry to see us, not until I explain things to him. Joe was a little peeved about it but it's the only way I'm going to go with him, so he agreed. Henry called on me about an hour ago, most likely to find out how my night with the girls went. I didn't answer, I can't face him just yet. My heart feels burdened every time I think about him. I don't deserve him at all. He means the world to me, but I don't know — what I did was not right, but it felt exhilarating and the thought of spending the evening sat in Mr Flint's front room yet again feels tedious. Henry detests his brother, so I know what I have done is unforgivable even more so, not just in his eyes but also if anyone found out I would be frowned upon, but committing a sin felt adventurous! Joe didn't seem to judge me for it either, his sweet kisses this morning told me that. I will have to break the news to Henry sooner rather than later. It is going to be so hard, I know that, and like I said, he doesn't deserve any of this; he is the most genuine person I know and without him I would have struggled. Maybe I am making a mistake after all — Henry has done nothing wrong and the thought of him hating me hurts, however, the unknown of what this evening may bring is intriguing. I feel so grown up and overly excited about where Joe is taking me, and truth be told I am looking forward to seeing him again. I best be off its five minutes to five now.

Chapter Ten

11th December 1957

Dead is what I am, well and truly dead. Mam and Dad have locked me in my bedroom, Henry won't talk to me, and Walter is beyond angry with Joe, actually everyone is angry with Joe.

When Joe took me out the other night it was a better night than I had anticipated, I have never felt so alive. We headed to a hidden bar beside the railway bridge in Durham. As I am underage, I imagined there was no way on earth that they would let me in, but Joe was friends with the bouncer at the door as well as the bartender and they just let me in, no bother, just like that. I felt like a grown up on a night out. I wondered if Mam and Dad used to go out to bars at one time, I know Nana and Grandad had many nights out in their early days. This bar was not like the type of bar that Dad and Walter visit on a Sunday afternoon down the road. This one was dark, there were no windows and a big stage at one end with a band playing and a great big, long black bar. The seats were blue and red velvet. Each wall painted black with dim red lights scattered around. The place quickly filled up and before I knew it, I was rubbing shoulders with lots of people on the dance floor with a gin in my hand.

"Welcome to my world!" Joe shouted above the music then smacked a kiss onto my lips.

I loved every moment of the night and met lots of Joe's friends; there was Ed from the farmhouse, Mark who I often see Joe hang around with and his girlfriend Kitty who looked like a model. She had long red hair tied into a ponytail, perfect make up and wore black cigarette capri trousers and a white blouse with a big pussy bow tied at the top. I envied her and was pleased to see her besotted with Mark, besides Joe never left my side all night. Then there was Pepe, an Italian whom I could barely understand a word of, but he was a smooth dancer.

We were having so much fun that we lost track of time and realised it was already half nine. We were on the other side of town, and I knew we would never get back at a reasonable time.

"Fuck it, let's stay," I said to Joe as he freaked over the time.

"Your dad will kill us both. I think he wants to punch me already."

"I will lie, I'll say I am at Carol's or something. Let's stay. I don't want to go; I want to stay here with you."

Joe smiled. "You're wild Charlotte, like me."

The note I left had told them that I was off to the cinema with the girls, I had a lot of explaining to do and tried to come up with a convincing story to cover my arse. Nothing however was going to prepare me for what happened when we did reach home.

Everyone, and I mean everyone, I know was hovering in and around my house. My parents, Walter, Mr Flint,

Cathleen, Rupert, Molly, Carol, and of course Henry, whose face is etched in my mind as he noticed me walk down the street with Molly's heels in one hand, side by side with Joe who looked as equally as rough as I know I did. It didn't take much to realise that we had been out together.

"She's here!" I heard him call out in a tone of voice that told me all I needed to know. He was pissed and I deserved whatever he thought of me now. I felt myself panic and all I could now see was Henry, and all I wanted to do was explain to him.

"Henry," I began, "we need to talk."

Henry shook his head and looked down at me like I was dirt on the bottom of his shoe. "No, I don't think we do, Lottie." There was a hiss in his voice, and it brought tears to my eyes as he proceeded to walk into his own house.

"Henry!" I called back about to follow him when I felt hands pull me back.

It was Joe. "Let him go Charlotte, he'll get over it."

However, I didn't want him to get over it. Despite my wild nights, and sin with Joe that my body thrived on, Henry had done nothing wrong, and I had hurt him just by hanging out with Joe. He didn't even know the half of it.

"Get off my daughter!" Dad pulled me off Joe. "Where the hell have ya been Lass?" he yelled. "We've been worried sick!"

"I was just…I was just out."

"She was with me, Frank. It's all my fault. I bumped into her and convinced her to come to a party. She didn't want to go, she knew you wouldn't allow it, but I told her I would get her home in time, but I got carried away with the time. Charlotte has been worried, but I was too drunk and then hungover to bring her home and she didn't know where she was to get home herself. Please, don't punish her, it was all my fault." Joe stood behind me with a protective hand on my shoulder, taking the blame.

My dad took a step forward. "I told ya to get off my daughter, if I didn't respect your dad so much, son, I would knock you off your feet. I never want to see you anywhere near her again, do you hear me?"

Joe didn't reply nor did I feel his hand slip off me if anything it gripped harder. He was heading for trouble. "I can't stop seeing her," he bravely said.

"You what? I wasn't asking ya; I was telling ya!" Dad pulled me away from Joe, pushing me towards my mam, who was stood at the front door. Everyone was out watching now, even Henry had come back out. I really wish he hadn't.

"Frank, I'll sort it," Walter said as he stepped between my dad and Joe before Dad could hurt him.

"I want him to stay away from Charlotte. She's a good kid and he's trouble, Walter. I won't have him taking advantage of her, she is still going through a grim time."

Henry glanced at me, if my mam had not had a grip of my hand, I would have run to him; then there was Joe who was being a muppet, yet kind of romantic. Like Romeo and Juliet.

"I know, I'll sort it. Joe get in," Walter tried to nudge his son towards the door, but he didn't move. "Joe, get in. Now!"

Joe looked over at me, I wasn't sure if it was the hangover, but his eyes were glistening, then he smiled at me. "I love you, Charlotte. This is not the end, I promise."

I didn't know how to react. Should I have said it back. Should I have told him that I loved him too? Should I have tried to get to him? I had never told Henry that I loved him, nor had he said it. How did you know if you were in love? When did feeling good and happy with someone become love? How was Joe sure of this already? If we had been alone my reaction would have been different; as I was not, I said nothing. Cathleen tutted. Henry shouted, "bullshit!" And Molly clapped, receiving an unpleasant look from my mam.

"Why don't I put the kettle on," Mr Flint said, heading indoors.

"Good idea, I'll come and help," Rupert followed.

"No games lad, if I see you two together, I will kill you," Dad pointed at Joe.

"Frank," Walter said, surprised at my dad's words.

"I mean it, Walter. Make sure he stays away. Mavis, get her inside."

I took a quick look at Joe who was still smiling smugly, and Henry who looked like he could be very capable of murder himself.

All evening I was fired questions from everyone and told

the same things over and over:

> *How could you be so stupid?*
> *Where did he take you?*
> *Where did you sleep?*
> *When did you become so irresponsible?*
> *You're only fifteen, you shouldn't be drinking.*
> *What if something happened to you?*
> *We've been looking everywhere.*
> *How could you be so selfish?*

The result was staying in my room until my shift at the library tomorrow and if I am caught going anywhere near Joe Hollister or any parties again then I can say goodbye to the little freedom I have left. I fear I have messed everything up between what was good with me and Henry. It wasn't until I saw him again that the thought of never speaking to him again frightened me, he holds a place in my heart that I can't describe; yet I've ran from him, far from him to a world I never dared to be part of but one that has pulled me in like a magnet. I have hurt him, I know this, and I hope I can make it up to him. I am just not sure how at the moment. As for Joe, he loves me. He said so himself in front of everyone and looked proud as punch. Do I love him? I have given myself so easily to him and it felt so right, it felt like a need, an explosion. Is that what love feels like?

16th December 1957

For the past week I have not entered the doors of the little
high street library, not even once, instead I walk to the
bus stop where Joe picks me up on his motorcycle and we
go anywhere but work or home. Sometimes we just drive
until we find a nice cosy cafe or pub to hide in, other days
we have hung out at his friend Mark's flat. I have loved
spending time with Joe, you never know what the plan
will be for the day, it is all spontaneous. The world is ours
he always tells me. He has a small job a couple of nights a
week at a pub in Chester-Le-Street, and sometimes he
works with Mark's oldest brother, David, I'm not sure
what it is that they do, Joe just says it is good money and
with the extra cash he can treat his girlfriend...me.

He always puts an arm around me when we walk and
kisses me at any opportunity. I love it when we pass girls
my age, he makes me feel like I have won the jackpot, he
is definitely a looker.

We had not done anything more than kiss since the
night of the party, but I wanted to. I wanted him to take me
in his naked arms and have me again. Not a night has
passed by that I have not thought of it, reliving it in my
mind. Joe has not mentioned it, but I'm not too worried as
his actions show that he is into me, and he tells me he
loves me every day.

"I love you too," I whispered back a few days ago
when we parted ways behind the community hall away
from our lane. His smile could have lit up all of Durham

during a power cut. When I was not with him, I yearned
for the next touch, the next kiss it was torturous lying
each night with a wall between us. As for Henry he will
not even look in my direction. Joe said it is his loss
because he did not make me his nor did he fill my world
with excitement as he ought to. I do miss his company,
but I will not stop spending time with Joe, which I know
he will ask me to do, plus how can I be a friend to Henry
now when all I want to do is run to his brother's bed, not
sit around in Mr Flint's allotment with cups of tea and
iced buns. I need more than that and Joe gives me just
that. Today we were walking around the city centre of
Newcastle, a home game at St. James Park was playing so
the town was heaving. We travelled by bus as it looked
like it may snow.

"What would you like to do?" Joe asked, tucking my
gloved hand under his own linking us together. "We can go
and have lunch, take a walk along the Quayside."

"I want you," I replied more boldly than I had
anticipated.

He looked at me a little puzzled. "You have me baby."

"No, I mean I really, really want you. Like before on
the hill." Joe's eyes widened. "But if you don't want to
that's fine."

I felt my cheeks heat up despite the gentle falling of
snow and began to head up Northumberland Street not
sure where I was heading. I heard Joe's heavy feet walk
behind my own. He didn't try to stop me or say anything
for that matter until we passed a phone box.

"Wait here," he instructed as he stepped into it with his back to me. I stood outside in the cold for what felt like ages before Joe stepped out of it and grabbed my hand hastily. "Let's go."

"Where are we going?" I asked, trying to keep up with his long legs, careful not to slip.

"Mark's place."

Joe hailed a passing taxi and we jumped into the warmth of the tin car leaving the city behind. Joe didn't say a word to me in the car, I had begun to worry that I had upset him somehow. He stared out the window and fondled with his zip on his coat.

Outside of Mark's house was Anthony, the middle brother of the three, finishing off a cigarette, he smirked at Joe. "You owe us, you soft shite."

Joe playfully thumped him on the arm before we headed inside, the flight of stairs leading to the flat was immediately before us. David poked his head out of the living room upon hearing us. "They're here, Mark!" he shouted.

Mark popped his head out of another room from the far end of the landing. "All good," Mark said appearing from the room, closing the door behind him. At this point I was so confused as to what was happening, why we were there and what everyone was talking about.

"Thanks," Joe said. He turned to look at me and held my hand gently in his.

"Right then, well we will just be in the pub round the corner, you have got two hours max love birds,"

David said, grabbing his coat off the hook.

"He only needs about ten minutes," Mark chuckled, also grabbing a coat. "Have fun." With that the brothers headed out laughing.

"Next rounds on you, Hollister!" David called up the stairs before the door slammed behind them.

"Right, what's happening?" I asked Joe the minute they left.

Joe took off his coat and hung it up and then began to undo the buttons of my own coat and slowly removed it not taking his eyes off my own. A feeling of urge from deep inside me exploded as his lips pressed down onto mine dropping my coat on to the floor as his hands reached for the frame of my body. "You said you wanted me," he whispered in between kisses.

"I do."

He suddenly stopped, his hands tangled in my hair, I looked up to him, his breath was rapid at that point. "I want you too, I've wanted you every day since the first, but I wasn't sure how you felt, and I didn't want to just do it anywhere. You deserve better than a grassy hill on a frosty night or an abandoned house. It should be special."

Joe kissed me gently and led me to the room that Mark had been in at the bottom of the corridor. As Joe opened it my first glance of the room was darkness until I saw the flickers of lights from the candles that had been lit on the chest of drawers and one on an old wicker stool.

"Are you sure you still want me? You don't have to. I know last time we had quite a bit to drink."

I took in the room, the thoughtful gesture, and the gorgeous lad beside me. I would be lying if I said I was not nervous — my legs had turned a little into jelly — but this is what I wanted, I had to feel that explosion again, I had to be close to Joe.

Now as I write this back at home, in my childhood bedroom that I feel I have now outgrown, I can't stop smiling. Joe was everything I imagined and afterwards we lay naked, tangled in bedsheets and each other. I can't wait for tomorrow.

20th December 1957

Never did I imagine that I would be climbing out of my bedroom window, but that is how I escaped my boredom, down to Joe's great plan.

"I thought you could pop in and see Mr Flint this morning," my mam said as she buttered some toast for Peter at the table. "You haven't been round for a while, I'm sure he needs some help."

"He has Henry now," I replied not looking up from my own plate of toast and scrambled egg.

"Cleaning is no job for a boy, Henry has other things to be doing. Walter and Henry have a lot on at work. Go and do as ya mam asks," Dad piped up.

I rolled my eyes, cleaning Mr Flint's gritty little house or hanging out with Joe. It's a no brainer.

"Can I come?" Peter asked me.

"No."

"Why? I like Mr Flint," Peter said with a mouthful of toast.

"Mr Flint's house is no place for little boys."

"Can we go to the library after then and pick some new books?"

"No."

"But I need new ones."

"You have loads, I brought some the other week for you."

"That was ages ago," Peter said. He may be right; I can't actually remember when I last brought him some new books. "You don't read to me anymore," he sulked.

Mam poured him some milk, "Now, now. Charlotte's been busy that's all. She will take you this afternoon."

"Yay!" Peter shouted shaking the table in excitement.

"What! I didn't agree to that," I exclaim. "I have plans."

"Like what?" Dad asked quickly.

"Like…writing and stuff." It was my turn to sulk.

"You can do that later. You have all day," Dad said not daring to look me in the eye. If he had he would have seen the rage in me. Mr Flint's house and the library? Besides how was I supposed to waltz into the library with Peter when I hadn't been there for bloody weeks?

"Finished Charlotte," Mam said looking down at my plate, eager to start tidying up. She removed it before I even answered, to be honest, no I was not finished and would have liked to have eaten more.

"Right, Mr Flint is expecting you at half nine. Your

dad is going to walk you there as he needs to pop to the shops."

I looked at Dad who put his folk down, a mouth full of food and another plate not yet finished. "Oh, yes. Come on then, Lass."

I chuckled to myself. Really, this is what it's come to, being baby sat and escorted to Mr Flint's in case I wonder off with Joe. Little do they know that me going off to *work* didn't keep me away from him either.

Mr Flint's was a pigsty. His smoking has increased dramatically, the ashtrays tell you that, and the stench of the place was enough to make me want to be sick. I had let myself in with the spare key and didn't know where to start. The table was covered in letters and newspapers amongst other things I sighed as I took in the bin outside filled to the brim.

"Jesus!" I said out loud.

"You know you shouldn't say the Lord's name in vain," Mr Flint said, entering the living room in his dressing gown and slippers. "Tea?" he asked.

"No thank you, I've just had one."

"Suit yourself," Mr Flint said putting on the kettle. "Was canny of you to come on your day off."

"I didn't have much choice," I said through gritted teeth. Mr Flint didn't answer, and I felt instantly guilty.

"How are you doing? Not seen you in a little while?" he called from the kitchen.

"Just work," I lied, beginning to pile up the letters sorting them into piles of importance and rubbish. There was a letter from his nephew with news of the family, an overdue electricity bill and a letter from his doctor enquiring about a missed appointment.

"How are you?" I flapped the doctor's letter in the air as he sat at the table with his tea placing it onto a copy of the Daily Times.

"Oh, that's nothing, I'm fine. Bin it," he replied.

I would, I thought, if I bloody had one. To make things even better, the door slammed shut and in came Henry his face snuggled into a big coat.

"Got your paper," he said to Mr Flint before realising I was there. He immediately dropped the newspaper on the table on top of the overflowing pile. "I will pop round later," he said, turning to leave again.

"Not so fast, Lad. Come on now, look at my mess, give Charlotte here a hand while I go and get dressed. It's about time you two cleared the air. That was a demand by the way." Mr Flint shuffled off upstairs leaving us behind in an awkward silence.

I returned to my papers not knowing what to say. I had already apologised endlessly, what more could I say to him. It was now up to Henry if he wanted to speak to me or not. He turned his attention to a pile of clothes that had piled up on a dusty chair by the window. We both got on with our jobs in silence, I looked over to him now and then. His face looked angry in its quiet state, his friendly expression replaced with one of hatred — no words needing to express it at all. It made an uncomfortable knot in my stomach as I stood close to him. It felt unnatural to not have him smile at me or allow me close to him in a warm embrace while he played with my hair twisting it round his finger as he often did — of course that would be strange for him to do so now. He never dared look at me and acted as though I was not there at all which hurt. I don't deserve Henry's kindness, but I do miss it. If I didn't already know of the rejection I would receive if I approached him, I would have given him a big hug and begged him to forgive me. In a moment's thought, as I watched him carefully fold up a white shirt, I thought I might be brave and give it a shot, not the hugging or the begging but the asking for forgiveness part for I had nothing to lose.

What could be the worst that could happen, he already had stopped speaking to me.

"Henry," I sounded like a mouse. I wasn't sure if he had even heard me. "Henry," I repeated a little louder. Henry carried on folding the clothes ignoring me. "I know you don't want to talk to me, and I get it, I've upset you massively. I can't take anything back, but I am so sorry, I really am. Maybe not now but one day I hope you could find it in your heart to forgive me. I miss you, Henry."

Henry then gave a little laugh. "I bet you don't miss me when you're shagging my brother."

The word struck me to the core. '*Shagging my brother.*' How would Henry even know such things?

"Don't say that."

"Why, it's true. There is no need to deny it, I share a room with him remember and he drinks…a lot. All his secrets spill."

I didn't know what to say; should I deny it and make out that Joe was lying or do I just lay down and admit defeat? I decided to go with the latter, too embarrassed to say anything more.

"Bit quiet over there, Lottie," Henry said looking at me for the first time. As our eyes met, I felt my eyes water.

"I'm sorry," was all I managed to say, feeling awful.

"Don't be, I have realised now that I had a lucky escape. No one wants a tart for a girlfriend now do they?"

"Henry!' I exclaimed, shocked by his words.

"Let's not pretend, you go out for one night with the girls and come back forty-eight hours later looking like a brass after a long night's work hanging off Joe's arm.'

"We didn't do anything," I defended.

"Ha didn't but not haven't," he tapped his nose. "Your secrets safe with me, little Lottie."

"Henry, it's not like that." I felt confused because I was apologising for something that I was now aware that he knew all about, yet I still couldn't admit it – I didn't want to believe that I was capable of hurting him like that. I quickly approached him, grabbing his arms. "Henry."

"Get your filthy hands off me!" he shouted, grabbing my wrist. "Don't you ever touch me again."

"I'm sorry Henry, I just want you to know that I'm really sorry. What can I do to make it better?"

"Better, there is nothing you can do to make it better.

You're a whore, Charlotte Ridley, and I am so glad that you are no longer mine."

I pulled my wrist away, anger replacing my sadness and guilt rather quickly. "Yours, I was never yours. You were never man enough to ask me to be yours."

"Really, are you kidding me?"

"No, not once did you refer to me as your girlfriend or take me out to meet your friends, or anything to show people that I was yours."

"This is a fucking joke right. You were my only friend! You and that old man upstairs. I didn't realise that I had to make a claim on you, that I had to pronounce to the world that you were my girlfriend, I thought my actions would have let you and any fucker else who wanted to know see what you meant to me."

"A little clarity would have been nice," I hissed.

"A little clarity." Henry walked away from me leaning on the littered table. I could feel his rapid breathing and noticed his clenched fists turn white as he squeezed them tight. "You know what, Charlotte. Fuck you. I'd have done anything for you and if you couldn't see that, then maybe Joe is the right lad for you."

He grabbed his coat, and my body was thrown into begging mode as I lunged forward grabbing his arm once more, he tried to shrug me off as I pleaded for him to stay and sort things out.

"Do one Charlotte, you've got what you want now, someone who wants to show you off, take you dancing, someone who takes you away from your boring life. The truth is, me and Mr Flint aren't good enough for you anymore. We never were, we were just here to fill the void until you moved away to live out your exciting life in London."

"That's not true!"

"But it is true and deep down you know it. One way or another you were going to leave me one day and forget all about me and you, like we never even happened. You want this big, exciting life and I don't fit the bill. Good luck is all I have left to say to you and goodbye."

Henry pushed me back with his arm, not needing to make much effort and slammed the door shut behind him, and I cried — my goodness did I cry. Pain gushed from everywhere, I cried for Henry, I cried for the state I had left the house in for Mr Flint, I cried for ignoring Peter, and I cried for my nana. The pain still feels as raw as ever, just as it has for a little while now, I have told myself that crying isn't good for me and I have to get on in life, like those around me, but today I couldn't and letting a release of emotions go for Henry led to a heap more pouring out from the gaps of the trap I had tried to hold them in. I hadn't even realised that Mr Flint was holding me, all I knew was that I had fucked up.

"Now, now, Lass. Let it all out now. You need to let it all out."

My body rocked slowly as Mr Flint rocked me back and forth like you would to sooth a crying baby and it brought comfort to me.

"I have made a mess of everything," I sobbed. "I am

sorry I haven't been around to help you."

"Oh, you have been missed, but you are not to be sorry. You've got a little lost that's all." Mr Flint's jumper smelt of tobacco and a slight tinge of mould, but I did not mind at all, for his words meant a great deal to me.

"Henry hates me. He thinks terribly of me."

"He doesn't hate ya Lass, the complete opposite in fact. I'm not gonna lie you've hurt him big, but he is nothing but miserable nowadays without you. Give him time he'll come round."

"You really think so?' I asked with so much hope.

"Of course, I do. There is something special about you two, that I know for sure."

I found that this made me smile but the smile didn't last long because the large figure of my dad stood outside the window with his face pressed up against the glass.

"Home! Now!" he shouted.

It didn't sound good, I remember thinking, and it really wasn't. While I had been over at Mr Flint's, back at my house I had a visitor. It was none other than Mrs Morgan enquiring about my health and letting my parents know that she felt that the position at the library was no longer suited for me as my attendance and attitude to work had slipped. Leaving her with no other choice but to hire someone to replace me. This left my parents confused and beyond angry. It also left me in big trouble. Dad pretty much dragged me home, I could barely keep up with him, my feet were dragged along the snow, he had a hold of me by the scruff of my neck as if I were five again.

"Get in!" he shouted as we reached home. Mam was sat on a chair by the fire knitting baby clothes for a baby that Cathleen was no longer having, in hope that she would someday. She had called round two days ago in tears that she had lost the baby. I hadn't known how to console her so left Mam to it as I escaped to my room to get ready for Joe. Mam gave me a disapproving look as I sat opposite her.

"Where have you been, Charlotte?" she asked quietly.

"Mr Flint's," I replied. I knew it wasn't a smart answer, but I didn't like how they were treating me and either way I was in trouble so I may as well try to fight my corner.

"Don't get cocky, Lass. Where have you been instead of work?" Dad asked while stood behind Mam's chair. Two against one.

"Just out and about," I replied.

"Just out and about?" Mam repeated.

"Yes, Mam. I haven't felt like going to work recently. I don't like it anymore. It's not for me, I need to find somewhere else."

"Oh, so your job hunting now," Dad said. "You know I didn't want to go to war, but I did. Your Cathleen didn't want to go to church some Sundays, but she never missed it."

I couldn't help but chuckle. "I'm sorry I can't be as perfect as Cathleen, and I don't think you can compare me missing a couple of shifts at work to war Dad."

"The point I'm making is you can't just not go

because you don't feel like it. It's your responsibility. As for missing a couple of shifts, Mrs Morgan said you haven't been in for a few weeks. So, again, what have you been doing?"

"Nothing just wondering around," I lied.

"Show her Frank."

Dad dug deep into his pocket and lay down on the small side table a bus ticket to Newcastle for two, a napkin with the name of the chip shop from South Shields with my lipstick smudged across it and a ripped corner of a newspaper with the words *'You are so beautiful'* written on it in Joe's handwriting.

"So, Lass, where have you been…and who with?" Dad asked again.

A lot of shouting followed, the three of us yelled at each other. I was angry that they had gone through my stuff. They were angry that I disobeyed them. I was physically dragged to my bedroom; it was for my own good; they said that no good would come from Joe Hollister, that he was a waste of space and Uncle Albert would get me, and I would see then how quickly Joe forgot about me. Dad stormed over to next door, and I heard more yelling follow, my dad was furious. I heard the back gate of next-door slam shut and I ran to my window only to see that Joe was legging it.

"Joe!" I shouted from my window.

Joe ran back to outside our yard quickly. "Your dad's going mental in there, Charlotte."

"I know, he found out about us. The library snitched on

me, and they went through my stuff. I'm sorry."

"Don't be daft, the guy hates me." Joe was still in his slippers as he stood out in the cold staying out the way of my dad.

"Did he try and hit you?" I asked him scared of the answer.

"No," Joe laughed, "I legged it the minute he stormed in the house. Knew it couldn't be good news for me. Did he hurt you?" Joe suddenly asked, stopping his cold tip toeing dance.

"No, just yelled. Dragged me around a little. I am banished to my room till the end of time."

"They can't keep you in there forever," he smiled.

"I wouldn't put it past them this time Joe, my mam even suggested I go to London to give me time to come to my senses," I said quoting her with my fingers. "Really it is just another way to get me away from you."

Joe looked at me seriously. "You don't think they really will, do you? Send you to London."

"I don't know, Mam was probably just angry. She's never sent me to London as a punishment before."

"Yeah, but it never was a punishment, now though, well it's different, isn't it?" Joe looked around and quietly entered my back yard, standing right beneath my window.

My heart raced as I listened out for footsteps. Joe climbed our joining back wall and climbed up the drainpipe to my open window.

"They can't take you away," he said as he placed a

kiss on my lips sitting on the window ledge. I found the whole scene romantic, but also terrifying, all it took was for my mam to walk in or my dad to storm outside and see us. "I won't let them take you, I can't be without you." He hugged me close to his chest. "You make me feel normal, Charlotte." He scattered kisses all over my head and then he said the most berserk thing I had ever heard. "Run away with me," he whispered.

I laughed thinking he was joking but he wasn't. He spilled out a plan as if he had thought of it already. We would pack a small bag and head to Mark's until we find a place of our own.

Somewhere where no one knows us.

Where we can be together.

He told me he would get more hours at the pub and help David out more whenever he could. He reckoned we could easily afford a flat. "It will be just me and you."

"They will look for us, Joe. They will call the police."

"We will lay low. We will be off the radar, out of town, we could go to Northumberland, Tynemouth, anywhere."

I know it all sounds crazy, but I was contemplating it. The idea of me and Joe running off into the distance on his motorbike and the world becoming our oyster was inviting.

"We could leave now."

"Now?"

"Yes! What do you say, baby? We could leave now and leave this place behind us? Then no one can take you away. I will look after you."

I know it's berserk and I know we could get into a

heap of trouble if we got caught especially Joe, but I am tired of being told what to do, I am tired of being the one who has to be there for everyone else, Peter, my mam, Mr Flint. What about what I want? I don't want to be stuck here in Durham forever. I don't want to be parted from Joe, he is the only person who understands me and takes me away from all the pain that sits heavily on my heart. He makes it disappear. So, I made the mad decision to go with him, to run away there and then. I grabbed my old school backpack which I keep my journals in and shoved some clothes in, it wasn't much, the bag filled up pretty quick, but it would do, and Joe said he would buy me more, then with the bag secured on my back I carefully followed Joe out of the window, down the pipe ever so slowly; I dared not look down.

"I'm here, don't worry," Joe whispered ahead of me. He helped me down the wall into my yard and we quietly but quickly left the yard of my childhood home behind. My mind was full of crazy thoughts of Peter being upset, my mam and dad going out of their minds with worry but next to me, with his hand held tight in mine, was Joe who made the runaway worth it. We were going to be happy. Joe couldn't stop smiling as we headed out to the back of our lane.

"You're in your slippers, Joe," I said.

"It's fine, I'll buy more stuff later. My motorbike is parked outside my house, I am going to have to get it if we are going to get away fast. I'm going to have to sneak in and grab my keys, they are by the front door it shouldn't take me long."

"Ok, well meet me outside Mr Flint's, I want to just see him quickly one last time."

"Don't tell him we're leaving," he warned.

"I won't."

With a parted kiss I ran to old Mr Flint's and burst through the door into his front room, he was sat at the table with Henry who must have returned not long after I left. They both stared at me with my sudden appearance and lack of breath from running.

"Charlotte? Are you alright? What was all that about earlier? Your dad sounded furious," Mr Flint asked me concerned, as he always had been for me. He really was the kindest man and it hurt to be leaving him. "Sit down Pet, come and catch your breath."

"I can't, I don't have time," I said rapidly. "I just came to… I just came to say… thank you. Thank you for being such a good friend to me and to my nan." I looked at Henry who was looking at me with such intriguing eyes that I feared he could read my thoughts. "And to Henry."

Mr Flint blushed a little. "You two are good to me, I am a very lucky man. What's brought all this on anyway?"

"Nothing, I just wanted you to know." The lump in my throat grew. Henry was stood up now and approached me carefully. His face became inches from my own, it was the closest he had been to me in weeks and my body suddenly ached for his touch.

"What are you up to?" he whispered in an almost angry

tone of voice.

"Nothing."

"You're lying," he accused, and with one swift hand he grabbed my backpack, which I must not have closed properly in the rush of packing, and he pulled out a blouse. To make matters worse, Joe pulled up outside the house his motorcycle roaring with anticipation. Henry need not look outside to know that it was his brother, his face softened and was replaced with a face I could only describe as anxious. "Where are you going, Lottie?" he asked.

"Nowhere," I lied again, pulling my blouse from his grip, anxious to leave but also partly wanting to stay.

"You're running away, aren't you? Please tell me I'm wrong."

"What's going on?" Mr Flint asked.

"Nothing, I'm sorting it," Henry replied sternly holding onto my arms. "Please Lottie, tell me I'm wrong."

I shook my head tearfully. Henry lowered his head and to my surprise rested it onto mine pulling me closer into a warm embrace. I wasn't prepared for the reaction of feeling completely lost. I was running away with Joe who made me feel alive but there in Henry's arms I felt at peace.

"Stay," he whispered. "I need you."

I wrapped my arms around him as tight as I could. I wanted to feel him as close as possible as I fought back the tears.

"I'm sorry about what I said this morning, I didn't mean it. If anything, it's me I hate, not you, I hate myself for not going to that stupid dance that you begged me to go to."

I felt immense guilt hearing Henry apologise, the night of the dance changed everything between us, for the three of us even, but it was me who had done the most awful thing.

"I'm the one that's sorry, I really am." I was sorry for hurting him, I was sorry for leaving him and I was sorry for not realising just how important he was to me.

Joe thumped on the front door, his knocks sounded desperate, and I knew I had to leave quick. As soon as my parents realised I was gone, Mr Flint's would be one of the first place they checked.

"Don't go, please," Henry held my face up gently. "I tell you this because I love you not for any other reason — my brother will hurt you."

The words *I love you* stayed with me and have played on repeat in my thoughts all evening. I ignored his warning against Joe, just as his older brother knocked again. I looked at the door anxiously and tried to pull away from his arms, but Henry shocked me when he suddenly gave me an unexpected kiss, making me stumble a little on my feet. His kiss told me to stay, it told me he still cared about me, it told me that I was forgiven, and it frightened me because I did not stop him, yet I knew once our lips parted that I would leave him.

I never looked back to see his face as I left Mr Flint's house not knowing when I would be able to return, it hurt too much. I marched over to the motorcycle, walking straight past Joe, and hopped on the back without a word. I don't know how long Henry stood there or if any words were exchanged between the two, all I know is that my heart felt like a chunk of it was being left behind.

With the cold winter breeze on my face, the tears fell silently and slowly as Joe and I rode off into the unknown. With my arms clinging onto Joe, I had to put thoughts of Henry aside, as hard as I was finding it. Joe said he would take care of me, and I believed him. Running away together was his romantic way of making sure that no one could separate us.

So here I am writing in my journal with Joe laid beside me sound asleep on his side with a protective arm around my torso. Mark has kindly offered us his bedroom until we find somewhere of our own. I wonder how long it took for Mam and Dad to realise that I was gone. Now that I am here, I know somewhere in a small lane in Durham people are out searching for me full of fear. They will know I am with Joe without a doubt and will expect me to come home tomorrow deep down, but I won't be home tomorrow or any other day for now I know I will be sent to Uncle Albert for sure. I just hope they will all in time forgive me.

Chapter Eleven

14th August 1958

I never slept a wink last night. I don't believe Joe did either, not with all my tossing and turning. When the alarm clock signalled his day had started, he did not appreciate it.

"I could sleep for days more," he moaned in a muffled voice into his pillow. I ran my fingers across his bare back and laid gentle kisses of apology. He moaned as I reached the back of his neck. Joe lifted his head from the pillow, hair stood on end messily, the bags under his eyes matched mine. "I best get used to it," he said turning round and pulling me into his arms. Joe gently placed his hand on my rounded belly. "Not long now, baby. Then we will never sleep again."

I laughed at the thought, it scared me a little too. Joe saw this in my face and rubbed his nose against mine.

"You're going to be the best Mam ever." With Joe working at the pub most evenings and out with David every other hour of the day I don't get to see much of him as I would like but he brings in money each week which we need to keep the flat and things for the baby.

It's been five months now since we began to rent our little home in Gateshead. It's not the biggest place but it's ours. Joe said as soon as he spotted the flat sitting above a book shop, he knew it was meant to be ours. Mr and Mrs

Gregory who own the shop downstairs have been nothing but kind to us. Mrs Gregory is always knitting baby Hollister a cardigan or tiny booties. They never ask us any questions either, Mr Gregory said our business is nothing of theirs as long as we pay the rent on time and even then, if it's a little late, they don't mind too much. Mr and Mrs Gregory are all heart, they always check we have food in and if Joe must work a Sunday, they invite me round for a Sunday roast. They don't have any children of their own, so I think the Gregorys are a little excited to have the sound of tiny feet above their shop. It does make me think of my own parents, if they knew where I was and realised that they would be grandparents in a matter of months, how would they react? Would Mam be sat by the fire knitting booties of her own as she did for Cathleen? Would Dad and Walter go to the pub to wet the baby's head when he or she arrived? Then it saddens me to think of the others too. I won't get to enjoy seeing Peter become an uncle and carefully hold the little one as though it were made of China. Would our baby upset Cathleen and Rupert? Then there's Henry, dear Henry, who I can only imagine would be deeply hurt to see me and Joe with a bairn, or perhaps by now he has long forgotten his love for me.

It's too late to go home now, Joe said. He said no one would support us and the decisions that we have made. He believes he would be arrested the moment we stepped into the lane, and he would never get to see our baby grow. Without me, jail would kill him. I do miss home more than I imagined. I always wanted to get away as far as possible, but the thought of Mr Flint's garden sitting in full bloom right now aches, as well as the fleeting thoughts of Henry's face that crosses my mind often making me feel guilty for leaving him and guilty that I think of Joe's brother as much as I do while carrying his baby. Whenever I feel like my mind is pondering too much, I look at Joe and our home and think of the lengths we went to so we could be together. Baby Hollister may not have been planned but Joe is going to love our little one so dearly, he is always coming home with baby grows that he has passed on his way back and has painted our bedroom bright yellow on behalf of the arrival of our baby. Everything he does is for us, and each day I do feel like I love him that little bit more.

18th August 1958

I had a visitor yesterday — Kitty woke me bright and early looking fresh and gorgeous as always. She is so pretty she makes me feel so much fatter and, well, pregnant!

"Morning," she said cheerfully arriving with bacon sandwiches. Kitty and I have become quite good friends since living with Joe. She tends to pop by to see me every now and then to make sure I'm doing okay. As I've grown bigger and become more tired recently, she sometimes stops by to do some cleaning for me which I hate, but she insists and makes me sit with a magazine while she potters around chatting about Mark and his brothers. Kitty is close to all three of the brothers having dated Mark since they were about eleven. She is always staying over at their place and partying.

"I may know them well but there is one mystery that always baffles me," she often says. "David's job, I have no idea what he actually does, he tells me he does odds and ends, window cleaning, gardening. He is up to something that one is. No one goes away, sometimes for days, to clean windows. Joe works with him; what does he say they do?"

To this day I have no idea what it is that Joe and David do to be honest. I have asked Joe and he says the same — odds and ends. What I do know though is that when he is working with David, he comes home quiet and reserved another reason for our argument last week, he tells me it's because he is tired but that it was worth it as he gets triple the money he receives from the pub.

Kitty was full of beans. "I saw Joe yesterday; he said you were beginning to feel like a trapped bird."

"He did?" I asked.

"Yes, and I don't blame you, being stuck up here all day, so he has given me some money to get you some new clothes fitted. He thought it might cheer you up a little and then we can have some girlie time."

"Girlie time? I don't know about that Kitty." I really didn't, it was nine am I was tired, standing in the hallway with one of Joe's t-shirts as a nightgown and only just covering my dignity, may I add, and not feeling the greatest.

"I insist, I'm not taking no for an answer. I've called my aunt and she is going to fit you in this morning and then I am meeting up with my friends, Shirley, and Lizzie, whom you've met before. I promise you; we are going to have fun! Now get dressed!"

Kitty's aunt was a seamstress and had made me a couple of dresses before when I first grew out of clothes, she will do anything for Kitty. Having brought Kitty up when both her parents were lost in the war and with no children of her own, Kitty is her world. As for Shirley and Lizzie, yes, I had met them before when me and Joe were living at Mark's, they came round a few times for a drink, and both were well acquainted with Joe. Shirley had dated Joe for a little while before Betty died and when he went off the radar and ended up sleeping with Lizzie, both girls had a lot of hatred for each other before concluding that Joe was a dick! Of course, I can see why they came to that conclusion but as Joe's girl now, those encounters were far from friendly, Ice Queens were how I described them to Joe, who found the whole thing hilarious. I decided if I was going to have to endure a day with the two of them, whilst the size of a balloon and with large feet may I add, then Kitty's aunt best work some magic on me.

After our pamper my new floral dress was swishing from side to side sitting perfectly over my bump as we headed to Ronnie's bar. I had agreed to stay for a little while before making my way home. The Ice Queens were already seated in the corner in tight fitted dresses with red lipstick on. Shirley was brunette like me, and Lizzie's hair fell straight and copper. They were both good looking girls and my Joe is a very good-looking chap also, so it comes as no surprise that he was once interested in the pair. As I walked in, I placed a protective hand on my stomach with my Nana's ring clear for all to see, I didn't look at anyone for fear that they were staring back at me which would surely make me blush. The girls who spotted us couldn't help but glance at my protruding bump I didn't know whether to feel embarrassed to be sixteen and pregnant out of wedlock or proud to be carrying Joe's child.

"Charlotte, wow you're looking well!" Lizzie exclaimed as I took a seat. "I love the dress!"

"Thank you," I replied with a great big smile.

Shirley, I could see, was staring me up and down making me feel a little uncomfortable as she took a sip of her drink.

"You look ready to pop, how long have you got now?" Lizzie asked, not taking long at all to ask about the baby, but who could blame them, it was in everyone's face almost literally.

"Eight weeks left if she or he comes on time. So not long now." I rubbed my stomach and felt for the first time as though my baby was keeping me company, I was in a room seated with fake people but this ripple of movement inside me was a part of me, my family, a part of Joe, who although was not physically with me, I had a part of him here. A part of us. I was not alone, sat there in Ronnie's, I was sat with my baby, who I hope was listening and backing me up.

"Having a baby is a massive thing, especially for someone so young," Shirley began. "How are you and Joe coping with it?"

"We are coping fine; Joe is excited as am I."

"He really is, I bumped into him yesterday — proud as punch. I'll get us some drinks," Kitty said heading to the bar.

I couldn't help but smile at Kitty's words especially with the look it brought to the Ice Queen's faces, especially Shirley who had been with Joe for some time.

"I never did see Joe as the fatherly type; he was always so…free spirited. I guess people change," Shirley grinned.

"Yes, people do change," I grinned back at her, the type of grin that told her that I found her a total bitch.

"Oh, my goodness!" Lizzie almost shouted across the table, causing Kitty to look over her shoulder from the bar. "Are you and Joe engaged?"

Lizzie grabbed my hand and pulled it closer to her, gazing at my nana's ring. Kitty rushed back over at once.

"You both kept that one quiet," Kitty said, also examining the ring. "Blimey that looks expensive."

They had no idea how expensive, neither did I, but I know that most likely if everyone in the pub put their money together it still wouldn't cover the cost of this ring.

"We wanted to wait until the baby was here so we could celebrate properly," I found myself saying.

"This calls for a bottle of champagne; I am

bridesmaid by the way!" Kitty exclaimed as she returned to the bar.

So, I lied, but it wasn't a complete lie. Joe and I have discussed marriage several times before, he said he wanted to save up for the wedding I deserved. Yet tonight we were engaged, and I was loving every second of it. Shirley and Lizzie were constantly exchanging glances. I took a sip of my coke that Kitty bought me, after the champagne bottle was empty. I had only had a small amount and spat it back out.

"Vodka, Kitty?"

Kitty laughed. "You are here to let your hair down Charlotte."

"I don't think I should be getting drunk; I have to head home soon."

"Why, is Joe expecting his tea on the table?" Shirley asked sarcastically.

"No, because I have to head home on the bus and…"

"Girls come on, we're forgetting Charlotte is just sixteen. She shouldn't be here at all really, she's just a kid," Lizzie said.

"Nonsense, I've seen this girl knock back vodka like its water — drink, now. I'll get you a taxi later." With all three girls staring at me I felt reluctant to have the drink. One more drink won't hurt I told myself, then I would leave.

With the vodka down my throat, my lovely bladder, which must be the size of a pea at the moment, had me rushing to the toilet many times.

"Right, Kitty, I am off now. I've had enough." The drink was already beginning to affect me; I hadn't had a drink in a while, the last time was a toast to me and Joe to celebrate the new flat. That was in the comfort of home not a half an hour bus trip away.

"No stay," Shirley said. "You won't get to come out after the baby comes. Have another while you can. The next round is on me."

"Oh yes, that is true Charlotte," Kitty said pulling me back down to my seat. "Please stay, I miss getting drunk with you."

"Just one more Kitty," I firmly said.

"Sounds like a mam already," Lizzie giggled.

Shirley brought over a tray of cocktails. I am not sure what was in them, all I know is after that glass everything changed.

I can remember the noise in the room becoming so loud, the girls were chatting and laughing hysterically about something Kitty was saying. The room was spinning, and I felt so light, like I was somehow lifting out of my body. When I tried to go to the toilet I stumbled and a large hand, I don't know whose, grabbed hold of me to stop me from falling. The whole bar looked fuzzy, I felt like I had drunk so much more than I had. When I reached the toilet, I heard laughter and after a while I realised it was my own. It took me ages to pull my knickers off, I kept missing them not able to grip the sides and almost fell off the seat making me laugh more. Shirley walked into the toilets as I attempted to wash my hands. Baby

169

Hollister was kicking strong, I grabbed her hand and placed it on my stomach. "Feel Joe's baby," I said to her, then I remember nothing else.

Last night I woke up in a bed that was not my own yet was familiar. The room smelt of sick and I could hear shouting from another room. My head felt heavy like someone was pushing it down onto the pillow.

"Anything could have happened to her!" It was Joe who was shouting I realised. I felt so vulnerable that I wanted to shout for him but couldn't find the strength. "I can't believe you let her get that pissed! She's pregnant for fucks sake!" Joe's voice was followed by another two, I tried to make out who they belonged to but drifted back off to sleep.

When I woke again the window was open allowing air into the room, my whole body felt hot and sweaty, but my head felt a little easier to move. I slowly sat up and recognised that I was in Mark's bedroom. My yellow dress spread across the sheets, still on me, with stains that looked like blood, or perhaps more vomit, I couldn't quite tell in the dark. Beside my bed was a glass of water and a plastic bowl that I later found out was for my vomit, which I was told there was plenty of. Joe apparently watched me all night for fear that I would choke on it. I have no recollection of what happened after I was in the toilet or how I had even got in that state in the first place, I had only had three drinks and come to think of it I am not sure that I even finished the third. Joe entered the room and closed the door gently behind him. Seeing him stood there before me, looking worn out, and us there in Mark's house told me that everything was wrong, and I burst out crying.

"I'm so sorry, Joe, I don't know what happened. I didn't even want to go out or have anything to drink at all, honestly. I am such a bad person."

Joe climbed onto the bed and gave a sigh as he held me. "I'm just glad you're okay, you had me so worried." He sounded as though he might cry himself. Neither of us spoke for a little while we just lay there and held each other. Joe, who was exhausted, began to drift off but suddenly sat up not allowing himself to sleep.

"Joe, sleep. You need it."

"No, I need to get you home. We can sleep there. How are you feeling?" he asked me.

"Awful." I couldn't lie my face said it all. My head was aching, and I know it wasn't the baby that was causing my nausea.

Joe nodded. "I'm not surprised, baby, you were off your head."

I was shocked to hear this. "I only had a few, Joe. I wanted to come home. Oh God." I began to get upset feeling so confused. "I don't understand, one minute I was fine and then the next everything was spinning, I can remember going to the toilet and that is it."

"I know baby, Kitty said the same, although I may have blamed her at first. Apparently, you knocked yourself out in the toilets, Shirley said she found you on the floor with blood against the wall. She shouted for Kitty, and they brought you back round. Kitty said you were delirious after that. Screaming at them to leave and to get away from you."

"I know before that I felt like I was extremely drunk, how did they get me here?"

"A struggle, you were adamant you wanted to stay, apparently. Kitty said your head was bleeding and she suggested ringing an ambulance, but Shirley convinced her not to, she said underage drinking with a baby on the way would bring the social on us. So, Kitty ran over here and luckily Anthony was in, he seemed to calm you down enough to get you here." Joe paused and stroked my face. "You gave everyone a fright Charlotte, Anthony said he got you to the top of the stairs and you just collapsed, he said your eyes weren't fully closed. He thought you were dead for a moment."

I recalled none of this and couldn't believe that this was actually me that Joe was speaking of. Joe went on to tell me that apparently Anthony carried me to bed and was about to call an ambulance when I came round; delirious, shouting, and desperate to escape the room. Anthony struggled to keep me in the bed and stay still enough for him to try and patch me up. Then I slept for hours, meanwhile, Joe had gone home and was surprised to see Mark waiting on the doorstep. He thought perhaps I had gone into labour but instead was told I had gone mad. Joe said when he reached me, I was awake, crying about my nan in-between vomiting. All night he held my hair back and made sure I stayed on my side.

"I don't remember any of this; I am so sorry Joe. I don't know what happened."

"It's ok baby," he hushed me and kissed me gently. There was something else, I could tell.

Something that Joe wasn't telling me.

"What is it? What else happened?"

"Nothing." He was lying I thought.

"There is something, tell me, please."

"You said something through the night. You woke up and you began pacing the room. I was worried you were in pain; that the baby was coming early. You were with me, yet you looked right through me, and you kept saying over and over," Joe stopped, he looked down before continuing, "you wanted Henry. You kept asking for him. *'Go and get Henry, please get Henry.'* I know you weren't in the right frame of mind, but it hurt, you know."

My heart was suddenly racing, why would I say such a thing? Why ask for Henry, he would surely have given me some kind of lecture and thought me idiotic to get myself into the situation I had. I felt the urge to grab the vomit bowl as I recalled Joe's words. How could I be so stupid, to hurt Joe like that, he was my world and Henry really needs to fuck off out my head now.

"I love you, Joe; you have to know that."

"I know," he said like a small child, his head cupped in my hand, which he held to keep my hand against his cheek.

"I picked you, I left with you. It's me and you, forever."

"Forever," he repeated, my breath must have tasted

173

awful, but we kissed anyway, we kissed like lovers who have been parted for some tragic reason and reunited once more. The night must have been long and traumatic for Joe, I believe he was relieved to have me back to normal and his Charlotte once more.

"Should we go to the hospital, the baby Joe?" I asked worriedly.

"The baby will be fine. I want to get you home. Where you will be safe and can rest. The hospital will take you back to Durham, Charlotte. I could have lost you tonight. I don't want to risk losing you again."

"How did Shirley say I fell again?" I asked as we lay in our bed when we got home this morning.

"She didn't say, she said she found you on the floor."

"No, that can't be right. I remember her being there." I racked my brain. Had I seen her or had I imagined it. Perhaps it wasn't her. "No, it was her because I let her feel the baby. The baby was kicking, and I put her hand on my stomach. Yes, she was already there, so she must have seen me fall."

Joe looked at me seriously. "You're certain about this?"

"Yes, I remember because I wanted to fuck her off."

"Then why did she say she found you, surely she would have witnessed you fall?"

We both stared at each other, deep in thought. The same thoughts most likely, yet neither of us wanted to make such a big accusation. Joe's body was tense beside me.

"I will get to the bottom of this, leave this to me, baby." I was too tired to chat much more, and together we slept all day.

Joe is now off to work at the pub and now that this journal is all updated, I think I may find that I can sleep some more. I was so frantic before Joe left, wondering if I had harmed our baby somehow last night. I felt so guilty and ashamed, but Joe reassured me, as he felt a hard kick, that our baby is fine. As much as he wanted to get me to hospital, he is worried they will see us as incapable parents and involve the social services and return me home. He may be right as of now I am being kicked like a football.

Chapter Twelve

<u>25th August 1958</u>

I wonder what age you must reach for everything in your life to fall into place. When you wake up in the morning without a worry in the world, when the day rolls out how it should, when you can sit back, relax, and think this is good.

Joe decided to take some time off, which pleased me greatly. It has felt like such a long time since it was just the two of us.

"Close your eyes," he said, approaching the bed with a tray that smelt of bacon.

I giggled. "Why?"

"Just close them," he said.

I closed my eyes, still fighting the urge to giggle, which made Joe laugh. He was close to me, I sensed; if I reached out my arm, I would be able to touch him.

"Right, you can open them," Joe said with a slight stutter. The tray of cooked breakfast was on the floor as was he, crouched before me as I had suspected, but he was on one knee and in a blue velvet box he presented me a gold ring with a small diamond sat in the middle of the band.

"I know we are young; I know we have made crazy rash decisions and have a baby joining us soon, but I don't regret any of it. I love you, Charlotte Ridley. Would you please make me the happiest lad alive and marry me?"

"Of course!" I squealed and lunged forward knocking Joe from his position and onto the floor. He jumped into bed beside me, and carefully slipped the diamond ring onto my finger.

"I love you, Joe."

"I love you too."

Engaged! Yes, I am engaged to the gorgeous Joe Hollister. He could have the pick of any woman, but he has chosen me, Charlotte Ridley, to be his wife!

So, all was well and exciting. Joe proposed, we are ready for baby Hollister's arrival, we were happy and then Joe, in his true Hollister way, unintentionally may have fucked it up. Causing my fuzzy head of excitement to switch to anxious thoughts instead. David called on us this evening asking to borrow Joe for a little while, together they left for a few hours only for Joe to return with a cut face and bloody knuckles. He was angry, I could tell, and said nothing as he made his way to the fridge for a beer.

"Joe," I said from the doorway, wanting to allow him his space. His energy was negative, and he was impatient with the beer bottle cap that he could not open. His fists were black and blue. Endless thoughts crossed my mind, taking in his wounds. Only a few hours earlier we had been on the sofa laughing about things we did to each other when we were kids. He wasn't half as bad as Henry had been, but he was a tease all the same. My thoughts cleared as Joe smashed the bottle into the sink causing the brown liquid to splash around the sides.

"Fuck's sake!" he shouted.

"Joe, what's happened?" I questioned, holding back my fright.

"I'm not a good person, Charlotte," he said as he tried to clear everything with a tea towel. "I — I don't deserve you."

"What are you talking about, of course you do, we both deserve each other." I crossed the small kitchen and held onto Joe's arm. "Look at me Joe, I think you're amazing and I couldn't be without you."

Leaning my head onto his arm, I asked him again what had happened. Why was my fiancé stood in our kitchen in this state?

"I'm scared you'll hate me if I tell you, you might see me differently."

I was adamant to know and wouldn't settle until I had the truth. Kitty had her suspicions about David and over time I had begun to feel that she had every right to. For an odd job man, he had plenty of money, he owned a flash car and was often spotted with a black eye or a bust lip — he fell he would say, or he had an accident with a lawn mower. Joe was perfectly fine before David borrowed him.

"I told David what you said about Shirley, about her already being in the toilets with you when you fell. The way you were behaving that night, baby, was not through alcohol alone. I've seen you get wrecked and never have you acted like a nutter. Anthony thought you died on him for fuck sake." Joe slouched down to the floor, his head in his knees he reminded me of the boy who was so lost back when his mam died. "You had taken something else, a drug. Now I know you're too clever to take anything like that, so someone snuck it in your drink. It doesn't take a genius to guess who it was either."

"Shirley?"

"Jackpot."

"But why? What would she gain from that?" I felt my rage building as I imagined Shirley sneaking a drug into my drink, I know she was pissed about Joe, but drugging me was another level of jealousy.

"That's what I had to find out, funnily enough Shirley's been away for a while since your girlie night out and she returned today. I had to see her Charlotte, she tried to hurt you and I had to know why."

"Did she tell you? I bet she denied it, she isn't going to admit to that is she?"

Joe looked away from my gaze once more. "She didn't have much choice. I was so angry. She acted all miss innocent, but I can tell when she's lying. So, once her neck was pinned to the wall and she couldn't breathe she was willing to tell all." I grabbed my own neck recalling the time Joe once had me pinned to the wall. I remembered the look of anger in his eyes and how a part of me believed he didn't care about the consequences if he had killed me.

"My biggest regret is hurting you; I was in a bad place, and I hated myself afterwards and I would never lay a finger on you again I swear it, but Shirley…" Joe wiped away a tear as I slowly lowered myself to the floor opposite him, frightened of what he was going to tell me. "I wanted to hurt her, really hurt her. I saw red, she was responsible for going out of her way to hurt my girl and my baby. I wanted to kill her and if David hadn't stepped in to pull me away, I think I would have."

I was lost for words, but despite his confession of wanting to murder the girl who drugged me, I still wanted to hold him. It may sound crazy; some may see it as a warning sign, but I saw it as protection. In my heart I believe Joe would do anything to take care of me and our baby. Both me and my child could have died because of Shirley's meddling; just like that Joe would have been left alone and I can't bear to imagine what kind of man would have been left behind. I know he needs me. I'm not saying I wish for him to kill people for me, being locked up is no good to any of us either but hurting her she deserved. I am glad David stepped in when he did though.

Joe may not see it, but I believe he wouldn't have gone through with it even if David weren't there; the three of us need to be together. Joe wouldn't chance that.

"But you didn't Joe and that's the main thing," I told him. "What did she tell you?" I was more than intrigued to know.

"She got the drugs off her cousin, Bill, he's well known for his drug dealing, her aim was to do anything to hurt me the way I apparently hurt her, whether that meant causing injury to you or our baby. She pretty much didn't have a plan and once the bitch went through with it and pushed you causing you to fall and hit your head, she shit herself. The girls deranged."

"That I believe, your hands Joe?' I questioned as the reason behind their state was not yet revealed.

"I had a fight with David, he didn't approve of my approach with Shirley. He's worried that I've brought trouble to us all from Bill."

"Have you? Brought trouble to us all?" I asked worriedly.

"We will be fine," Joe said, not sounding completely convincing. "I'm going to go to bed." And with that he got up to leave, leaving me alone on the cold floor wondering what happens next. Only for Joe to return minutes later to lift me to my feet. He looked as worried as I did, but in his strong manner told me that he would keep us all safe.

28th August 1958

Through the night Joe woke up, the room was dark with a small light coming from his bedside table when he woke me. He was topless beside me looking annoyed.

"Charlotte!" he called, shaking my arm.

"Yes, I'm awake Joe, what's wrong?"

"You were talking — dreaming — talking in your sleep thing again."

My heart was racing, and I felt my body clam up. Oh no, I thought, feeling instant guilt. He must have heard me calling for Henry in my sleep, it wouldn't be the first time and his expression said it all.

"Sorry if I woke you. What was I saying?" I asked innocently.

Joe said nothing, he scanned my face and then sat up rubbing his eyes. "Couldn't make it out really," he said. "Just shouting." He rolled over to his side turning off his lamp and without a word he went back off to sleep.

I lay there for a while listening to my heartbeat slow down before I must have drifted off myself.

Today, Joe was gone before I woke. I never heard his alarm or felt his goodbye kiss. I am worried that I have upset him. This is the second time Joe has heard me mention Henry in my sleep. It is as though my subconscious is punishing me, turning me in for my thoughts. I decided to cook us a meal for tea, to remind him of how much he meant to me and my love for him. I am not the best cook; I just made a simple cottage pie. Only he didn't eat any because Joe has not returned home. I was expecting him to be home around half six, yet he is not here, and it has just gone ten. I am besides myself with worry.

Did I upset him that deeply that he doesn't want to be around me? Has he had an accident on his bike? Perhaps he had been asked to do an extra shift? I keep pacing around the house, just waiting like a lemon. You know what I'm going to just go to the pub myself and find out otherwise I will worry myself ill.

Chapter Thirteen

1st September 1958

Everything has changed and it's all my fault. Every dream we had is shattered. Every plan we made together, gone for as long as I can see. Our baby's life is now shadowed with questions, loss, and burden.

It's been three days since I last saw my Joe and I just keep waiting for him to walk through the door, pick me up and tell me everything is going to be all right. Every time I think about him my heart breaks again, like a fresh wound over and over. If I had ever felt lost before, never did I feel it as much as I do now.

I went to the pub to find that Joe wasn't there after all. A middle-aged woman behind the bar said he had left with a mate who had one too many. She was caked in makeup and her hair was in the biggest beehive I had ever come across however once she was aware of who I was she gave me a glass of lemonade for free before I headed back home

"I'm not having you leave on your own at this time in your condition," she kindly said. "My Uncle Ted's a taxi driver he will take you." So, with the free lemonade and the lift home I was quickly back, and then seeing our front door open made me overjoyed that Joe was back too.

To my horror I couldn't have been more wrong. As

I reached the top of the stairs to our flat, I couldn't believe what I saw before me. I was not met with Joe like I thought I would, no, instead I found the flat in a state, pictures smashed on the floor, tables flipped over, every plate and cup lay in hundreds of small pieces, the doors of the cupboards hung off their hinges, and my greatest sorrow was the hacked cherry wood that was piled up in a heap in my bedroom. I sunk to the floor and cried as I held the specially carved wood of my baby's cot that Joe had so proudly made himself. I didn't understand why anyone would do this. We didn't have anything worth any money to be stolen. Most of the flat was furnished by Mr and Mrs Gregory. The cot was the most precious thing that we owned…they even cut up the mattress. Our home was destroyed and everything we owned along with it. In eight weeks we would be welcoming a baby to a home with nothing, not even a drawer! I didn't hear Joe return home through my cries, not until he ran into our bedroom.

"Charlotte! What's happened? Are you hurt?"

I shook my head, too upset to speak as he cradled me in his arms. I was relieved to have him home and feel his affection but very much still in shock at my surroundings.

"Baby, I'm sorry I wasn't here," he apologised while rocking me back and forth. "I took Mark home; he was pissed again. Had another argument with Kitty. Fucks sake, I should have come home first." I relieved him of his sorry state, explaining to him that I too was not home when the house was trashed. I thought this would make Joe feel better but instead it made things worse.

"It's not safe here, Charlotte. If you had been here, it would have been a lot worse. They'd have beaten you. Taken you. Killed you even."

"Killed me, I think they were just robbers Joe, not murderers."

Joe shook his head. "Let's not pretend baby, you know as well as me who this is all down to."

Bill.

I know Joe had been worried about Bill, but I never thought he would come to our home in Gateshead. How would he even know where we lived?

"He can find out anything he wants. He has people all over working on his behalf, all over the Northeast. He is a dangerous man, I'm on his hit list Charlotte." Joe's words were frightening, and my strong confident fiancé became a scared boy.

"What will he do to you?" I asked, not wanting to know the answer.

"Imagine the worst thing someone could do to you. Then triple it. You think Shirley is crazy. He's a nutter! I've never met him before, purely because he's been in prison. It's a wonder no one has come for me before this."

Joe and I sat on the floor for a while, lost in our own thoughts. I could feel his heart beating rapidly against my cheek. We had built the flat into a home, now it was all destroyed and not by just anyone but by a psychotic killing drug dealer. That was not the only thing that Bill destroyed either as the next sentence that came out of Joe's mouth will stay with me for the rest of my life.

"I have to run," he whispered, "and you have to go home." I pulled away from him at once, staring at him blankly thinking it was just said in the moment, a stupid suggestion maybe. A study of his face, however, told me he meant it.

"No." I tried to get up, but I was too weak, I felt like my heart was missing beats it was going so fast, panic rose, and I could hardly catch my breath.

"It's the only way." Joe grabbed my hand with both of his, and holding back tears of his own, continued with his stupid plan. "Bill will be back with his gang and this time it won't be the flat that is smashed to no repair. I can't protect you from him here, it's not safe."

"No, Joe."

"Yes, baby. Listen to me. We must go now, before they return. Baby, look at me." Joe sat up onto his knees and grabbed my face. "You need to go home."

Bill knew where Joe was, and he wanted his revenge. Yet I couldn't face the truth because it hurt too much. I leaned in and kissed him; I pulled him closer to me kissing him like my life depended on it and in return his hands tangled themselves in my hair as he brought me as close to him as I possibly could.

"We have to pack baby," Joe sadly said as he gasped for air.

We packed frantically, bringing with us all that we could muster. The baby's clothes, blankets, bottles, and nappies went into a bag. Like before, I packed into a backpack my diaries and a few clothes, Joe did the same. As I looked around the panic rose inside me once more.

"I can't do this Joe, why can't I come with you, why do I have to go home?"

Joe sighed. "I don't want to do this either, but if you come with me then that puts you and the bairn in danger. My life is over Charlotte, I'm going to spend it running from one place to the next. That's not a life I want for my family."

"Let's go to the police then, they can protect us."

"The police are corrupt, never trust the police."

"Well, we can go down south, we can go to my uncle's. When everyone sees how serious we are about each other they will help I'm sure of it."

"Charlotte, baby, everywhere I go now I put anyone with me in an equal amount of danger. There is nothing stopping Bill from hunting me down. I've heard of him finding guys who got on the wrong side of him in Bournemouth for fucks sake. I'm sorry baby. I hate all of this as much as you. I want nothing more than to be with my family. Are you ready?"

I reluctantly nodded. My legs felt like jelly, but they were also grounded to the spot. The baby began its late-night routine of kicking me, reminding me that I had someone to protect; but alone, I'm not sure I can do that without Joe. Joe noticed the ripple of my stomach, then a prominent lump stuck out making me gasp, a head? A hand? A foot even? I wasn't sure.

"Come, quick!" I shouted.

Joe was on the opposite side of the bed and quickly came to my side and stroked the baby's body part. That will be the closest he will ever get to seeing his child.

"I've let you both down." He collapsed onto the edge of the bed inches from where I'd sat not so long ago when he proposed. He asked me to be his wife. We were going to be one big family; we were going to be so happy.

"You haven't, Joe. All you have ever done is love us. I shouldn't have let Kitty take me out. I didn't even want to go. I should have come straight home from her Aunt Lorna's, then this would never have happened."

Despite Joe telling me that I wasn't to blame I have blamed myself ever since. We sadly crept away in the night leaving Mr and Mrs Gregory a note in their shop letterbox. We thanked them for everything and apologised for the mess of the flat. It broke my heart to leave our little home above the book shop. The high street was dark and empty with the only sound coming from a distant pub. Joe's motorcycle roared its engine and drove us away for good.

Before going back to our old village Joe made a stop. We parked up the bike at the bottom of a hill and made our way up, Joe supporting me and bump. The top of the hill was the very spot we came to the night our unneighbourly relationship became somewhat more. The view below overlooking the lights of the city was just as breath-taking as it was the first time we came here. We were drunk as skunks, confused, and so lost in life and here we were once more on the brink of becoming parents, engaged to be married, yet saying goodbye. Joe wrapped his jacket around my shoulders to protect me from the summer nights breeze. I sat between his legs taking in every touch and kiss on my skin.

"Joe, what do you really do with David?" I asked curiously, for now I could know without backlash or worry.

I thought I heard a slight laugh from him. "We sell dodgy gear for a guy called Mick out of his lorry. Sometimes we visit people who owe money to him, and, you know, warn them."

"Threaten them more like, Joe Hollister," I corrected.

"Ok, that sounds more correct."

"Will we ever see you again?" I asked, afraid of the answer.

"I honestly don't know baby, I would like to think so."

I gripped his arm closer to mine holding back the tears. "I will tell our baby all about you. How you saved us and how much you loved us both."

"I will love you both forever, I'm so sorry that I can't be a part of your lives."

I don't know how long we sat up on that hill. Hours passed us by, I believe I even nodded off before Joe said we had to make a move. He wanted me to go to Walter's as I was much too afraid to head home. I cannot see my parents being happy to have their runaway daughter turning up pregnant and out of wedlock. I can't say I was so happy about seeking refuge from Walter either.

"I don't want to be a burden to him Joe. I can imagine things are hard enough between our dads."

"He will help you; I know he will. You and the bairn."

"And Henry?" I asked, before jumping back onto the motorcycle.

"What about Henry?" Joe asked avoiding eye contact.

"He isn't going to like it. I left him for his brother, which I don't blame him for not appreciating, and now I'm going to waltz back in asking if he minds giving up his bedroom for us. I don't think I can. There has to be somewhere else I can go. Molly's perhaps or even Evelyn's."

"No! That's not good enough. You have to go to my dad's Charlotte. Only there will I know you are cared for. Henry will come around. Let's face it, we all know he will do a better job at looking after you than I will." Joe looked hurt by his own words and helped me onto the bike.

"You know that's not true, Joe, otherwise you wouldn't be protecting us now."

"If I didn't have such a temper on me, I wouldn't have to be protecting my family like this at all."

The ride back to our old home was a quiet one, I held on tight to Joe inhaling the smell of his jacket, leather with a hint of tobacco. Each mile closer, each building I recognised, brought me so much pain.

When we reached the end of our lane Joe turned off the engine. It must have been about half one in the morning, we didn't want to make too much noise and potentially wake anyone who may recognise us.

"You can't hide forever, baby," Joe warned, referring to my parents, as he once more helped me off the vehicle.

"I know, but right now I'm not ready to face them." Joe nodded. His eyes sparkled under the streetlight.

"Baby." It was now Joe's turn to break down. I tried to stay strong for him, holding back my own emotions, for he was about to go on a harder journey than I. I would get to live a life with our child, at least, and family around me. Whereas he would very much be going solo. "I don't know if I can cope without you."

"You're strong," I trembled. "We will always be here." I placed my hand over his heart. "I am going to tell our baby all about his daddy every day."

By now my own tears had well and truly escaped.

"You're going to make the best mammy, I'm sorry I won't be around to help."

I pulled him closer kissing his tender lips, which tasted salty from our tears. If anyone passed us from behind, we would look like teenage lovers, but another angle would show you a vastly different story. The kiss was as passionate as our first. I felt like Joe might never free me from his embrace. I hoped that he wouldn't, that the kiss would make him reconsider, that maybe our love was strong enough to go on the run together. We could

make it work we could go far, however Joe did release me
— and his mind had not changed.

"I will wait here until you're in the backyard," Joe said
pointing to our old back lane. I looked ahead and I could
feel the loss of air in my lungs once more.

"Joe."

"Baby, you have to go. If not for me then for baby
Hollister. Please, just go."

I slowly let go of his grip and we reluctantly parted. It
was now or never. I took the first step away from him and
then another and without a word I kept walking until I
reached Walter's back gate. I took one last look at the
figure at the end of the lane, the figure looked back and
quietly but swiftly I entered the Hollister's backyard and
closed the gate behind me. I pinned myself against the
back wall and stood still listening out for the sound of
Joe's motorcycle. It took a while for the engine to roar
again. I had almost hoped he had changed his mind but
when the engine grew quieter, I knew he was gone. I
thought of him driving off in the night to a secret location.

I thought of how long it would take for him to notice
the small gold ring hidden in his pocket with the quick
note I'd scribbled out:

"A part of me to take with you. Never forget. XX.
P.S if you ever need to sell it for money please do. XX"

I burst into tears, holding my mouth to muffle the sound of
my cry. The black windows before me belonged to the

people I knew, the people I had left behind. From my spot I could see Henry's window and my own next door to it on the other side of the wall. My window was firmly shut tonight. Beyond the walls were the sleeping bodies of family and friends. I didn't want to wake anyone, nor did I want to see them, so I made a run for it. Joe wouldn't have been pleased that I had left but he was gone now, so I made my way to the only place I felt was best for the night.

"Bloody hell, Lass!"

I was awoken early the next morning, begrudgingly, having had barely a wink of sleep. Mr Flint's blankets were not cut out for a comfortable night's sleep at all. No matter how much I tossed and turned I just couldn't get comfortable. My back truly ached. My eyes felt like they were battered.

Mr Flint stood in the doorway of his shed in disbelief. I can imagine the sight of me was a shocking one. Realising I was to face my first day without Joe, the sight of the grubby old man was comforting.

"What ya doing in here?" he asked puzzled. I really didn't know where to start. I cradled my bump and wept. Mr Flint looked around outside before closing the shed door behind him.

"I didn't know where else to go," I cried.

"Where's Joe? Done a runner has he? Left you up the duff? He'll kill him when he finds out ya know."

"Who will?" I hadn't heard Mr Flint speak so abruptly

before. He sat himself down on a stool.

"Henry, he'll kill Joe when he finds out he's dishonoured ya like this," he said pointing to my bump, before casting his eyes elsewhere. "And then leaving ya high and dry."

"He never left me high and dry. I had to come back. Something happened, something I can't explain right now. As for Henry, please, Mr Flint, don't tell him I'm here."

"He's gonna see for himself in a bit Lass, he's coming here this morning."

"No," I was horrified. I wasn't ready to see Henry. "I need to go."

Mr Flint looked alarmed as I struggled to get up from the floor before giving me a hand. He was very hesitant in letting me leave with nowhere to go so insisted that I stopped with him.

"Here's a key for the house, ya can stop in the spare room. Hurry now if you don't want to bump into Henry. You will stop by and see your folks at some point won't you, only it doesn't feel right knowing you're here and what not."

"I will, I promise. Just not yet."

Mr Flint nodded. "Yes, well, go and get some sleep Lass, ya look like ya need it."

"Thank you, Mr Flint." I gave the old man a peck on the cheek and made a dash to his house.

Mr Flints spare bedroom looked like it belonged in a museum. I had never been upstairs before; it was only ever the downstairs that Mr Flint had wanted cleaned. It screamed out the Victorian era. The walls were papered in pastel coloured floral paper with a thick green border along the top. The furniture was a heavy looking mahogany set that overpowered the bedroom. Yet over in the corner stood a rather dusty white cradle. The white bedding and the cotton canopy had yellowed over time. I rocked the cot gently and it let out a small squeak, but it was a pretty little thing. Mr Flint hadn't ever had any children, but this little treasure told me that children were once something he either wished for or lost. Either way the little bed left behind in an old man's house brought sorrow to me.

With tiredness over taking me I collapsed onto the bed. I knew the sheets had laid there unused and unwashed for many years — Mr Flint's nephew was his last guest and never in my time of coming to the house had I met him — so, I skipped jumping into the sheets and instead opted for sleeping on the top and it wasn't long until I drifted off.

I've been with Mr Flint ever since. He's asked me many questions, and I have given him the answers. I trust Mr Flint and it's important to me that he doesn't think badly of Joe. I'm not too sure on his verdict exactly; Joe's temper, as he liked to point out, was what had left us in this mess. That may be so but his love for me was real.

In the past, being at Mr Flint's meant giving him a hand with the cleaning and decluttering, but everything has flipped around now; the old soul doesn't allow me to do a thing.

"Let me get that, Pet."
"Oh, leave that, I'll see to it."
"Come and sit down and I'll make ya a cuppa."

I don't know whether it's a joy or not. He even fluffed up a pillow before I sat on the sofa today. I can't say I've been the nicest guest; my emotions are on fire. I have snapped a few times, unintentionally, at the poor man and then I have cried, many, many tears. I try to stay upstairs as much as possible, in my own space; I am struggling to accept that Joe has gone. He is God knows where! Oh, why did I go out with Kitty! I should have gone home. I should be in my bedroom right now in the arms of Joe. Instead, I'm sat here in a time warp too anxious to step foot out the house. We were meant to get married. Every time I picture his face I feel as though I need to throw up. I keep peeking out the window hoping I'll see him come riding down the road declaring that Bill is now back in prison or even dead and we are free once more. I wonder how far he is now; does he have enough money, a place to sleep. I miss him, I miss him already.

6th September 1958

I was seething yesterday when there was a knock at the door. Mr Flint was out getting a few essentials at the shop, and I slowly began to tiptoe down the stairs. It could be anyone I told myself, the postman, a neighbour, someone from the allotment. That was all wishful thinking, for it wasn't long before the letterbox opened. I froze to the spot. Holding onto the stair railing not daring to move.

"Are you in there, Charlotte?" It was Walter! Anger rose at first, I cursed Mr Flint for telling him I was here, for blabbing when I had asked him not to. I was not ready to see anyone. "Please, Charlotte, if you are, let me in Lass. I just want to make sure you're all right." I thought if I ignored him, he would go away. "Joe sent me a letter."

Joe. Hearing his name made my chest tighten. I slowly crept down the remaining stairs and opened the door just enough for only Walter to be able to see. He smiled when he saw me, it was a sympathetic smile that made me feel all the worse.

"Are you alone?" I asked.

"It's just me, Pet."

Walter made tea while I read the letter Joe had sent him over and over again, so much so that I remember every word.

Dad,

It's Joe. I know I've let you down and I have brought nothing but trouble to your door since Mam died, but I beg you to please help.

If everything went to plan this will be no shock to you but I can't help but worry that it has not.

I am in big trouble, so much trouble that I must go away. Do not worry about me though I can look after myself, but I am asking that you look after my family. Charlotte is expecting and it breaks my heart to leave her behind, but it is for the best.

I left her with you knowing yourself and Henry would both take good care of her and the bairn. If she did not seek help from you, please find her. Please help her. She is precious and needs you both, I know I was not a good son to you, but she deserves the world. I hope my child will bring a smile to you all.

Joe

I wept as I read the words, running my finger over the paper. He really was gone. Walter was ever so kind, he invited me to stay with him, but I refused. To live on the other side of the wall to my parents does not sit well with me. My parents will have so much to say about everything, they will control everything.

"They will find out at some point. You can't hide here forever. You're going to have a bairn, pet," he gently said over his cup of tea. "I know Mr Flint's been good to you and all but," he stopped and looked around, "but this is no place for a baby".

I knew he was right. The smell of tobacco lingered in my hair and on my clothes. There was not an adequate nor clean space in sight for toys and bottles and what not. The house needed a complete refurbishment and that would mean taking Mr Flint's home comforts away.

"I can move you in tonight if you prefer," he went on. "That way you won't be seen. Then you can tell ya mam and dad whenever you're ready."

The thought of clean cutlery and a floor that wasn't sticky swayed me. My mothering instincts were telling me to go and stay at Walter's. So, I nodded in agreement, although I still felt a little uncertain.

"You don't have to be alone Charlotte. You are carrying my grandchild. Joe asked me to look after you both and I will," Walter choked up. "Sorry Pet. Despite Joe being a pain in the arse he's still mine and Betty's boy." He dabbed his eyes with his sleeve. "I just hope he's alright."

"Me too," I quietly agreed.

Walter stopped a while. I filled him in on our months away and the trouble we faced. I also filled him in on the good parts, Mr and Mrs Gregory's help, Joe bringing in enough to support us all, our little flat, his proposal and the beautiful cherry tree cot he built himself. Walter was most impressed, and I could see a sense of pride that I wished Joe, who always doubted how far his dad's affection stretched, could also see.

Before Walter left to, in his words, *'sort out the house,'* I asked him a question that had been burning ever since it popped into my head halfway through his visit.

"Walter, how did you know I was here?"

"Henry guessed this is where you might be."

"He knows then?"

"I had to tell him, Pet."

I nodded in agreement.

Mr Flint did not mind me leaving to go to the Hollister's, in fact he thought it was a great idea. Relief that others knew of my existence here showed on his face. Henry had kept him at the allotment while Walter had spoken to me earlier. I think Mr Flint was beginning to feel burdened with my secret.

"How was Henry?" I asked, preparing for the hours to come.

"Quiet, he was really quiet. The lad loves ya, Lass. That's plain to see."

Walter did as he said he would and picked me up once it was dark, quietly sneaking me in through the back. I didn't have much to take with me — a few bags and a pram Mr Flint got from a charity shop. I was panicking myself rotten to see Henry but to my utter surprise he was there waiting for us with a cup of tea and a Victoria sponge. I was waiting for the *I told you so* but no, he was more than welcoming with a sweet smile on his face. I couldn't help but notice when I saw him that he looked a little bit older than the Henry I saw a little under a year ago. His shoulders were a little broader and his face looked as though he had been shaving a little above his upper lip. He cut us all a generous slice of cake and commented on how kind it was of Mr Flint to take care of me and that we should all thank him with a small gift, which Walter agreed to. The chat was easy, the Hollister's updated me on work which seems to be going from strength to strength, Henry said that there were rumours that Carol was getting married, with her dad's blessing, to Gareth, the butcher's son, which had taken everyone by surprise, and Peter has taken an interest in the trumpet, which currently doesn't sound too great at eight o'clock in the morning. The conversations were pleasant enough, but I couldn't help but feel like I should butt in with some much-needed questions. I was like an elephant in the room, a great big one. You couldn't ignore my rounded stomach, my constant shuffling in my seat to keep comfortable, or the fact that my shoes could barely fit because my feet were slightly swollen. Yet no one said a word.

"Right, I best be off to bed. Got to be up early in the morning." Walter wished us goodnight and retreated upstairs for the night leaving me and Henry.

"I best be off too. You are to have my room," he said. "I will stay on the sofa."

Henry stood up without another word and left the kitchen. He most likely isn't happy about this arrangement, and how long can he stay on the sofa for. I began to wish I were back in Mr Flint's Victorian bedroom, at least there I knew I wasn't taking up anyone's bed or bringing up bad wounds with my mere presence. I didn't move from the kitchen for a while. I sat in silence with my thoughts, worrying about my next steps, angry at how I got into this situation,

201

frightened by how alone I really was.

Chapter Fourteen

11th September 1958

Just when I felt like there was no hope left in the world, Mr Flint showed me that in the darkest of days there can be some light.

This morning as I made my way downstairs, there was a new addition to the Hollister house. In the middle of the living room stood a white cot. It was the same cot that I had spotted in the corner of the bedroom at Mr Flint's house, so I knew right away that this was down to him. The cot however looked much brighter than before. The yellowing of the cotton canopy had been replaced by a white laced material and the cot itself had a fresh coating of paint, so new that I could still smell the paint. Inside was a layer of foam with a white sheet placed on top, at the bottom a yellow knitted blanket was rolled up with a written note left on top.

This cot has laid empty for far too long, please accept this gift.

Rufus.

I tapped the side of the small cradle and it gently swung without a creak. My emotions are everywhere, and the kind gesture brought me to tears. It wasn't the grand cherry oak cot that Joe made but it was the prettiest cradle, and it too came from the heart. I had not noticed Henry step in and found that I felt embarrassed by my tears as I hastily turned away wiping them.

"Sorry, I left my sandwiches," he said turning a shade of pink as he scurried to the kitchen. On his return he hung by the front door. "Do you want me to stay?" he asked nervously. "We are not too busy today; my dad can manage without me."

His kind offer brought out more emotions which I tried to keep buried within. "I'm fine, honest," I choked out.

Henry left and I let out a gasp of air, letting out all my tears, collapsing onto the couch. I felt the couch sink a little as he sat down next to me and carefully placed a hand on my back gently moving it up and down. He must have crept back in, or the sound of my own crying drowned the noise of his arrival. I turned towards him and leaned in for a much-needed cuddle. He could have pushed me away, but I didn't even think about it I just knew I needed his comfort. Henry embraced me, much to my relief thinking of it now.

"I'm such a mess, Henry," I wailed. "I'm so scared."

I felt what seemed to be a gentle kiss on the top of my head followed by a quiet, "shhh."

"And I can't stop crying," I continued, wailing into his overalls.

"That's because you're having a baby." Henry had never mentioned the baby before, so this comment surprised me. "It's just your hormones."

"My what?" I asked, sitting up and wiping away my

tears.

"Your hormones," Henry repeated and quickly taking in my expression realised I hadn't the foggiest about what he was talking about. "It's a chemical inside your body that changes when you're expecting. It can make you emotional."

"Like when I'm on my monthlies?" I asked.

Henry looked a little embarrassed. "I suppose so, yeah."

I nodded, knowing nothing about my hormones, however, it didn't stop my sadness, it just brought on so much more. "I know nothing, Henry. I'm a failure, I'm going to fail this baby."

"No, you're not," he quietly stated. "I believe you're going to be a great mam. You're just emotional, Lottie, and being stuck in here can't be helping either. You need to get out."

"I can't," I cried.

"Everyone's going to find out you're here at some point, you know. You can't hide here forever."

Why does everyone feel the need to remind me of this. I didn't reply to his comment, I knew they were right, but I wasn't ready to do anything about it just yet. Instead, I stayed silent. We both did in fact. The Hollister's have a small TV now, I haven't put it on for fear of my parents hearing it from next door and wondering who is using it during the daytime. Now that Henry was home, I felt comfortable with it when he put it on. All day we sat there. Over time I began to get fidgety, Henry offered his lap as a place to rest my head to allow me to stretch out my legs.

"Here," he offered me a small cushion, "place this between your legs you'll be more comfortable." The cushion was ideal and with the rhythm of Henry's hand stroking my hair I began to feel a little sleepy.

"Henry, do you hate me?" I asked, my eyes closing with a sting. He did not answer straight away. It would not surprise me if he did, but I hoped that he did not. I know Mr Flint thinks he loves me, but I heard that the line between love and hate was a fine one.

"No," he eventually said. "I've tried to hate you, but I can't."

And on that note, I drifted off to sleep.

The room was dark when I woke up, the TV was off, but a small creak of light came from the kitchen along with the chitter chatter of Walter and Henry and the strong smell of vinegar. I tried to return to my slumber, but Henry had other plans. In he strolled with the kitchen light now blaring into the living room carrying a wrapped parcel easily identified as fish and chips.

"Ah good, you're awake," he said. "I'm taking you out for some fresh air."

"What? No." I sat up, so quickly that the baby must have been alarmed by my sudden movement giving me a great big kick.

"It's fine, it's dark now. I will keep you hidden until we get to the van. No one will see us, I promise." After struggling to put my shoes on and finding that my coat was as good as a shawl, Henry placed his cap on my head.

"And wear these." He handed me a huge pair of sunglasses. "Perfect"

I couldn't help but laugh, I looked ridiculous. I don't even think Joe would recognise me. Especially with the added touch of a scarf wrapped around my neck and mouth and an umbrella. Henry, as promised, got me to the van unseen by anyone. I assumed Walter was going to be driving but it was Henry who took the driver's seat.

"You know how to drive?" I asked impressed.

"Yeah," he smiled at my surprise. "I'm seventeen now, my dad's been giving me lessons. Well one lesson but I know what I'm doing." I shot him a look of terror before he laughed. "Relax, I've had many. I drive all the time."

We were heading to the allotment and what should have been a short drive turned out to be a very, exceedingly long one.

"Henry, why are you driving so slowly?" I asked him.

"I don't want to upset the baby, some of this road is bumpy." Henry continued to drive at a slower pace looking very seriously out of the windscreen, I honestly could have walked faster.

"I came here by motorcycle; you can drive faster."

Henry gritted his teeth. "Idiot," he muttered.

"Excuse me," I gasped.

"Not you, it's not safe to be in a bumpy vehicle it can cause problems; and a motorcycle, God's sake what were you both thinking. Did your midwife not tell you anything?"

I could have retaliated to the insult at Joe, but I didn't have the strength to, and Henry may have had a point. I can see why it could be dangerous, and it left me feeling a little bit ashamed for not knowing better but in my defence how could I have. "I didn't have a midwife, so I wasn't advised on what transport was safe and not safe."

"Your doctor then."

"I never had a doctor either."

The van came to a complete stop, the engine died down leaving behind silence and a stunned Henry. "Who have you seen, medically?"

"No one, just Mrs Gregory."

"And she is?"

"A book shop owner."

"A book shop owner," he repeated. "For God's sake, Lottie!" he shouted, making me jump as he hit the steering wheel. "Why you picked him I will never know."

"What's the big deal, Henry. Look at me, I'm ready to pop, I'm fine!" I shouted back.

"The deal is you haven't been cared for properly. Joe should have made sure of it."

"I was cared for. Joe knew if someone saw me, they would take one look at my medical records and bring me back here. We had no choice!"

"That is Joe thinking about himself, not you! He is selfish, anything could have happened to you!"

"Well, it didn't!" I screamed, thinking of the night I was drugged and how we didn't seek any help afterwards to make sure the baby was okay. I felt guilty at the thought of neglecting medical care so that I could carry on living with my boyfriend. Did that make me a bad mam? An immature mam even.

"Let's go back, Henry."

"Lottie, don't you see. You did everything that he asked of you all the time, and now where is he?"

"He had to leave us, for our safety. You know this."

"He left you because it was easier."

"No, that's not true. It would have been dangerous."

"More dangerous than carrying a baby for nine months at such an immature age. More dangerous than driving her around on a motorcycle and leaving her to pick up the pieces in a world where she will be forever judged."

"Alright, I get it Henry, please! Let's go back to the house."

We made an abrupt turn and were back quickly with the speed of the driving at a faster pace. I carelessly made a quick dash into the house before Henry could help me disguise myself and took myself straight to my room. Well Henry's room, nothing here is really mine at all.

"Charlotte are you alright Pet," Walter called after me as I passed him, to which I rudely ignored. I am sure Henry will fill him in. Henry is wrong about Joe. He did care for me. He did what was best for us both. He did care, I can't believe anything different.

12th September 1958

I was up, dressed and waiting for the front door to close

before I made my way downstairs this morning. I was going to forget about last night and have a good day by myself. Maybe I could hunt out a book to read I thought or sort out the baby's clothes and see what I need to buy. All plans of my day however were quickly tarnished when I was met with Henry eating toast at the table.

"Morning," he said glumly.

"Morning," I replied, helping myself to a cup of tea opposite him. I could hear Betty's cuckoo clock ticking loudly as we sat miserably. Me and Henry always find a way to fall out. We can escalate from being cheerful to a full-on shouting match in minutes. No matter how many times we get angry at each other, I can't help but feel sad by it. I hate Henry being pissed with me; it makes me yearn for his kind spirit all the more.

"I'm sorry," Henry apologised, "I didn't mean to upset you yesterday. I just get so wound up."

"It's fine, I'm sorry too," I replied honestly, I had to hide a small smile of relief. I knew we were going to be okay, in the end we are always going to be okay.

"I've got something for you." Henry reached into a sideboard cupboard and pulled out a bright pink book. He passed me it, taking a seat closer beside me. I was surprised when I read the title *What to Expect When You're Expecting - A Housewives Guide.* Below it was a picture of a new-born baby in the arms of a woman.

"Where did you get this?" I asked.

"I'm not proud, but I stole it from the library. It tells you everything that's going on with your body each month and what will happen when the baby is ready to come." Henry took hold of the book and flicked through it until he found the page he was searching for. "And at the back here, it has tips and things on how to prepare a bath or a bottle."

I had been going through this pregnancy in the dark, love had gotten me through it so far. I knew nothing of swollen feet and night sweats until they came to me, and I most definitely did not know what to expect when the time would come for baby to arrive.

"Have you read it?" I asked curiously.

Henry handed me back the book. "I've read it. I got it when I knew you were coming here. I wanted to be prepared but I've come to realise that I know more than you."

"Is it scary?" I flicked through the book, pictures jumped off the pages of illustrations and body parts making me feel rather faint.

"You've already gone through the majority of it now."

"But the end...is it?" Henry looked at me with his piercing blue eyes that told me that it wasn't going to be pleasant. "I don't think I want to read it. It will frighten me; I've come this far without knowing. I will just deal with it when the time comes."

Henry nodded. "Well, I'll be here."

I rested my head on Henry. I believed him; I knew I could rely on him.

Together we spent the day getting things prepared, Henry made me write a list of what the baby needed so he could ask Walter to go shopping once he returned from the cemetery visiting Betty. He carried the cot up to the bedroom and with great difficulty wrestled with an armchair up the stairs.

"I don't see why I need an armchair."

"For the night feeds."

"I can sit on the bed."

"You'll want to be sat upright correctly and you won't want to be too comfy and fall asleep."

"You do know I will have to come downstairs to make the bottle. I could sit in the chair then."

Henry who was still pushing with all his might sweating buckets stopped for a second. "You will wake me up then," he said with a cheeky wink.

"Oh, so this isn't about me or baby it's ensuring someone gets their beauty sleep."

"Priorities, princess."

"You're going to either break your back or the chair."

Thankfully neither were broken and I am now the new owner of a floral (rather old) armchair which Henry thought would be nice sat overlooking the window at the bottom of my bed.

"You can watch the world go by from here."

I laughed at his vision looking down at the grey shade of yards and brick walls of the back lanes.

"One day perhaps you will have a better view."

14th September 1958

I must write this before I forget any detail at all. The

house is quiet, everyone is sleeping, and the birds are singing ready for a new day and what a beautiful day it will be.

Last night Henry tried once more to get me outside. This time he was successful. He offered me his arm to link as we walked slowly to the allotment from the access path where the road ends.

Anyway, when we arrived it was like a scene from a movie, the garden was lit with candles and blankets were laid out in the centre with a hamper.

"Thought we could have a midnight picnic seeing as you're a vampire nowadays." Henry guided me to a spot and plated up some food for us. It smelt delicious.

"We have cakes, sandwiches, crisps, and the best sausage rolls in the world. They may be cold, but I picked them up from Greggs on my way home from a delivery in Gosforth today."

The candles and the picnic under the stars were wonderful. When we were stuffed, we lay down and tried to find constellations above. I was a little bloated and began to think maybe I had eaten a little too much as my stomach began to ache.

"I feel fine," Henry said once we gathered that it couldn't have been something we ate.

"Oh, it's ok, it's not so bad now. I've clearly been a little too greedy."

Henry carried on telling me a story about the stars when my pain began once more. "Oh, Henry I think we should go home, it's real sore."

Henry, being the gentleman that he has always been, sat me in the shed on a stool while he packed away our picnic. "We've had a lot of good times here, haven't we?" Henry said. "The three of us breaking a sweat, sharing stories…sharing kisses."

He looked at me as he said sharing kisses and it brought many memories to my mind of me and Henry in the mist of our teenage romance, our first love, sneaking off for kisses and sharing glances across the plants while Mr. Flint chatted our ear off about the good old days. It was innocent back then and I did not realise just how nice that felt. "We will be able to bring the little one here one day," he continued with his projected thoughts.

"I would like that very much."

"Right, we are ready to go. My lady." Henry pulled out an arm for me once more. I stood up ready to leave when I felt a sudden dampness between my legs.

"Oh my God, Henry!" I exclaimed. "I think I've peed myself."

"What?" Henry said, looking puzzled down at my dress.

"Don't look, Henry. Oh my God, how embarrassing." Another wave of stomach ache then hit me only this time it knocked me for six. I gripped onto Henry's arms terrified that I would lose balance and fall.

"Lottie?"

"My stomach it's really sore, Henry. I think I need to — Ahhh! Ahhh!"

I couldn't finish my sentence but as though he heard my thoughts Henry scooped me up and sat me back down. Quietly I could hear him repeat the word *"shit"* over and over. He quickly threw some blankets onto the floor.

"Henry!" I wailed. The pain was too much. Henry slowly moved me over to the blankets and sat me down.

"You haven't peed yourself Lottie. I think you're in labour."

"No, I can't be. I'm not ready, I still have a month to go."

"You must have worked it out wrong."

"Noooooo!" I yelled as another shot of pain ran through me across my back and into my stomach.

"I should fetch a midwife. I can call one from the phone box."

"No! Don't leave me Henry. Please don't leave me." I gripped onto his shirt keeping him close to me. "I'm scared."

Henry stayed, and he was a saint looking back on it now, for I was crazy! We must have been there for hours, and the pain shocked me every single time it snuck back around. Henry said it was called a contraction and that it was my body getting ready to let the baby out. He kept telling me to pant every time one came.

"I'm not a dog Henry," I shouted at him. "I don't want to pant."

"The book said it will help."

"I don't give a fuck about the book, this is real life, and I don't want to bloody pant!"

It didn't stop him for reminding me for the next couple of hours to bloody pant. Anger was not my only emotion throughout the ordeal, because I also went into a state of panic.

"I'm going to have a baby; I'm going to be a mam. I'm sixteen, I don't know how to look after a baby. I helped with Peter but it's not the same, is it?"

"You're going to be fine, Lottie. I promise."

"You can't promise me that. What will people say about me, about my baby with no dad? What will become of us? I can't do this, Henry. I'm not ready."

"It's a little too late to undo things now darling but listen to me, you're not doing this alone. You have me and my dad. Your baby will have a family who loves them, and if anyone utters so much as a bad word about you or the bairn then they will have me to answer to."

I wailed when the next contraction came, Henry allowed me to squeeze his hand as hard as I needed to. "I'm scared Henry!" I shouted.

"Marry me!" he shouted back, I think in that moment even my contraction stopped in shock or maybe my mind was taken just by complete surprise. "Marry me," he repeated.

"Henry, you don't mean that."

"I do, I love you, Lottie. I've never stopped loving you. Marry me, I will look after you always and I will be a dad to the bairn. I know I'm not Joe, but I promise you both that I will never let you down."

I felt as though I was beginning to feel a little faint as

well as nauseous. Henry was always the knight, the one to pick me up when I was down and yet I returned his love with betrayal, a betrayal that I'd regretted at times so much over the last year.

"I'm no good for you Henry. I'm damaged, I'm just no good. You can have anyone you want."

"I want you. Marry me. I know you love me too."

Henry's words knocked me back and right into a pain screeching contraction. I had thought of Henry many times during my time in Gateshead. I had longed for him even, his company, his embrace. I missed his face and our long sunny days together, but I never thought that I loved him, I was with Joe that would be wrong.

"You can't deny it," he said with confidence, "you love me."

I shook my head.

"Yes, you do."

"I don't Henry."

"Yes, you do, you're just too afraid to admit it."

"What makes you think that?"

"Because if you didn't, you wouldn't scream my name at night or kiss me back when I kissed you."

I had no words, only screams. Is it wrong to love two brothers at the same time? Is it wrong to be pining for one while enjoying the company of another? Is it wrong that I still dream of Henry and ache for his touch every time I am around him? I have not wanted to admit this, not even to myself, but Henry was right. I love him.

Towards the end when I began to get the urge to push,

Henry had no choice but to help me. I never imagined I would ever give birth in an allotment shed with a Hollister playing nurse between my legs. Yet together we did it.

"We should be going to the picture house or to a dance," I remember saying as I got exhausted.

"It was dancing that got you into this shed, Darling. Come on now, keep panting, hopefully it won't be much longer."

I chuckled at his snide remark which was quickly followed by a scream that I'm sure all of Durham could hear.

Eventually, she joined us in this world, my daughter. All the fear and pain went out of the shed door the moment Henry placed her in my arms and I gazed at her for the first time, her dark hair, her button nose, and tiny fingers. She is beautiful, I felt instantly like I have to do anything and everything I can to make sure she has the best life. Henry sat beside us and covered her in a warm blanket. He placed an arm around me, and my girl snuggled in.

"Thank you, Henry," I whispered.

"No need to thank me, just call me Dr Hollister from now on."

I looked up at him as he sat with his eyes closed probably trying to forget everything he saw during the labour; blood stained his hands and his pale blue polo top. He was only seventeen, he didn't need to be here with me trying to make my life better. He really would do anything for me, Henry doesn't just say he loves me, he proves it, he is pure and honest. After everything I've put him through, he still wants to be with me. That must be love or just plain craziness. Either way I am glad he loves me for I know I have always needed him, always loved him. I thought I needed more in life — the busy streets of London, the theatre shows and afternoon teas. Having my daughter lay in my arms, that isn't what I wish for her, I wish for her to be surrounded by her family, to do well at school and make great friends, to spend the summer building sandcastles at South Shields beach and to meet Henry after work every Friday for fish and chips.

"Yes," I whispered.

"Yes what?" he whispered back.

"I will marry you."

Henry's eyes shot open and met my gaze. He didn't say anything, but his kiss said it all. I have thought about Henry's last kiss constantly, no matter how hard I tried to fight the thought. I wanted it, I know that now, or at least I can admit it to myself now. Our blissful moment quickly turned to an intense argument when Henry wanted me to go to hospital before the afterbirth and to have a check-up. I of course refused; we had just delivered a baby we could do anything ourselves now.

So, the world is magical once more. We made it back to the Hollister's just before light broke. Walter is still sleeping so has no idea yet that he has a granddaughter. Henry gave her a bottle just before the two of them fell fast asleep. Now my baby girl is wrapped up in her cot while Henry sleeps on the empty bed opposite. I feel blessed and emotional.

I know Joe would love to see her, I wish he could, to see how tiny his daughter is, I wish I could give him some sort of sign to let him know that she was here, but he is gone, and I must move on from the stress that came with being suddenly left on his dad's doorstep, for her sake. I will tell her all about him and the sacrifice he made to keep us safe as I am sure Walter will too. Joe has given me the greatest gift in the world, and he will always be loved.

Henry makes me happy, and I know he will love my daughter as his own.

I can't stop looking at her, she is so precious. I hope I can be the best Mam possible. I hope I can give her all the love and stories that her Great Nana Florence gave to me, I hope I can provide her with the care that her Nana Mavis gave me and the patience that her Nana Betty gave to both Henry and Joe. I want her to have it all and I am excited that I get to spend the rest of my life loving her.

My daughter, my little Betty Florence Hollister.

Chapter Fifteen

21st September 1958

I must have done something terrible in a past life, or perhaps even this one, to be dealt such an evil blow. No matter what you do, whether it be good or bad, you hope that deep down your parents will be there to support you, to love you, and tell you that despite everything they've got your back. Not mine. I know me and dad were never close, he made that clear the day he arrived back home when the war ended. My mam has never been one to show much emotion, but she told me in her own way how much she cared. Nana Florence once told me the whole house cried the day I was born, yet the day I almost died the whole house hatched up a plan instead.

I was rushed to hospital when I lost too much blood and became unconscious. Legally my parents were informed, there was no reunion, no explanations, or tears shed. I woke to an empty ward to be told by an emotionless doctor that my parents were the legal guardians of *the baby* — he didn't say, *your baby* he said *the baby*. I was too young he went on, still a child and a foolish one at that. My parents are allowed to make all the decisions of parenthood for me, I have no say in the matter at all. They just took her like you take a pup from its mother. The doctor wished me a good life and left. A week I was left on the ward — no one came, I was under strict instruction to see no one. It didn't stop Henry from trying every day. I could hear the commotion on the other side of the double doors of the ward as he shouted for them to let him see me. He would shout he loved me hoping I could hear him. I didn't have the strength to shout it back. I'd lost the chance to fight for my daughter before I even had a chance to fight. Every time I tried to leave the ward or even cry out for my baby someone would come and sedate me. The days and nights rolled into one big haze, my breasts were sore, my stomach was like smashed jelly, yet I had no baby in my arms. I had no baby at all.

They took her from me, my own parents have destroyed me and tore my family apart. I know they must have been devastated when I ran away with Joe and equally so when they were told of me and Betty. They were my parents though, they carried out their plan without a word to me, sneaking her away while I lay unconscious. How could they? I am their daughter. I could never inflict pain such as this on Betty. I can't get my head around their cold actions, and they didn't stop there either. This morning my Uncle Albert arrived at the hospital looking glum.

"I've come to take you back with me, kiddo," he said, looking uncomfortable. He wasn't wearing his usual attire of a suit, but instead looked casual in a pair of brown linen trousers and navy top.

"They hate me that much," I spoke.

"Your mother thinks it's for the best. I just want to

keep the peace." He always was, forever being bossed around by women my uncle, he was a mammy's boy, then pushed over by his wife and now he is a part of my mam's awful plan. I pity him really.

"I have your bag packed in the car; Henry ensured everything was there for you."

"You saw Henry?" I asked, desperate to hear of him.

"Yes, lovely chap. He wanted to be here himself, but he has a restraining order keeping him from being anywhere near this hospital."

"Then take me to him, Uncle. Let me say goodbye to him. Please," I begged. "Please I must say goodbye to him, take me home let me see Betty, she needs me. I am her mam."

"I'm afraid I can't do that. My orders are to take you straight to London."

I laughed at his pathetic words. "Your orders! Are you a man or a mouse?"

"Mock me all you like, but you have worried this family sick for the last year with your runaway. Your mam was ill not knowing where you were. I think getting away from both brothers is for the best. You always wanted to move to London. Now you can. Forget about them, Charlotte. Start again."

"My baby," I managed to say with a tremble at his rant.

"She is going to grow up loved and looked after by adults. You're a child, so be a child."

A week ago, I became a mam to the most precious little

thing. I didn't even get a day with her before she was cruelly taken against my will. I will never forgive my family for this. Now I sit in the back of a car going towards a place I once longed for, all the while I want to scream to turn around and be taken back to Durham, back to her. Joe would never have let this happen if he were here.

22nd September 1958

My bedroom at Nana's has lost its old charm. It's lost its feeling of adventure and childhood dreams. It now feels like my new prison cell. In fact, the whole house does. I'm not bound to my bedroom, I can roam free, but I do have *rules* to follow, which Auntie Emily was quick to dish out last night. We were having tea in the downstairs dining hall. I really was in no mood to be gobbling salmon and baby potatoes, yet she insisted for I looked *surprisingly* terrible.

"Right let's start how we mean to go on shall we, now that you are to be living here, Charlotte, let's go over some rules."

"Mother," William, who was home for the weekend, protested. "Is this really necessary?"

"Quiet William, Charlotte needs to know her boundaries."

I honestly didn't know where to look, my uncle said nothing but took a great big sip of his wine, so I carried on playing with my food.

"Firstly, you will have to find a job."

"What!" William shouted across the table. "She's just had a…"

"William, please, everyone has to pay their way in the world. Food and board are never free. Secondly, you must be home before eight each evening, unless work permits otherwise; then your uncle will retrieve you."

Uncle Albert gave an over-the-top smile from the far end of the large table, clearly following orders again.

"Thirdly, no boyfriends or even male friends."

"Mother!" William protested once more.

"William, please go and pack for school. Your train leaves early in the morning."

"Father, tell her she must not speak like that."

"Listen to your mother, go and pack William," My uncle replied, taking another large sip of wine. William threw down his cutlery causing a clatter, before storming off upstairs.

"The fourth rule," Auntie Emily continued, "and one I think all parties will agree with, is there is to be no communication with anyone back in Durham." My eyes widened as I heard the rubbish spill out of the witch's thin lips. "If your parents wish to get in touch, they will do so. As for your neighbours and that scruffy fellow, well, I think it's fair to say it's time to close that chapter of your life. There will be no letters or phone calls whatsoever."

I had no words to say to her, I just glared at her hoping it would make her feel uncomfortable. All this no communication crap was just another way of keeping me in the dark, keeping me from any form of knowledge or contact with my daughter.

"Is that understood?" Auntie Emily asked firmly.

"Very," I replied.

"Good, well now that is out the way, pudding anyone?"

William was sat at the top of the staircase after I was excused from the table. My scoop of ice cream well and truly melted; I had been sat for so long. William apologised for his mam. He told me he was embarrassed to hear her pathetic rules.

"It's fine," I replied, heading to my room.

"It's not Charlotte, we all do things on compulsion, we all make mistakes. It doesn't mean you should be punished forever for it."

I didn't know which direction to take William's comment, did he mean my relationship with Joe? My rash decision to run away and potentially scar my family in the long run or did he mean having my sweet little girl out of wedlock? Betty may have been an unexpected surprise, but she was not a mistake, she was a gift. All the high-end education in the world, however, could not explain that to my cousin. I sat beside him on the step and questioned him about his life. He himself was taken in by my auntie and uncle at just two when they adopted him, thinking of Betty now in the arms of others made me wonder about her future. Did she sense that they were not me? Did she listen for my voice? Was she ok? Would she be happy? Would they love her properly, how my parents were meant to love me? Any love given to her would surely be less than my own for I love her more than anything in the world.

"Did you ever wonder about your biological parents?" I asked him.

"Not really, they were both killed during the war. My birth mother died in the blitz, luckily at the time I was with my great-aunt in a country house belonging to my parents. My biological father was an officer in France and died on the frontline. My life could have been so much different but the one I have is the only one I know. To be honest the only one I want. I'm sorry they took your baby."

"Betty, her name was Betty. Cathleen left me a brief note in my suitcase, she sounded saddened by everything but also incredibly supportive of my parents' decision, which is typical of her really. Always thinking she knows what is best for me. Just like everyone does."

"Well not me, if you need anything, anything at all, just let me know," William offered before we departed.

"Thank you, William, but I'm fine at the moment." He can't wave a magic spell and give me back my baby can he. What else could possibly help me now, until it struck me like a thunderbolt.

"Actually, there is something you can do, if you really want to help."

William listened carefully as I quietly asked him a

favour, which he happily agreed to. I thought it would take a little more persuasion. It seems William has been growing his own wings since I last saw him, my uncle should take note. With my cousin on board, I immediately got on with writing a particularly important letter.

Dear Henry,

It is me, Lottie, as you know I am here in London. My parents have all but disowned me and stolen Betty as well. How could they do this? I'm their daughter, my dad talks of pain and loss, yet they torture me with a life sentence of grief. I don't even have a picture of her.

If you ever see her, please describe her to me, how she looks as she grows, describe her cries you hear through the night, the songs she falls asleep to. I need to know every detail. I can only imagine her angel face and the feel of her soft skin.

I'm a mother without a child, Henry.

I'm sorry I couldn't say goodbye, my uncle outright refused, he along with the rest of my family want to keep me away from you. I miss you already. I must have you in my life that is why we need to be careful. My cousin, William, is going to post my letters for me, you must reply to the address that will appear on the front of the envelope. This is the address of his school, address it to Master W Anderson. I will be able to receive them each weekend. Please write to me Henry. I already feel like I'm losing my mind.

Mel Higgins

Love you always, your Lottie xxxx

Chapter Sixteen

6th March 1959

Today's shift at the hotel was torturous, we are
unbelievably busy at the moment; I can barely catch my
breath. I swear I have lost tons of weight simply from
walking from the kitchen to the guests' tables. It is
nonstop, so I am grateful that tomorrow is my day off.
That is if Auntie Emily doesn't give me a list of chores,
that witch thinks I can work around the clock. The pay
isn't even worth it, once my auntie takes her percentage
out each week. I receive enough to get myself something
nice from the chippy or at a stretch a sneaky drink of wine
from Laurence the bartender. Not from the hotel bar, God
no, I would have to work ten years to afford one of those!
Laurence has quite a collection at his flat which he
sometimes allows me to buy enough to fill my grandads
hip flask that I found in a box of my nana's belongings.
Some days I just need a drink to take the edge off. It's not
always wine, sometimes its gin or even vodka. Laurence is
an expert in his field, and a sweet friend, a mischievous
one at that, I am forever getting in trouble for taking too
long on my break when Laurence is about. He is a very
pretty boy, I don't fancy him though, of course I only have
eyes for my Henry but to be honest I don't believe I or any
other woman would be enough for Laurence, if you get
my gist. Of course, I would never say anything to him or

anyone else; that would get him into heaps of trouble and it's none of my business anyway. Nana used to say that there were many men like Laurence around London, and in her eyes, they were fabulous! Sadly, the world does not see it that way, therefore, to admit it would lead Laurence to a punishment that he would not deserve.

Before I left for home Laurence asked me if I wanted to head out tomorrow to his cousin's, Danny Porter, who was a newly qualified policeman following in the footsteps of his uncle, Laurence's Dad. Every week he wanted to celebrate the fact that he was now a Bobby — any excuse for a piss up I believed. I liked Danny, he liked to party but knew when to stop, he liked to take the piss out of people but had been there a handful of times when I needed a shoulder to cry on after one too many. He was a policeman who knew to follow rules yet had also helped me escape in and out of the Anderson household one too many times. He is a good friend, and everyone knows that he is in love with me, at twenty-years-old he is wise beyond his years. All the girls want to get to know Danny, what's not to like; he has blonde floppy hair, dark hazel eyes, and large muscles. I can see how attractive he is, I am not blind, but I care for him only as a friend. Even then I don't know how capable I am of caring for anyone, my heart is so broken, I think I mistake the feeling of needing the likes of Danny and Laurence to stop me from doing something stupid. Henry tells me to hang on, to make friends and try to enjoy my life because I can't change what has been done. This doesn't stop the nightmares of my baby being taken from me or having to avoid every baby on the street as it hurts too much to see. I ask myself why I don't save up and buy a train ticket to Durham but what is the use. They would send me back and besides my baby is no longer there as my last letter from Henry informed me that Cathleen and Rupert, who have legally adopted my sweet little girl, have moved to France. France! Clearly, they wanted to get as far away from the Hollisters, and even possibly me, as possible after all I can only be forced to stay in London for so long. By the end of the year, I will be eighteen and I will be going home. Me and Henry will then marry and have as many babies as we like, and my parents will not even know their names.

"If you change your mind, we can pick you up at six," Laurence said, grabbing his coat. By picking me up what he really meant was they would meet me across the road as I climb out my nan's old bedroom window. Numerous times I have crept in and out this way, it isn't always easy though, especially if my auntie or uncle are hovering on the first floor. A few weeks ago, I had to slither down the drainpipe from the middle floor lounge. Although my auntie has these rules, she isn't bothered about me once I am home so escaping is easy, it's the return that is more difficult because I need to be extremely quiet creeping back up to my floor. William, the rebel that he is nowadays, accompanies me at times, he meets us a little later, as his witch of a mother will never let him go off to bed without a goodnight kiss. He sometimes rallies up some of his own pals and we will drink and dance, and in my case drown my sorrows into a bottle or a glass.

I sometimes imagine that Henry is with us too, he would be sat relaxed on the couch letting me have a fun time while watching my intake and looking after me. I would slither next to him and tell him that the room was spinning. He would laugh or give me a lecture and take me home with him, stopping for chips on the way.

"I'll think about it," I teased.

We both knew I was going to go, I had nothing better to do with my day apart from walk around the house wishing my life away or crying into my pillow which felt too exhausting.

As today is a Friday it means only one thing, William is home, along with a letter from Henry.

Dear Lottie,

I hope you are good this week, and everyone is treating you well. I miss you terribly, I know we have parted before, but never have I craved to be with you as much as I do now.

I have fallen out with my dad; we had an argument because I suggested coming down to London next month when I turn eighteen. I thought maybe I could get a job somewhere as a carpenter and rent out a room. That way I could see you. My dad thinks it's a stupid idea, he believes we are best off to wait and that I would be throwing away big opportunities at Walter and Sons. He said I would be better off putting money away for us. I know what he really wants to say is that he needs me to work for him because he can't do it on his own. I love my dad and I care about the business, but December is so far away Lottie, I can't bear to be apart from you that long. I'm crumbling.

I hear your stories and I want to be there. I'm glad you're making friends and trying to move forward but I can't help feeling left behind. My day is the same day in, day out. I'm just waiting. Waiting for you. Waiting for our life to begin.

Sorry, I'm just rambling now. My dad has wound me up. I look forward to your letter, that always cheers me up.

Love you always, H xx

I can't help but feel terrible. I've always felt like I was the only one suffering. That I was the one who had their child taken from them, I was the one betrayed by my family and I was the one forced to live miles away. I know Henry misses me as I do him, but I always thought he was ok. He was at home with his dad and their business is growing. Whenever I am out trying to take my mind off everything, I always wish Henry were with me, but never did I imagine he was at home crumbling. He has never sounded this down before; he is always upbeat but maybe that was just for my benefit. I must write to him and send him as much love as possible through ink and paper.

Chapter Seventeen

4th April 1959

Today is Henry's birthday, he is eighteen and a free man but then he already was free. Today Henry becomes a man and yesterday I was celebrating Danny's twenty-first, it's all fucked up. Danny had a small gathering at his flat with our friends, his mam and Laurence's dad, whom for his age was still in particularly decent shape, I have to say. His mam — Rosemary — put out a spread and it was nice enough, but my heart was not into such celebrations, although I still attended with William as a goodwill gesture. It was his birthday after all, and he personally asked for me to be there. Yet the whole time I was there I thought back to all the celebrations that the Hollisters had in their home for Henry and Joe's birthdays over the years. Betty always made the cake herself, but she was not the best at decorating, yet she always tried; it became the annual joke of the party. Those were the days, even if Henry did fling cake at me one year with his new catapult, I mean why on earth would you have bought Henry of all people a catapult, let us not forget how much of a shit he was. One year, his seventh I think it was, I blew out the candles while he was making his wish, he was so angry and I got such a telling off, but it was worth it, it was payback for pulling the string on my party hat and letting it fire back onto my face — how we fell in love is a mystery, I am sure we were destined to kill each other.

Rosemary approached me in the living area, where I was stood in a corner trying to not get anyone's attention. The evening was late, I had drunk too much, and I did not really want to be there, however she found me — lucky me. She is quite a plump woman with grey hair tied tight into curls, her face was kind making me feel guilty that I really did not wish for conversation.

"You must be Charlotte; I am Danny's mum, Rosemary," she beamed.

"Yes, yes I am," I nodded, giving a small smile in return.

"I have heard everything about you, my Danny is always talking about you. I am glad I can put a face to the name now. I have been wanting to catch you all night. Well, I can see why he fancies you, love, you're gorgeous." I blushed at Rosemary's comment while noticing that Danny, who was in deep conversation with William, kept glancing over at us. "I had a great aunt that lived in the Northeast, Hexham. You know of it?"

"Yes," I replied, "yes I do know of it."

"It was lovely there; I remember visiting as a child. It was so peaceful, so green. Nothing like London," Rosemary continued, looking happy as she thought back to childhood memories. "But this is home, and now yours too I've heard, I bet your house is ten times bigger than our flat in Mayfair."

I blushed again.

"Yes, but it's not mine. I live in a small terrace house back home." I did not want to sound as though I was better than her as I am far from it. My cousin may speak like a posh politician, but I come from a humble background.

"Well, I hope you are settling ok, and that son of mine is treating you well. Oh, he does like you very much."

"He is very kind to me, Mrs Porter."

"Oh please, call me Rosemary. I think we are going to be good friends, and I have good feelings about you two — are you all right love?"

I am not sure whether it was the alcohol or the conversation that stirred something inside me that caused me to want to vomit. I held up a finger and ran to the toilet to be sick. With my head in the toilet, I felt two hands pull my hair into one grasp away from my face.

"Better out than in," I heard Danny say.

"You should leave," I said quickly.

"Believe me, this is not the first time I've seen you vomit, Charlotte, remember that time outside Dukes when you projectile vomited all over that woman with the crazy hair? And the time you spewed on William's shoes."

"Shut up Danny!"

He laughed and let go of my hair as I pulled my head away from the loo. Danny sat on the edge of the bath opposite me and pulled away a strand of hair that was stuck to my sticky face. It came to my attention that I was also a little teary.

"Hey, it's just a bit of sick, happens to the best of us," Danny said wiping away a tear.

I grabbed his hand and gently pulled it away from my face. "Your mum, Danny, she speaks of us as if we are a couple."

"Don't worry about her, my mum is just a big romantic, probably why she had me with an American soldier she met during the war. She was swept off her feet and then dropped on her arse when he left her with me. She just wants to see me happy that's all."

I thought back to the smiley woman I met a few minutes ago, I know from experience how frightened she must have felt being left alone with a new life to look after.

"Did your family help her?" I asked, wiping away my tears that were still appearing despite trying to stop them.

"My grandad wasn't happy, but he blamed the war for heightened feelings. Her parents told everyone that her husband died in the war, and I was lucky I guess; I grew up with a good family. My mum has been all I've ever needed."

"Your family sound great."

"They're a good bunch, come here you, this is meant to be a party." Danny pulled me up for a hug looking confused by my sadness. "Is the thought of being with me that awful that it reduces you to tears?"

"No, sorry. I just had some stuff on my mind that's all."

"Henry?" he guessed.

I nodded. "It's his birthday tomorrow and I'm…"

"Here with me. Why don't you visit home?" he asked, a

question that many have asked before. Why don't I visit my betrothed? Why doesn't he visit me here in London?

"It's complicated."

"Well, Charlotte with a complicated life, thank you for spending my birthday with me. If it were my choice, you would have been the only guest here."

I gazed up at his hazel eyes as he took my hands into his own, he really was an extremely pretty man. I could see the muscles of his arms poke out of his tight t-shirt. His perfect face was inches from mine and just as he moved closer to my own all the alcohol I had consumed seemed to evaporate in an instant and I quickly pulled my face away, placing Danny's surprise kiss on my cheek instead.

"I'm sorry," I said as quickly as Danny pulled away from me.

"It's fine, I get it. I should get back to the party." He left the bathroom without a second glance, and I could not help but feel awful yet at the same time angry with him. He knows I am not interested in any romance. I found William and we made our excuses. I feel embarrassed every time I think about it.

But on another note, whatever you are doing Henry — Happy Birthday.

6th April 1959

I had a visitor outside of work this evening, Danny Porter, of course, along with a bouquet of purple and peach tulips.

"An apology for the other night," he said nervously, handing the bouquet over. "I hope you can forgive me."

I smiled. "And what If I do not?"

"Well, then I will just have to arrest you of course," his voice steadier.

"That doesn't sound very lawful, but just in case you are allowed to do that then yes, I forgive you."

"Thank God, I haven't stopped thinking about it. I was foolish I know, but you were just — I love you, Charlotte," he said passionately. I am used to the sarcastic, joking Danny but today he sounded serious. "I am in love with a girl who belongs to another which has to be the saddest love of all. I know you do not feel the same, Henry is a lucky guy, but please may we stay good friends? Please can we spend time together just the two of us and I do not mean getting pissed all the time. I just want to share your company if that is okay with you?"

With his desperate plea how could I say no, he is in love with me, and I do not repay that love at all, the least I can do is give him my time, it is not like I have much else to do here so I agreed, much to his pleasure.

"Great! Okay well I am off work on Saturday if your free, there is somewhere I want to take you that I think you will enjoy. Are you free?" he asked. "I can pick you up from here at say two o'clock?"

"Yeah, Saturday is great."

11th April 1959

Dear Lottie,

I hope you are okay and not having to pull P.C fucking Danny away anymore. What do you think the level of punishment is for punching a policeman? I know I want you to have friends down there but be careful as not everyone has such good intentions. You are young and vulnerable, I hope no one takes advantage of that.

Please, Darling, remember that alcohol does not solve our problems it only masks them for a short while. Picturing you leathered out in London does not sit well with me. What if you end up hurt or someone does something to you that is unforgivable? I am your partner, but I cannot protect you. Every time you have a day off you are on the end of a bottle, and I am worried Lottie. Alcohol and trauma are always a bad concoction, and I am sorry, but what kind of policeman condones underage drinking anyway?

Thanks for the birthday message, my day was okay, Dad took me for a pint after work. I think you did all the celebrating for me.

Love always, H xx

Dear Lottie

Dear Lottie,

I regret the letter I wrote you yesterday, I was angry. I miss you so fucking much that it hurts. I do not wish to lecture you, I just want you to be safe. I just want to be with you and the truth is I am jealous of those around you. I am jealous that someone can be so close to you, that they can kiss you, smell you, touch you. I want all those things.

Sorry, I hope this letter reaches you in time. I know my last will have your heart racing for all the wrong reasons.

I love you Lottie, I will always love you. H xx

Well, that is me told! You know that is so typical of Henry, quick to tell me what I should or should not be doing but his second letter has saved his bacon. Now I must cancel my meeting with Danny, I did not realise how much my friendships were hurting Henry, and of course they are, I would be completely the same. Going out has been my coping mechanism. I do not think Henry has one, he is braver than me and faces each day bare, he does not hide behind anything and feels every emotion as they come for him, while I run for the hills, and like he said the end of a bottle, out in London with P.C fucking Danny.

Chapter Eighteen

18th April 1959

Dear Henry,

I hope this letter finds you well. I wish you were here Henry; I do not know how much longer I can cope with all this. I know you may feel that I am doing fine with William and the people I hang out with, but they are not what I really want, they just let me escape from my prison because that is what being here is...my prison.

Me and William were at Laurence's yesterday when Rosemary popped in with her neighbour's daughter for whom she was babysitting. Henry, she was a baby, such a beautiful baby. I did not know what to do, I instantly felt like I wanted to die. Everyone was cooing over her, William tried not to, but even he could not resist her infectious giggle and tiny fingers. I treated her like she had the Spanish flu for I was frightened that I would not be able to put her down even though she is not even mine. Rosemary made a comment that one day the living room would be filled with all our babies, and I made such a show of myself, and I ran, I needed air and I could not stand to be around them all and that pretty, little doll — Betty would be around her age now, laughing and grabbing fingers. It's not fair that I should be trapped here while my sister enjoys my baby for the rest of her life. I do not know what to do Henry, the pain is too much. I need you and I need my Betty.

Also, I don't know how you feel about this, but I think you should know, I saw him — I saw Joe. I was running and ran into him coming out of a pub. He does not look well Henry, his hair was long, he had a scruffy beard and he looked exhausted. We did not talk long, and I cannot say the exchange was very pleasant either. It was not long before William caught up with me and he dashed away. I thought your dad might want to know that he is at least alive.

I feel like I cannot breathe...
Lottie x
P.S love you always

What were the chances of Joe Hollister running into me like that, or was it chance? I thought I spotted him the other day when I was at the pub but thought that it was too unrealistic.

Maybe a part of me ran in that direction on purpose, hoping to find him. What good timing as well, for I needed someone to blame everything on and he was the perfect candidate, I ran to him as soon as I recognised him. The time apart just vanished and I immediately began to scream at him, banging my fists on his chest, as hard as I could shouting, "this is all your fault!" I could tell he was taken aback; course he would not have expected to bump into me.

I forgot how strong he was when he grabbed my arms and pulled them away from him, keeping them in his grasp as he spoke, "Charlotte, stop!"

Last time I set eyes on Joe was when he left me on the doorstep of our old lane. There was never a letter thereafter, or a sneaky visit, he was dust to the wind. I could see that he had not had it easy since but neither had I.

"What are you doing here?" he asked me, looking both annoyed and concerned.

"They took her," I cried. "They took our little girl, our little Betty."

Joe pulled me into his chest and squeezed me so tight, I felt his body shake as he cried about how sorry he was. At first, I tried to pull away from his clutches wanting to give him more grief, but I did not have the strength mentally or physically, so I allowed the comfort of his familiar arms to wash over me. He smelt awful but the leather jacket against my face made me feel at home, even if it was only for a small moment.

"Do you know where she is," he whispered gently.

"France with Cathleen."

Once more we may have looked to passers-by, like two young lovers in the dark of the night, a quarrel may have been guessed between us not two parents with no child, no identity, and no home.

"William's here," Joe whispered in my ear, slowly dropping his embrace. William approached us panting his eyes fixed on Joe who would not have been recognisable at first sight. "I have to go," Joe said picking up a backpack that I had not even noticed off the floor.

"Where are you going?" I asked, secretly not wanting

him to leave so quickly. I wanted to tell him all about our girl, but Joe had a nervous look about him.

"I am not really sure to be honest, I normally just decide once I get to the station." Under the streetlight I could not help but see that Joe's face had aged, his eyes were red, and the end of his nails were filthy.

"Don't worry about me, I will be fine," he said catching my gaze.

"Hey Will."

"Hey," William replied awkwardly.

"Take good care of her please, she's special, this one," he said, tucking a strand of hair behind my ear. I closed my eyes taking in his last touch. A small kiss was placed on my head.

"Of course," Will replied.

With that he turned around and walked away, out of my life like a flash once more. He didn't even turn around to glance back at me, I stood rooted to the spot watching him walk away until I could no longer see his dark figure. In that moment I felt worlds away from my body, numb to the core.

24th April 1959

Dear Beautiful Lottie,
Your last letter left me feeling hopeless. Hopeless that I cannot carry you when you fall. Here, the house, the allotment, they all hold memories that you once walked the cobbled streets and lay on the blades of grass on

summer days yet are no longer with me. I see you smiling in the allotment and your dress floating in the wind as you walk down the street. I may be free to go as I please but there is nowhere but you that I wish to go, so I too can feel imprisoned.

You must hold on, Darling, you have come so far, and you are so much stronger than you think. There will be times when you are reminded of Betty, but you must not give up. You have a beautiful life ahead of you, I will ensure that. One day we will both leave our cells and start a new life, just me and you, and we will be free to do whatever we want, I promise I will never let you down. Please hold on, we are halfway there.

Love always, H xx

Oh, as for Joe, I passed on your message to my dad. He is grateful to you for letting us know, I think knowing he is alive gave him great comfort. I cannot say that I have much care for it, but I know you understand why. He may be my brother, but I cannot help but feel anger at the chaos he has left behind. Sorry if this sounds awful. I just know with me; you are going to be taken care of properly.

1st May 1959

Dear Lottie,
I have not stopped thinking about you. I could not help but notice that your last letter was quite brief. Darling, please tell me that you are okay, I am worried about you. William

*wrote to me; he tells me that you are not seeing anyone.
He is concerned, you have people that care about you
Lottie. He said he has mentioned that you should write
again, even making you an office, I think this is a great
idea, but you must not feel pressured. Everything will
come at its own pace and if it turns out that writing just is
not for you anymore then that is okay too, more than okay
in fact. Florence will want you to be happy most of all. I
can look after us while you find your passion in life, you
can do anything.*

*I know you are desperate to come home, I want you
here with me too. We will be together soon, and I am
going to hold you so tight and never let you go. Please
write back and let me know you are okay.*

*I love you with all my heart.
Love always, H xx*

8th May 1959

I have not written for a while; I have not wanted to do
anything to be honest. I think the changes made to Nana
Florence's bedroom into an office where I can write may
have been made in vain. I am no writer. I am not a
mother. I am nothing. Forever I am going to be reminded
of Betty, not just when I see babies in the street or born to
people I know, but when I have more babies myself one
day. Will I be able to love them without guilt that they

have a sister that they will never know, or that I get to be there when they wake up from a nightmare or clean their grazed knees. I will never be able to do any of those things for my Betty.

Society makes me act like someone I am not each day that I breathe, I am made to live each day with normal conversations, I have to always smile at guests and colleagues. The Andersons hide my big fat secret as do I, for I know I will be judged for the decisions I have made, and they will follow me forever, whether they are visible or not. No one realises that a simple smile can cover a hundred cracks beneath.

Henry has given me so much love and I have not always deserved it, anyone would be lucky to have such a wonderful person. He puts me first over and over again and is suffering for my decisions. Joe is running for his life alone, in fear because his anger took over, because I did not say no when I really should have. I let others pressure me.

Life is a mess. Henry cannot save me from the thoughts that run through my head. William cannot always be there when I have had one too many. Danny and Laurence believe we are friends, yet I could walk away from them both right now and not mourn their company.

Last week after my late shift, I made the conscious decision that I was not going to head back to the house. I thought screw my auntie and her stupid rules, I never follow them anyway. What could she possibly do to me?

Instead, I snuck a few bottles of vodka from the bar and headed upstairs to an empty room. It was all far too easy, most of the staff have watched me grow up. There I unloaded everything, I freed my mind from all the suppressed pain, I cried for my baby, I cried for Henry, my nan and Joe. I had loved Joe, very much, and witnessing what his life has become hurts me and I am partly to blame for that. Who knows what our life would be currently if things hadn't gone terribly wrong? Would I have always loved him and ignored my love for Henry? We would be living in our little flat with our gorgeous girl, watching her sleep each night in her cherry wood cot loved by both parents devotedly. The vodka passed my lips and burnt my throat just as my parents burnt me, just how my own sister did. Growing up she was always trying to do what was best for me, but I think robbing me of my child because she lost hers was a step too fucking far. I cried for Peter who I will never see grow to be a man and for Mr Flint whose garden will hopefully forever bloom. He had the kindest soul. I drank until the first bottle lay empty on the floor and the next one was opened.

Some may call me foolish, some (my auntie to be exact) may say it was for attention, but I call it being lost. So lost that I did not know what else to do. I am in so much pain that each day is a constant struggle. I wanted to feel something else, I wanted to feel free, I wanted to suck the thoughts out of my mind and for some time I did.

I woke up the following day in hospital, turns out I drank so much that I knocked myself unconscious but not before hitting my head off a bedside table. My uncle said I was lucky I made such a noise to rouse the room adjacent otherwise I may not have been found. My auntie however was more concerned about the bottles of vodka.

"She's nothing but a thief!" she shouted on the ward. I had just woken at this moment and as well as my auntie's shrill voice, I was aware of my uncle's hushed chatter close by "We took that girl in when no one else wanted her! She is trash," my auntie continued.

"Hush now Emily, this is not the place for that. Sorry, Officer."

Officer? My head was in so much pain that I dared move it nor did I have the strength to open my eyes and engage in any sort of conversation with these people.

"If your wife can't calm down then she will have to leave," the officer replied. "Now that Charlotte is expected to be coming round, we will ask her some questions and take it from there."

"Well, I tell you now, she won't be coming back with us, you will have to contact her parents they can deal with her." I could hear steps walking briskly up and down the ward floor.

"Emily, please," my uncle's voice was strained — most likely suffering from an earache listening to that witch, however sending me home was not such a bad idea.

"We put a roof over her head, gave her a job at our

hotel, her nan's may I add. That carpet is going to have to be completely replaced due to the blood and the cost of those bottles will be coming out of her wages. I knew this was a bad idea Albert, did I not? But no, you wanted to give her a chance."

"She's family," Albert replied.

"Her own parents disowned her, banished her without a second glance. No there is only one reason you have a soft spot for that girl, don't think I don't see it too."

"What are you talking about, Em?"

"Please can we keep the noise down," the officer said, although it fell on death ears.

"She looks like her, like Joy. It is the eyes. You treat her like the most innocent little girl that she used to be here on her holidays, you gave her your mother's engagement ring, you gave her a place to *write*. You look for the good in her when everyone else knows its tarnished, because she reminds you of your first love."

I could feel my eyes switch and hoped no one noticed for I did not want them to realise that I was listening. My uncle's admitted love for Joy flashed in my memories.

"Enough, Emily, she is my niece. Mavis and Frank may be able to just toss her aside and treat her like you want to, but I cannot do that! Yes, she has made mistakes but who hasn't."

"And what do you mean by that exactly?" I could imagine the look my uncle was receiving right now was not a great one.

"Just leave it, go home and update William." I heard a

chair move a little at the foot of my bed and heard a loud sigh followed by a shuffle.

"Another one who falls for her charm. Honestly, the girl runs away from home and gets herself pregnant by a scoundrel, she is now in hospital because she got off her face on *our* vodka that she stole from *our* bar and yet you both see a halo shining above her head. I want her out Albert, I will write to Mavis myself."

"Ma'am, I am going to ask you to please leave now. I think you have said enough." This was another voice that had been quiet until then, it made my heart race as I knew it extremely well.

It was Danny. My heart began to palpitate. He had heard everything.

I must have gone to sleep for I do not recall much else, when I was able to open my eyes, it was dark; the ward was quiet with the distant hushed voices of nurses on duty. Gone was the pain of listening to my auntie, I believe my uncle's regret in life was marrying her although he would never admit that. It was Joy he loved, still to this day. My nana had said he lost a daughter as well, maybe a part of him can feel my pain for my own loss. I see my nana in my uncle — he has a good heart, just a shame he does not have her wit.

"Ah, you're awake," Danny said, startling me as he entered the ward. "Thought I would double check how you were before I headed off."

I nodded. I really was not in the mood to speak to anyone, not about my past or my mental state of mind.

Nothing.

"I imagine you're tired, so I won't keep you. I will let the nurse know you're up on my way out."

Again, I nodded looking towards the window.

"Charlotte, I may have imagined it, but I would bet a pound on it that this is not the first time you've woken. Earlier today maybe. I understand why you didn't want to let us know; your aunt has a gob on her does she not." Danny walked closer to my bed holding onto the bars on the side. I could smell his aftershave; he always did put too much on. "I want you to know that your uncle isn't going to press charges and, well, I think you're very brave. My mum was one of the lucky ones, I guess. I do not know all of your story, but I want you to know that to me it does not change anything. I still think you are wonderful."

With no response, Danny left quietly knowing he was not getting anything more than the small tear that sat on the edge of my eye.

William, who had arrived early back from school, was full of beans unlike his mother who was no were to be seen when Uncle Albert brought be back today.

"I have a surprise for you," he whispered once we were out of earshot. William ran up the staircase. "Let me grab my coat."

"Your coat? I've only just got here," I whispered loudly from the bottom of the stairs. All I wanted to do was go to bed and shut my door.

William ignored me and came back a few minutes later.

"Come on cousin, you are not going to want to miss this. You will thank me."

Together we walked a mile up the road. William was power walking much to my annoyance, countless times I asked him to slow down, reminding him that I had just come out of hospital. I do not believe I have ever seen William so animated.

"William please," I gasped stopping against a wall. "I don't think I can walk much further."

"Hold onto my arm, we are but a few steps away." William held me up linking my arm into his. "Come on, almost there, I promise." True to his word we had arrived at our destination.

"A phone box?"

"I don't know why I never thought of it before, I am a genius I know." William stepped into the red box and inserted change into the small slot and typed in some numbers written on a scrap of paper. I watched from the outside; William was smiling exchanging words with someone on the other end. I was puzzled to what this had to all do with me. William opened the door, phone still in one hand.

Smiling he pulled me in. "Its's for you," was all he said as he left me there in the box with the stranger on the phone.

"What the hell," I mouthed through the window. William pointed to the phone. "Erm, hello," I said putting the black phone to my ear.

"Darling is that you?" the voice sent my pulse racing. I

spun round to look at William in total shock who was smiling knowing that he was brilliant! "Hello, Lottie? Are you still there?"

"I'm…I'm here." My mouth went dry as so many things to say came into my head, yet none of them would pass my lips.

"Thank God, you're alright. I have been so worried. William told me everything." All my body could do was cry because it never fails to remember how to do that. "Oh, Darling, please don't cry. Talk to me, everything is going to be okay."

"I miss you, Henry."

"I miss you too, I am counting down the days to your birthday. I am going to get you the minute the clock hits midnight, and I am never going to leave your side."

"You promise?"

"I promise, I am going to make you my wife Lottie, and I know we are going to be so happy. I cannot change the past, but I will make sure that every day you feel loved and protected. You must stay strong until then though darling, you cannot be reckless just stay still for a while. I cannot lose you. Tell me you won't do anything like that again."

"I won't do anything, I swear. It just hurts Henry."

"I know it does, it hurts me too."

We chatted for some time; William must have put a generous amount of money in. It turned out that Henry was talking to me from a phone box outside our old primary school. The longer I spoke with him the more I felt the tightness in my chest ease a little. He told me that Mr Flint, who knows of our letters, has been anxious about me, Henry said he avoids my parents like the plague as does Walter. The bond between our dads may have been strong enough to cope with war but it was not strong enough to work through the difficulties brought to them by their children. When the phone began to beep, I was devastated.

"The phone is going to cut off!" I shouted, panicking.

"I love you, Lottie. Keep writing to me!"

"I love you too!"

When the line went dead, I placed the phone back on the hook with shaking hands. I could not believe that I had just spoken to him, my Henry. It was the closest contact I have felt since we parted. Our letters are amazing but hearing his voice was something else. It was special. As I left the phone box, I was overwhelmed.

"Thank you so much."

"It was my pleasure, I thought it would cheer you up, and Henry. Come on then let us get you inside."

"I think I need a gin after that," I teased.

"That's not happening. Not for a long time."

Chapter Nineteen

15th May 1959

Dear Lottie,
Your sweet voice has never left my thoughts since our
call. We must arrange another soon. I hope you are
feeling okay, my darling. I hope our conversation has
helped you in some way, if not then please let me remind
you that you are the greatest thing to ever happen to me.
When I was feeling lost in the world it was you who
picked me up and made me feel like it was okay to
breathe when my mam could not, that it was alright to be
happy. You know my mam always did like you, she was
always having a go at me to be nicer. How I wish I had
been from the start, the years I wasted tormenting the girl
that was going to be the only person that really mattered.
Seven months to go, then we can start again.
*   Me and you.*
*   My dad and Mr Flint both send you their best*
wishes for recovery. You are so brave Darling, more
than you may realise.

I love you will all my heart and more,
Love always, H xx

P.s one more wage and I will have enough to buy us a car
— I will be coming for you.

17th May 1959

I have not seen William very much this weekend, he was not home long on Friday before he was out the door again without much information on what he was up to, Uncle Albert and I have been teasing him about a secret girlfriend, as he was out the door like a bullet on Saturday as well. A dark horse I believe William is, he is full of surprises that one. I found a weekend at the house was in order, a night out was not what I needed; I have writing to do.

Auntie Emily was quick to notice the absence of William on Saturday evening: "I have barely seen the boy at all this weekend. Who on earth is he with?"

I glanced at my uncle who gave me a sneaky grin, to discuss a potential lover with my auntie would not do any favours for William. God help the woman who would become the daughter-in-law to this witch.

"Do you know who he is with, Charlotte?" she asked me.

"I have no idea Auntie, his school friends perhaps. I would not know with it being after my curfew, and you know all of William's friends are of the opposite sex. Your guess would be as good as mine."

Auntie Emily gave me a stern look before returning to her dinner in silence. My uncle gave me a look that said I should know better. The two are still walking on eggshells with each other since their intense argument at the hospital.

William has just stuck his head into the office informing me that he will not be home next weekend due to a cricket game being played in Winchester. Meaning I will have to wait a little longer for my letter from Henry.

"I will write to him and let him know to wait out for your reply," William said. "Sorry cousin."

"It's ok, good luck with the game."

"Thank you, well I best be off. You will take care, won't you?" he asked me, hovering by the door. "While I'm away."

"Of course."

"William, Dear, I will accompany you to the station," my auntie called from the hallway.

"See you in a fortnight."

"See you."

Oh, this is a disaster! It is going to be a long fortnight.

29th May 1959

The most anticipated day has arrived, I have not been able to sleep or focus on anything while waiting for William to return home only to be told that I had no letters — no letters at all.

" Stop teasing me William, I should have at least two now."

"I am sorry, but I am not teasing you, Charlotte. I really have had no mail recently. He hasn't written," William sat down beside me on the chair that I had collapsed into. "But I am sure there is a good reason. Perhaps he is overloaded at work, or his dad has taken ill, or that old man. He will write again I am sure of it."

"He always writes to me; he has never missed a week the whole time I've been here William. It just does not make sense. Did you check properly, are you sure you didn't forget or someone else could have taken it?"

"I checked every day, and I double-checked before I left. There was nothing."

Without a word I left the study and ran to my bedroom where I sobbed like a schoolgirl. Why? Why has he not written to me? I replied to his last letter and William also wrote to let him know that a week would go by with no reply from me. Why would Henry just suddenly stop writing, and without a word. I have reread his last letters and there is nothing but hope, love, and concern from him. He said he was buying us a car, he said he would come for me. He has promised me a life together, William is right, something must have come up, something so big that he has not been able to find the time to write. That is the only explanation.

6th June 1959

I broke my own rule, in fact I broke many. I gave in and had a drink, not a little bit either. Not so much as to wake up in a hospital bed but enough to drive my choices all on the wrong path. William returned home yesterday with no letters.

What do I do with that? I wrote to Henry asking him to please write, to give me some sort of closure to what is happening. I had written him a similar letter last week pleading for knowledge, a response anything.

"It's been three weeks William!" I shouted when he revealed that he had nothing to give me.

"I know, I have written to him also, I swear it," William replied.

"We have to do something, money — do you have any money. I could get a train up to Durham, see him and then return as soon as I have answers."

"That is absurd, you will only make your situation worse. Just wait it out, I know he will write."

"I can't just wait it out! I have waited long enough! What about that number you called, we could call it again? Someone will answer it and I could tell them to pass on a message or Henry might even answer. What was the number?" I asked so desperately.

"I don't have it anymore."

"God, you're useless."

It was then that I stormed out and made the bus journey to Danny's flat. A party was already in full swing as I gained entrance and poured myself a long-needed drink. People who consider themselves my friends, yet know nothing about me, welcomed me with hugs and cheery greetings. The feel of the vodka going down my neck and knowing it was not going to be my last gave me immediate joy. Charlotte was back and she was ready to party. I searched the small flat until I found what I wanted

— Danny was coming out of his bedroom and looked surprised to see me.

"Well, I wasn't expecting to see you here," he said, opening his arms for a hug. "A part of me thought you were never going to come back."

"I needed to let my hair down, nowhere better to go than Danny Porters, the naughtiest policeman I know," I replied, accepting his embrace. The strong smell of aftershave hit me in the face. "Let's get a drink," I said pulling him towards the kitchen.

He, of course, obediently obliged. Danny poured us both a drink and no sooner was it in my grasp, Laurence had taken it into his own.

"I don't think so little lady," he said taking a swig of it instead. "Water? A cup of tea perhaps?"

"We all know I didn't come here for a cuppa now, don't we," I said trying to grab the glass back only for Laurence to lift it out of my reach.

"No, I'm not kidding Charlotte, you don't need this."

"Come on, Laurence, it's just one drink," Danny said. "She hasn't had one for ages."

"Liar, look at her face, she's already had some."

"It was just a little one, I'm not going to do anything stupid. Anyways, you will look after me Danny, won't you," I said leaning into his muscley chest.

"Of course, I will," he said gripping my waist tightly against him.

"This is about Henry, isn't it?" Laurence asked. "It's Friday, he didn't write, did he?"

"No, he did not," I exclaimed, "but this is not about Henry Hollister! This is about me, if he does not love me anymore then I need to learn to live without him." I managed to snatch my glass back out of Laurence's grip spilling some in the process, then happily downed it in one. "Starting from now!" I added.

"You're making a mistake Charlotte, there will be an explanation," Laurence said, making me laugh.

"Forget about him Laurence, I am. I am putting all the Hollisters behind me today." I grabbed Danny's hand and led him out of the kitchen leaving Laurence behind. "Dance with me."

Danny was only too happy to, as I had expected, his hands never left my body as we danced along to Bobby Darin's *Dream lover* and Frankie Lymon and The Teenagers' *Why do fools fall in love*. Ironically, the last time I danced to this song was back at the community hall when I danced with Joe for the first time. Then I was devastated about the life I had lost here in London; Henry had refused to come to the dance, and I had listened to other people's comments about his lack of commitment too much. This time I was devastated that Henry had decided to walk away from us because why else would his letters suddenly stop. Maybe the thought of running off with me became a scary one, Durham is the only home he has ever known, his dad is the only family member he has and the business he has is already great, why give that all up for the girl who betrayed him for his brother. To be given a second chance with Henry was something I never believed I was worthy of yet revelled that I had it. He must have come to realise that I was not good enough, that uprooting his life for me was not worth it. Maybe my auntie was right, maybe I am trash, if so then I was going to do whatever the hell I wanted with whomever I wanted. Having Danny's hands move up and down my body drove me insane. I got a mad rush of pleasure, something I have not felt for a long time. I wanted his hands on me, I placed mine over his to not let them escape, he could see that I was enjoying it, his grin said it all.

Then I saw him, over Danny's shoulder I could see a familiar figure stood by the door, at first it was just an outline then the features all came into place, his dark hair, his piercing blue eyes, a disapproving look followed by the small frame of his slim build. He was dressed in his work overalls they had saw dust on from the working day. His hands looked rough, yet as the smooth hands of Danny's ran over my back my body repulsed and I pulled away. I looked back in search of the figure which was gone, I glanced around the room and found him nowhere to be seen. I ran out the flat in case I could catch him in the corridor, but it was empty. How would Henry even know how to find me? Why would he come to London now?

I decided not to return to the flat; I knew I would only end up doing something I deeply regretted. Hallucinating my fiancé told me that it was time I headed home. As I passed doors of families, I could hear other parties happening, families arguing, children crying, behind each door was another story, lives with love and loss, happiness, and hatred.

"Charlotte!" Laurence called, pulling on a jacket as he caught up with me. "I'll take you back."

In other places there was kindness.

Chapter Twenty

14th June 1959

My hands tremble as I write this, fear runs through every bone in my body, every strand in my hair. I am without a doubt the most awful human being. Everyone to ever know me should hate me to their core, yet they will go on to feel perhaps sadness instead. I know I have done things rashly before; I know I can be silly and my heart thinks before my head. My emotions control how I live my life, but now I have taken it too far, I have taken it beyond repair; nothing can fix this. I feel so frightened, and I do not believe I can be physically sick any more than I already have.

The drugs Shirley gave me should have killed me, giving birth should have killed me, hitting my head at the hotel should have killed me.

I will never forgive myself.

How could this happen?

When I left the party I went home, I felt fine, I wrote in my journal and tried to get to sleep but when I heard William return home from wherever he had been I could not settle. I could not accept that Henry had given up on us. There had to be more to it, something that I did not know, so I barged into his bedroom and demanded he tell me more. We fought, he did not want to talk to me about it, he said he was sorry and that maybe I should learn to get over it, he was worried about his mum hearing us, but I did not care and then he said it, he came clean with it all. He told me that Henry had wrote to him telling him that he would not like to receive any more letters from me, that he has decided that it would be best for us both to move on as it was all too difficult for both of us. This is when I saw red, I did not want to believe him so I…I grabbed one of his many trophies off a shelf and launched it at him. William fell to the floor and blood immediately began to flow from his head. I did not know what to do. I tried to shake him, I tried calling his name, he lay motionless on the floor, and I panicked. Instead of grabbing my uncle or calling for help, I ran. I ran like my own life depended on it. With only my nightgown on, I did not stop running until I reached Danny's flat. It might sound crazy to run to a policeman after committing a crime, but I felt like he was the only person who was going to be able to help me.

Danny took one look at me then dragged me in locking the door behind us, sensing that I was not there on normal terms. The party was over, and he was eager to know what was going on. I blurted everything out, I do not know if it made much sense, but I had to tell someone quickly, I needed him to help me, to help William.

Looking back, I do not know how he managed to stay so calm, I had just told him that I thought I had killed someone. Instead, he sat me down on the couch and casually poured us both a glass of whiskey.

"Now, calmly tell me everything again."

So, I went through the whole ordeal again, Danny

listened carefully not taking his eyes off me. I was beginning to think perhaps coming to him was a crazy idea. He was a policeman, his job was to protect people from the likes of me, to punish murderers. He had a duty, why would he help me, only hours earlier I had led him on and then walked out the door without a word. When I was finished there was a moment of silence before he stood up, put on his coat, and grabbed his keys.

"Stay here," he said sternly. "Do not open the door to anyone, do you understand?"

I nodded. "What about your mum?"

"She's on nights at the hospital. She won't be back until morning."

"Danny!" I shouted in a panic. "Are you going to the police station? If you are then just take me now."

"No one is going to the police station, Charlotte. Now stay here I'm going to fix this."

With Danny gone I was left alone in the flat, the incident replaying in my mind over and over again. Why did I pick up that God damn trophy? It was not William's fault that Henry did not want me anymore. William has done nothing but help me. For the first time since those school days I prayed, I prayed that God would protect William, that everything will turn out to be one big misunderstanding. I paced every inch of the flat and drank what was left of the whiskey before Danny returned alongside his uncle. I promptly stood up like a girl being taken to see the headmaster.

"How are you feeling, love?" Laurence's dad asked,

locking the door behind him.

"Sick, scared," I replied nervously, I now had two police officers before me; was this all a big trick I kept thinking, trying to read their body language. Danny sat me back down and grasped my hand tightly.

They told me that William was dead. I had killed him. They told me that the punishment for this was a visit from the hangman. They said they did not want this. They said they know I am not a murderer, that it was all a big accident, but that I would need to be protected if I was to stay alive. That is when their master plan was revealed to me.

"We are going to have to get you out of here, Charlotte. If we get you away quickly you can start fresh somewhere else but to do that we have to make sure no one is going to go looking for you," Uncle Porter said carefully.

"That means we have to make sure that everyone else thinks you are dead," Danny continued.

"Dead?"

"I know it's a lot to take in, love, but it is the only way. Me and Danny can go and set an old building on fire tonight and then in the morning we can make sure your family are made aware of the tragedy. That way you can be free to start again as someone else."

"Someone else?"

"Leave that to us, but you will need a new identity. You can't be Charlotte Ridley anymore if she is registered as dead," Danny said. It was too much, and it frightened me to the core. William was dead. I had killed him. Therefore,

270

unless I wanted to die too, I was going to have to pretend I was dead and become someone else. "You won't have to do anything, me and my uncle can sort it all out."

"It would help if you could give us something, something that can be recognisable as you. When someone dies a member of the family normally the next of kin would be asked to identify the body to confirm who has passed. In your case, we do not want that to happen. We can make out that you were so badly hurt that it would be pointless, an item of yours though could confirm it."

With nothing else on but my nightgown I tried to hide my nana's ring. Danny saw me and looked at me gently. "Charlotte, it will help you."

"I can't," I cried. "It's the only thing I have."

My finger is now bare as I had to hand it over, it broke my heart letting go of the only link I had to my nana. Everything was too messy, setting fire to buildings and lying to my family. I had committed a crime, I had killed my own sweet cousin, I should be punished; I should just hand myself in, but Danny would not hear any of it.

Everything after that happened so quickly. The pair of them left me to carry out the next steps and did not return until the early hours. My mind went from one awful thought to another. I cannot remember the last time I had a proper night's sleep.

Rosemary was informed when she returned, she was so supportive and rallied up some clothes for me, even trying to feed me, but I could not stomach anything. Everyone said

Laurence is not to be told, as an employee of the Anderson family they believed it was best for him to not be in on the secret. They believed his heart was too big to carry such a burden. Last night Danny presented me with a new birth certificate, my name from now on is to be Elizabeth Reid. I grew up with relatives in Northumberland after my parents were killed during the war. I am now moving to Croydon for a new job. I stood in the mirror, in clothes that I did not pick, practicing my introduction:

"Hi, my name is Elizabeth Reid." I did not recognise myself. It has come to my attention that Danny and his uncle may not be such good policemen after all, to pull off everything that they had done so quickly, however without them Charlotte would have died for real. I think I would prefer my family to think me dead from a fire than hung for killing William.

I wish I could take it all back, William had his whole life ahead of him, he was by far the cleverest person I knew, he was going to be somebody great, he would have made a great husband, a great Dad. I was the one to rob him of that. What sort of life do I deserve now? I wonder if anyone will put two and two together with me and William gone on the same night at two separate events, or will they believe it all to be one horrific coincidence. Auntie Emily and Uncle Albert will be destroyed; losing their only son, Uncle Albert does not deserve to have such a loss brought to him again, even Auntie Emily, despite her faults and hatred for me, I know William is her universe. When news reaches Durham will they care?

Would they have any regrets of their own? Good job Henry cut his ties with me already, I wish him only the best. He has been the love of my life and I know he will make someone incredibly lucky one day.

Danny came to speak to me while I was packing the last of my bits. He closed the door behind him for privacy.

"Just wanted to let you know that we will be leaving as soon as it gets dark. It's not going to be an easy adjustment, so we all agreed that it would be best for me to come with you."

"To drop Elizabeth off for her big adventure?"

"No, not to just drop *Elizabeth* off. I am going to stay there with her — with you. My uncle has managed to get me transferred over to the department in Croydon." Danny pulled my hands away from my packing and took them into his. "You don't have to do this on your own. I'm going to be there with you every step of the way."

My wings are well and truly clipped.

Dear Lottie

Mel Higgins

1960s

Dear Lottie

Chapter Twenty-One

23rd June 1969

Last night was a total disaster, I thought having the evening child free to enjoy a few drinks and adult conversations in a fancy dress would have been divine. We danced on the shiny dance floor filled with sparkly dresses and handsome uniforms and chatted to colleagues. All was well I thought, I had enjoyed the evening at the annual summer ball. I genuinely look forward to it, as well as the Christmas one, but the look on Danny's face in the taxi home told me that he had not.

"What is wrong?" I asked, feeling his negative energy.

"Nothing," he grunted, gazing out the window.

"Well, there obviously is, what have I done?" I asked, no point beating around the bush is there.

Danny turned to face me ready to give me the spiel. "Spike!"

"I have not done Spike," I tried to joke nervously.

"That's not funny, Liz. I meant he was all over you all night. He couldn't keep his hands off you."

"We were dancing, that's all."

"Well, I didn't like it and what was all that whispering at the table about. You should not let anyone get that close to you. You're my wife," Danny said gripping my leg.

"I know I am. You are looking at this all wrong.

277

Everyone was dancing with different people. People that were not their partners, Danny. It was a ball. I saw you dancing with Peggy and Sylvia."

"That's different," he butted in, "I wasn't all over them like a fucking rash. It was my work event, I invited you, you're there as my guest, my wife, and there are certain ways you should behave Liz. You are a mother, a respectable woman, remember that next time."

"I will. I'm sorry," I replied.

I have learnt over the years that there is no point in arguing with Danny, it's best to just apologise and move on as quickly as you can.

24th June 1969

Nothing to report today, just another typical day. We all slept in, so the morning was a mad rush as usual.

"Eat your breakfast."
"Quickly brush your teeth."
"Put your shoes on."
"Where're my socks mum?"
"Where's my shoes mum?"
"You've burnt my shirt."
"I'm going to be late if the kids don't get in the car now."

Arthur did not want to go to school again, the water works began at the door. "I want to stay with you Mummy."

"I will come and pick you up, okay. First you have to go and be a big boy and have fun with all your friends," I said wiping his sweet little cheeks. He is such a gentle boy.

"Arthur, now!" Danny shouted. "You mother him too much."

"He's only five."

"He'll be soft like Laurence if you keep it up." I could not help but laugh at the horror that fills Danny's head with the thought that his son would be anything but macho like himself. Heaven forbid if he grew to be healthy, happy, and like Laurence.

With Arthur in the car and the house empty it was time to get the marigolds on for a good clean, and food shopping was also on my to-do list. I knew it would not feel like long before the kids needed picking up and tea needed cooking.

Danny was out late again, so he had his tea reheated on the sofa. Me and the kids had eaten earlier at the table, full of discussions about their day at school. I love hearing about their day. Both the girls enjoy school and I know Arthur will get there eventually. I disappeared for an early night knowing Danny would stay up watching the television only for him to wake me when he got to bed. I had been hoping to avoid this. He crawled under the sheets, and my body froze, pretending to sleep. It did not take long before his hands began to caress my thigh sliding up my night dress. His kisses spread across my back.

279

"Not tonight, Sweetheart," I guiltily said. "I've had a long day. Tomorrow, I promise."

Danny sighed and rolled over to his side, our backs facing each other. Am I a bad wife?

27th June 1969

Today marks the day of our eighth wedding anniversary. A framed photo in the hallway shows the two of us stood outside a registry office, Danny dressed in his uniform, his smile beaming from ear to ear, while on his arm I stand with my large bouquet of flowers hiding my large bump. I was seven months pregnant with Flo and felt like a hippo in my white gown. I smile in the photo, but I remember feeling like we were embarking on this life for all the wrong reasons. Danny had been my rock and I had eventually fallen for his charm and ended up with a bun in the oven and a ring on my finger.

I had hoped for some recognition of the day this morning, but it was not noticed as it had not been for the last five years. At first Danny had showered me with roses and gifts to mark the day they united us as Mr and Mrs Porter. To say I was a little peeved may be an understatement and as the day went on my annoyance increased. I had hidden a card in Danny's packed lunch this morning, so thought he would return home full of surprises; I am not asking for gifts, just maybe, I do not know, just something! Anything! He did not even say anything!

Tonight's tea luckily had us all around the table, the chit chat of the day buzzed around the room. I had a bottle of wine for me and Danny. I watched on as they all tucked into their chips and homemade pork pie, deep in conversations. I picked at mine, taking more time on the wine. He has no idea, I kept thinking, I clean his house all day, gave birth to three of his children, put up with the endless shit that comes out his mouth every day, dismissed many of his drunken states, yet he cannot even remember the day that I signed up for it all. The day he calls – *'when he got the girl.'*

"Are you alright, love?" Danny asked, silence fell, and all four sets of eyes turned on me, I nodded and smiled guzzling the last of my wine before going to pour another. "You're a little quiet."

"Too much wine," Florence commented, rolling her eye "Debbie's mum at school is always drinking wine."

"Debbie's mum is going through a tough time; you shouldn't talk about people, Flo," Danny said.

"Sorry, Daddy." Florence's face flushed a scarlet red as she tucked back into her tea.

"Liz?" Danny said. "You, ok?"

"Hmm, oh yes, dandy," I said, our eyes met and Danny began to laugh.

"I think Dad's done something wrong, kids." He stuffed his face with a large piece of pie smiling right at me, I married a cocky bastard. "Come on Mum, tell us what Dad's done now."

"It doesn't matter anymore, it's pointless now."

"Tell us Mum," Nancy said holding onto my hand. "Then we can sort it." It always surprises me the head that sits on my seven-year-old's shoulders.

I began to feel foolish, that perhaps I had made a big deal out of nothing. Maybe it was less about the actual day it celebrated, and more to do with what I felt owed to me by Danny. "Well kids today is mine and Daddy's wedding anniversary." I felt a pang of guilt as the smirk on my husband's face left almost immediately. "Daddy forgot."

Now it was time for all eyes on him. He dropped his cutlery and looked deep in thought for a little while. Clearly thinking of a way to save his bacon. "Daddy has been really busy at work lately. I'm sorry love."

"I left a card with your lunch; did you not see it?" I asked curiously.

Danny gave a nervous smile. "I erm, had lunch over at Bridges today."

Typical.

"But I will make it up to you, I promise." Danny suddenly stood up with his wine glass. "Everyone, grab your glasses and cups and toast to your mum here. What would we all do without her? We all love you, Liz. To Mum!"

"To Mum!" the kids shouted, giggling as we all toasted our drinks.

"And when the summer holidays come, we will all

take a trip to the seaside!" Danny exclaimed, followed by an excited squeal of delight from the kids around the table. Danny sat back down and gave me a cheeky wink.

I let him have me tonight.

Chapter Twenty-Two

12th July 1969

I took the kids to the local library today. A treat we all love on a rainy day. I get a little lost amongst the books as we snuggle up in the children's section diving into stories of witches and orphans, dragons and castles, heroes, and villains. I love that my kids enjoy the adventures that a story can take you on, that they have the imagination to dive into another dimension. If there is one thing that I have given all three of my babies, that is the gift of books. Thelma, the librarian, has watched all three of them visit since they were just small bundles in their prams. Now between the ages of eight and five they walk in like they are visiting a relative.

"I'm going to get your mum working here one day," she always tells them. I always laugh it off, it's her mission in life I believe. I love the place, I love the books and I have worked in a library before, I know how it works, but I have the kids to think about, I need to be available to pick them up from school, to have tea on the table, and be available for the weekend. Danny would not take them for the weekend if I had a shift on a Saturday.

"You're a great storyteller, Liz," Thelma said today. "The kiddies are so engrossed. You should work here…I know, do not give me that look…I have some hours coming up that I think you will be interested in. It's part time for ten hours a week, spread over three days. Have a think about it."

"Have you just made that job up?" I asked.

"Maybe, oh, come on Liz. You know your perfect for this," Thelma pleaded. "Take this application form and let me know next week…tell your mum to fill it in you lot."

I folded the application form and put it in my handbag, a few hours over a couple of days would not do any harm. Nothing would be neglected, and it would be so nice to be able to work with Thelma and to basically be out the house and somewhere that is not the corner shop. It would be my job, my own independence. I would get all my earned money, now do not get me wrong I do not go without, but it is different from being able to make something of yourself. I wanted to wait until the children had gone to bed before discussing it with Danny but that did not exactly go to plan.

The moment he stepped foot into the hallway Florence ran into his arms shouting, "Mum is going to work in the library!"

"What gives you that crazy idea?" he asked putting her down.

"Thelma said."

Danny laughed. "That old bag has been asking your mum for years. Your mum knows she is too busy looking after you lot."

"She has a new position; It will be for just a couple of hours a day. I will still be able to look after the kids," I said hopefully.

Danny pecked me on the cheek. "You know you can't. Right, what's for tea?"

Danny had put me in foul mood all evening, when the kids were in bed, I had to say something; the anger was rising inside of me.

"Why can't I work at the library?" I asked.

"You know why?" Danny said, his gaze not leaving some awful programme on the TV.

"But I told you, I can still look after the kids."

"It's not just the kids, Liz. You don't have any references; you don't have any experience of working in a library."

"I have lots of experience," I said stubbornly.

Danny muted the television. "Charlotte has the experience," he whispered, "Liz does not."

Hearing my old name for the first time in years felt almost alien to me. I have been Elizabeth for ten years now, everyone calls me Liz. Even my own kids are not aware of my real name. It is surreal how hearing the name felt as though I was suddenly slapped across the face, but I remembered I was angry with Danny.

"Thelma doesn't care for references; she knows I've been at home with the kids."

"She works for the council love; she will have to ask for references from somewhere." Danny increased the volume on the TV, getting comfortable once more. I checked the folded application form in my bag and there in black and white was a space for me to put down reference details. To say it pissed me off was an understatement, I ripped up the application form and shouted at Danny with no regrets, may I add, for every word was true.

"I'm never going to be able to get a job, am I? Honestly, you managed to get me a fake birth certificate pretty quickly, but a fucking reference is just too hard!"

"Keep your voice down for God's sake!" he said shouting equally as loud. "My concern was keeping you alive, Liz, not whether you would be able to get a job shelving books!"

"It's independence I want, Danny!"

"You can have anything you want; I will give you it all." He tried to calm me by leaning in for a kiss, but I pushed him away. "You cannot work for the council. End of."

"I'm going to bed!"

Sometimes I think without the kids what would I do? What will my life be when they grow up? Danny says I cannot work for the council but if it were somewhere else there would be a different issue, I know. He wants to wrap me up in cotton wool, and it can be suffocating.

Chapter Twenty-Three

8th September 1969

I hope this will all make sense; I may have to write it
again because my head is about to explode and I have
just run for the first time in years — I am very unfit, but
somehow I got home without stopping. I need to write it
all down while it is still fresh so I can re-read it and know
that I am not going mad.

I was just out at the corner shop grabbing some bits for tea
when I noticed that every move I made, someone behind me
was making the exact same ones, now I do not mean I reached
out for a potato so they copied, I just mean everywhere I
walked, but I didn't dare look at them except from the corner
of my eye…I could make out that it was a gentleman wearing
sunglasses. I paid for my bits and then proceeded to walk
home, making sure I kept away from alleyways and parks. I
could sense that I was being followed; I do not know why I
did not stop and ask someone to help me, I think I just froze in
my own thoughts and began to pick my pace up, but he just
quickened his. Crazy thoughts began to go through my head,
was he going to attack me? Was he going to kidnap me? What
will happen if I am not there to collect my kids from school
later? Was it perhaps someone undercover coming to collect
me, to jail me for my crimes? I felt like I was going to have a
panic attack. I did not understand why he was staying so

silent. It was then that my heel stupidly decided it was the right time to get stuck in a drain that I did not notice. The seconds felt like minutes as I stumbled and attempted to free my shoe, why I did not just free my foot and leg it then I do not know. Foolishly the foot won and so did my predator.

My body was quickly forced up against the side of an end townhouse, the man pinned me there and I remember my own voice screaming, "I don't have any money!" The man did not listen. In fact, he did nothing at all. I opened my tight eyes that had closed in fright and saw that he was just looking at me his mouth slightly open, both his hands had pinned my arms to the wall, and he was dressed in an exceptionally fine suit. Too fine for a murderer, but then what does a murderer look like after all. His jaw line was tight, his shoulders were broad, and his teeth were perfectly white. My breathing was still rapid as I tried to work out whether I was about to be beaten or not. The grips on my arm were released but only for his hands to rest onto the wall either side of me so that I was still his trapped prey.

"Please," I quivered. "Please let me go."

The man put down one arm leaving space for me to run but I could not move, I stood there like a fool.

With one quick move, the sunglasses of the gentleman were lifted onto his head revealing his eyes. Two pools of blue looked back at me, the face now one complete picture; I was instantly blown away. Not only was he impeccably handsome but his face was one that could never hurt me but looked like it had been hurt a thousand times over. The eyes told me so, the sorrowful look deep within them that mirrored my own hazel ones.

"How?" was all that escaped his lips as I felt him stare deep into my soul. I wanted to touch him, I wanted to help his confusion, but I did not know how. I did not even know if I wanted to.

"I... I can't do this." And I left.

I walked away quickly picking up my pace into a run just in case he followed me once more. My heart was in my mouth and my hair had blown out of its beehive, I looked a mess, I felt a mess. I feel guilty that I just ran off, but I did not know what else to do.

How was I supposed to tell him why I am alive?

How am I supposed to tell him that the girl he once loved was a murderer?

How could I look him in the eye and reveal such secrets?

Now that I am back home however, I have gone back and forth with the idea. Should I have stayed and given him a well-deserved explanation, for he was obviously shocked; he had in fact seen a ghost today, or did I do the right thing.

I seem to have been away with the fairies today, I messed up tea, so Danny had to get some fish and chips from the chippy. I burnt the cottage pie to a black tray of charcoal mash and boiled the vegetables until the water had totally evaporated. The family all think I am sick and have made me come for a lie down, which you know I am more than happy to oblige with. Here I can think more clearly, in the quietness of my bedroom. I can close my eyes and see his face once more, a face that makes me smile every time I think about it, sending shivers down my body. It was a face I have seen a million times before in my dreams, yet it had ever so slightly changed. I always imagined the face of a boy but today I saw the face of a man.

Today I saw Henry Hollister.

9th September 1969

With barely a wink of sleep last night I made the decision today that I had to find him, I had to see him again; his expression of utter shock yesterday was playing heavily on my mind. As soon as everyone left the house, I got ready and made my way back to the corner shop, I knew he would not be there, it would be silly to think so however he could not be too far, right? I was about to look for a needle in haystack. I popped my head into every café, shop, and pub. It dawned on me that he could live here in Croydon, if it were a house he was living in then I had no chance of finding him, I checked hotels and guest houses. I looked in the park and all of the above again hoping by chance he would be somewhere at some point. Exhausted I sat down on a bench and laughed at myself. I must be a crazy woman, I thought, searching the streets hoping to find someone I had not seen for over a decade. What if he did not want to see me, I would not blame him if he did not. Then as if by some miracle I spotted a building site across the road with a sign that stood outside with the words *Walter and Sons* written across it in an emerald font. I found myself smiling, they had done well — Walter and Henry had expanded, exactly how they had always hoped. Without a second thought, I marched over to the site with its danger signs and barriers and ignored the lot of them. The building was but a shell held up by a scaffolds, the floors were uneven, and a plank of wood had been placed down for safe walking. Men were scattered everywhere in hard hats and emerald overalls.

"Oi, you can't be in here Love," one gentleman who was pushing a wheelbarrow said. "It's dangerous for the public."

"Sorry, I'm looking for Henry Hollister, is he about?" I asked.

"Boss is through the back, is he expecting you?" he asked staring me up and down suspiciously.

"Yes, yes he is." I smiled trying to keep my cool.

"In that case, please take one of these. Otherwise, you will get us into trouble, Miss."

The gentleman handed me over a hard hat that had been abandoned on the floor. I accepted the hat as I did not want to come across as rude or willing to get Henry's workforce into bother, but I was not going to approach him wearing a hard hat, so placed it down once the gentleman was out of sight. On I walked to the back of the building, my heart tucked up in my mouth at this point, until I came to a large back room, three men were huddled around a large piece of paper deep in discussion, Henry was pointing around the room taking lead. He had his own hat on but unlike the other men, he was in a perfectly clean suit. Once I was before him, I was unsure what to do, I watched on as he worked, the men were hanging off his every word. Back when we were young, Henry had very few people that he could openly speak to but today he sounded confident and had surely grown to be a man people listened to.

"So, in theory I want a new wall to be put here to split the room in two, one side will be much smaller, but it is only to store medication, then this room here is going to be split further, this time into two GP rooms with a narrow corridor separating them. That back door will be the fire exit as well as everyday access for staff then over here on this side will be...Charlotte!" he gasped. "I...er...wasn't...what are you doing here?"

It was awkward, he looked uncomfortable, and I realised then that I made a mistake and wanted to bury my head in one of the swivelling cement machines I had passed on my way in. All three men stared at me waiting on a reply. "Sorry, I didn't mean to intrude I just...I just really needed to see you," I admitted.

Henry handed his papers to one of his colleagues and quietly apologised before placing a hand behind my back and softly pushing me forward towards the exit. "Let's go outside," he said in a hushed voice.

Outside was bright and it took a second for my eyes to adjust after being stood in the dark building. Henry took out a packet of cigarettes and lit one up, taking in a long puff. "Sorry, do you want one?"

"No, no thank you. I don't smoke."

He inhaled once more, letting out a big puff of smoke that drifted away slowly like a freed bird. "What did you need me for?" he asked.

"Henry," I said slowly enjoying the very word on my tongue. "I just…well after yesterday I thought…" My words were stuck, and he was hanging off every word.

Fuck. Fuck. Fuck.

So, I thought fuck it and did what I had really wanted to do when I first realised who he was and I sprung at him and wrapped my arms around his neck, the skin from my face grazed the side of his and I held back every weak emotion strongly. I could smell his aftershave, feel the stubble on his chin and had his dark hair in my hands. At first, I think he was startled for he did not hold me back and I felt half like a fool and also a little proud of myself for if this were the only time, I was going to be this close to him then I would cherish it even if it were not reciprocated. It was then that I felt his arms wrap around me. I felt his body sigh and relax from his stiffened posture as he gathered me close. I could feel one hand tighten on my waistline while the other caressed my hair which was worn down loosely with a headband. I could feel him smell the skin on my shoulders.

"I thought I may have imagined you," he whispered.

An apology was all that I could muster. Henry withdrew letting me go, he looked suddenly annoyed, he turned away from me pacing up and down whipping his eyes quickly. "You have so much to explain, Lottie," he said pointing at me, I had never heard Lottie be spoken with so much anger.

"I know, and there is an explanation I promise."

He paced the backyard once more, lighting up another cigarette. "Not here, not today. I have a lot of important stuff to deal with, now is not the time to have a catch up with my *dead* fiancée. Are you free tomorrow?"

"Tomorrow, no." It is Danny's day off. "But I am on Thursday, I could meet you at the little café next to the shop we were in yesterday."

"Ok," he said almost unsure, "I will meet you at ten."

I am not too sure whether today was a success or a total disaster. I better go and collect the kids; I cannot wait for Thursday, and I also dread Thursday. Is that even possible?

11th September 1969

I was there for nine-thirty and instantly regretted my decision to go for the sexy look. I felt out of place in my mini black and white mod dress accessorised with black kitten heels. I looked like I was ready for a night out, looking around at everyone in comfortable looking dresses and trousers I wished I had opted for the sweet wife option. My peach dress with the full skirt was hanging on my wardrobe desperate to be worn. I felt like a fool, I had my hair tied up and my nails polished in shiny red, and I may have gone a little heavy on the makeup. I felt like eyes were on me from all directions of the little shop and who could blame them, I looked like I had just marched in from an all-nighter. I moved to a corner table that had become vacant to hide away my foolish attempts to impress someone who I hadn't seen for over a decade. Ten o'clock came and there was no sign of Henry, nor at five past or ten past or even quarter past, I thought he had bailed on me when in he waltzed at twenty past, no apology or explanation he just took his seat opposite me and said nothing at all.

"Hey, I...I didn't think you were going to show," I said shuffling uncomfortably in my chair.

"Neither did I," he admitted.

"I'm glad you did, coffee?" I offered, which he shook his head to. "Okay, Henry, I know you must hate me right now, but I can explain."

To my horror in walked Jennifer, mum of one of Arthur's classmates. She was always parading around with a big fluffy coat and sunglasses no matter what time of year it was. She spotted me right away dressed to the nines and rushed right over to our table, face beaming.

"Hello, look at you don't you look gorgeous!" she

exclaimed. "I love that dress!"

"Thank you."

"You going somewhere nice?" she asked, eyeing Henry up. "Oh, I saw your Danny this morning with little Arthur, screaming the playground down he was, the little tike. Refusing to go in." She added without letting me speak. It all came to me why I never speak to her much; she is a real gobshite! "Your hubby got him in in the end. He didn't look too pleased about it, but that is what men are like—no offence," she said to Henry. "We women are the patient ones; well, I will leave you to it, I have a day with the mother-in-law, so I am in need of a very strong coffee."

Jennifer left leaving an incredibly bad odour behind at our table, I did not know where to look, Henry's face was enraged. He grabbed my left hand quickly and then dropped it on the table. His fists clenched and I could see the lines in his forehead pop out.

"You're married to Danny? Please don't tell me it's Policeman Danny," he said through gritted teeth.

"Henry, please calm down."

"It is, isn't it? Danny the policeman. Oh my God, it all makes sense now." Henry placed his head in his hands. "You two planned all of this didn't you?"

"Planned what?"

"You faked your death so you didn't have to call things off with me, so you could be with Danny."

"What? No! Henry, you have it all wrong."

"Oh my God! All these years I grieved for you, you were here all along, playing happy families with him, with your kid. Is there anymore?"

"Two more but Henry..."

"Of course, there is more, I bet you live in a lovely home with a dog and family friends all popping round for barbecues at the weekends too."

"No, Henry..."

"I'm an idiot, I shouldn't have come here, I knew it would be a mistake." Henry stood up to leave, my instincts grabbed hold of his arm to try and stop him. I could not have him leave thinking I faked my death to be with someone else. I had loved Henry with every fibre in my body and I grieved for him also.

I pleaded for him to stay, but it only made things worse as he shrugged me off and yelled. "Get off me, Charlotte!"

The café fell silent for a few moments, causing my face to go a deep scarlet the scene caused gobby Jennifer rushing back over believing that she was some furry superhero.

"Are you alright, Liz?"

"I'm fine," I lied.

"That is no way to treat a lady, Liz here is a respectable woman," she snarled at Henry. "Shame on you!"

With one last look Henry took his leave, leaving me devastated. I wanted to run after him, but I could not be seen running after other men from coffee shops, I already knew I had to make an excuse about this whole encounter to Danny, once Jennifer made the whole school aware of it. So instead, I sat with Jennifer who insisted. Over our drinks I told her that I had no idea who the man was, he was a drunk who I had felt sorry for who had just lost his wife. I know that didn't explain my overdressed attire, but my mind was not entirely there in the discussion with her, it was with Henry and how awful I felt that he believed that I chose Danny over him.

"Thank you for the coffee, Jennifer, but I really must be off I have a pile of washing I must attend to." I got up eyeing up the door of my escape. "Have a wonderful day with your mother-in-law." I added leaving the table quickly as Jennifer said we should have coffee together again sometime. Over my dead body.

I stormed out the café in what appeared to be rage, I was angry that Jennifer stuck her ore in, I was angry that Henry did not give me a chance to explain, and I was angry that I was heading back home to clean a never-ending pile of washing and let my life continue as it was. My anger turned to tears as I headed home, I was not used to wearing my heels they were new and at that point they were already leaving blisters and causing me bother not even five minutes from the café. As I hobbled down the street a black car slowed to my speed, it was a very good-looking car, a Ford Mustang convertible I noticed. I tried not to make eye contact with the driver as my mascara was halfway down my face and I did not want anyone I might know recognising me. The car picked up speed and parked up on the side of the road about ten feet away, the driver stepped out and I stood still, as I felt both my feet begging to be freed from the tight shoes that captured them, the driver opened the passenger door and glared at me.

"Get in," Henry said. As I urged my feet to move a little faster, I jumped into Henry's car. He drove off at such a speed I gripped the door handle as an extra precaution. "Why did that woman call you Liz?" Henry said, swerving round the corner like a racing driver, he was raging. "Well? Why did that woman call you Liz?"

"Henry, slow down!" I shouted at him.

"Not until you tell me, and I want the truth."

"Henry, watch that car!" Henry narrowly missed driving into a parked car sending my heart into my mouth.

"TELL ME, LOTTIE!" he bellowed.

"OK!" I screamed; my hand white from its tight grip. "That is my name now, I had to change it. Everyone knows me as Elizabeth." Henry's speed did not die down, so I continued. "I had to change it to protect me because — because I did something awful and if I didn't change my identity and run, I would be dead now, for real." My head bounced off my seat as Henry did a sudden emergency stop, he managed to stretch his arm out in front of me before I went flying into the dashboard.

"What did you do?" he asked, his voice was urgent and both hands were clasped around the steering wheel ready to go again.

My hands were clammy, and I felt like the car had no oxygen as Henry asked me the question, I dreaded answering. "What did you do?" he repeated.

"I – I." My heart raced so fast I swore it would stop and then I would just die there without having to tell Henry my horrendous secret, the secret that keeps me up at night, the secret that haunts my dreams.

"I haven't got all day, so get on with it. What did you do that was so bad that you had to pretend you were dead?"

"Henry, I want to tell you, but I'm scared. I don't want you to hate me," I whispered.

"Look at my face, look at me. This is your chance to redeem yourself because up until a few days ago I remembered you as the angel of my life. The sweetest girl I have ever known who was lost to flames and I never even got to say goodbye. Now you're here right in front of me and all I feel is betrayal and rage."

I stared at a man I realised I no longer recognised, and it was all my fault. "I got into a fight with William." I rubbed my sweating hands on my dress and spoke with my gaze on my lap unable to look at him as he sat quietly beside me as I began unleashing my demon. "We were arguing about your letters, I hadn't received one in weeks, and I didn't want to believe that you had just stopped writing. I did not understand. Then he told me that you wished for us to go our separate ways and that is when I saw red. I threw a trophy off his head and it — it killed him. I killed him." My eyes were blurry, and my body felt like it had been only yesterday. "I didn't mean to kill him I swear." I turned to Henry who was staring right at me, I could not read his face he was even harder to read as he was when he found me, it was like he had been turned to stone. "Please, Henry. You must believe me. I loved William, he was my cousin; I did not mean to kill him. I did not know what to do so I ran which I know is an awful thing to do, I should have stayed and got the punishment I deserved but I was so scared."

"So, you went to him — Danny," Henry calmly stated.

"Yes, I didn't know where else to go."

Henry sat back into his seat, he pulled a hip flask out of his suit pocket and took a gulp before passing it over to me. The burning smoky liquid slid down my throat burning my chest but not enough to warm my quivering body. "Was it his idea? The whole fake your death plan?"

I nodded, sitting back into my own chair, the thoughts of Williams's body now at the forefront of my mind.

"I see, well that kind of makes sense. He must have wanted you really bad, more than your letters led me to believe."

Shockingly Henry lost his temper, he began to punch his steering wheel over and over until his knuckles were bruised, all the while letting out a yell. I was frightened by his anger, worried that this Henry might do something to hurt me, this was not his usual nature, his face was red, and his fists would not stop despite the obvious

302

discomfort in them.

"I'm sorry Henry!" I shouted over his cries. "I'm so sorry!"

"HE TOOK EVERYTHING FROM ME! HE TOOK EVERYTHING I EVER WANTED!"

"It's all my fault, I am so sorry for everything Henry. I should go," I cried.

"No! Lottie stay, I'm sorry, I didn't mean to frighten you. Please stay." Henry grabbed my face gently; he wiped away the tears from my face and in return shed his own. "You poor thing," he said slowly stroking the side of my face. "None of this is your fault, Darling," he whispered.

His gentle touch and tender words made me feel even more ashamed, I did not deserve his pity. I had done something unforgivable. "I am a horrible person."

"You are anything but, listen to me Lottie, and listen carefully. I never stopped writing to you. I never gave up on us, I wanted you more than anything in the world." I gazed at him confused. "Listen," he said before I could say anything, "I never stopped writing and you did not kill William."

"I did Henry, I saw him, I did. You might not want to believe that, I know I don't want to either, but I did — he's gone because of me."

"No, you did not. William is not dead, Darling. He is alive and I know this because he was the one who told me that you were gone."

The words leaving Henry's mouth were ones I could not

make sense of. I pulled myself away from him, opening the car door a little for some chilly air. "I don't understand. Why are you saying that? William is dead. They told me, Danny, and his uncle, they went back to check and told me he was dead." I could feel my breathing grow heavy and my head was faint. "Don't say such things to make me feel better, I am a murderer, Henry."

"You are not a murderer; you are guilty of nothing more than causing a few stiches to his head and that is all. William is alive, he sat on my couch in bits telling me that you had died in a fire. I remember his bump to the head, but I never asked him about it as, to be honest, I did not give a fuck. I did not give a fuck about anything after that."

"I didn't kill him?" I asked. "Are you telling me the truth?"

"I swear to you, I would never lie about something like this. You have done nothing wrong, Darling. You have committed no crime. You ran from nothing."

"I ran from nothing," I repeated in utter shock. "I'm not a murderer."

Henry tucked a loose hair behind my ear and smiled gently. Although his words had caused a sense of freedom at the thought that I never actually killed my cousin and he was away somewhere living a well-deserved happy life, I could not cope with the thought that my husband and the father of my three children had lied to me. That he had used my vulnerable state to trick me into a life without anyone but him. I fiddled with the rings that had sat on my

finger for eight long years, each one a trap all so that
Danny Porter could get the girl.

"Everything has been a lie," I said thinking aloud. "One
big fat lie. I hated him when we moved here. He was
trying to help me fit in and make a fresh start, but I was
constantly looking back. I remember feeling like I wanted
to die. I had lost everything and even though I believed
you did not want to be with me anymore I still wanted you
and a life without you was unbearable. I am so sorry
Henry; I am sorry that I was so messed up that I had to get
involved with Danny in the first place. I made friends with
a monster."

"None of this is your fault. You mustn't blame
yourself."

"I have to go home Henry. I need to be on my own."

"Let me drive you."

"No — no thank you, I can walk it isn't too far. I need to
just, I just need some space," I said continuing with my
quick exit.

"Lottie, what will you do? Will you be safe? Please let me
come." Henry panicked.

"I am not going to do anything — not yet. Danny has
proven that he is an extremely dangerous man, and over
the years I have come to know times that have shown that
he really is not someone you should be on the wrong side
of. I have to play it safe; I have three kids to think of."

"Meet me here tomorrow then, ten o'clock. I need to see
that you are all right."

To which I nodded in agreement.

Chapter Twenty-Four

<u>12th September 1969</u>

Henry was on time today, parked up in the street where we were yesterday. He was looking sharp in a grey suit while I had opted for the peach dress that I had quickly put on yesterday afternoon as well. Henry looked as though he had just as much sleep as I did. He was concerned about me and my marriage to Danny. What can I do though? I cannot just waltz in and tell him I am leaving him, that will never go down well, not in a million years.

"Why don't you go to the police?" Henry suggested.

"He is the police."

"Not every policeman is corrupt, Lottie."

"If he is anything like his uncle, then no one will go against him. This whole life here was sorted within a week, a flat, a job transfer for Danny, fake birth certificate, Charlotte's death certificate. To be able to have such things so easily tells me that they are a powerful piece in the force and a dangerous one for me."

"Do you love him?" Henry blurted out.

"What?"

"Do you love Danny? Are you happy?"

I felt somewhat uncomfortable with the question asked and not just because it was Henry asking me but because it was something I had asked myself over and over. Did I love Danny — was the fact that I wanted him to remember our wedding anniversary a sign that I did have romantic feelings for him or was it that he was all I had and the father of my children. Was I happy? I loved being a mum, was that enough for pure happiness.

"I don't know," I replied. "You don't happen to have that hip flask on you, do you? I could really do with a drink."

Henry smiled passing me his silver flask from his inside pocket. We took turns sipping the golden liquid as we sat in the car, people walked by getting on with their day, men in suits off to work and women pushing buggies and armed with shopping bags. All the while I was sat with Henry wondering how messed up my life was.

"I can't ignore your bulging muscles anymore, what happened to the scrawny bod?" I asked, moving our thoughts away from Danny.

Henry gave a bashful laugh, even blushing a little I noticed. "I've been boxing for a while now."

"Boxing! Well, I am impressed, I know you were once a toe rag but didn't see you as a boxer."

"My dad pushed me into it really, I stirred onto the wrong path once I lost you," Henry said gazing out the window. "He wanted me to put all my negativity into something else and to be honest it was a relief, an adrenaline."

"That's good then," I said guiltily, passing him the hip flask imagining a young Henry fighting his anger out because of me. "How is Walter?"

"He is good, really good. Moved in with his girlfriend only last week," Henry said with a cheeky grin.

"Oh well, good for him."

Silence filled the car once more, I racked my brain for things to say but I did not have anything that I wanted to talk to him about, my life had been consumed with ill thoughts of my crime, nappies, bottles, housekeeping, nothing that would be impressive or worth telling him for my family life I felt guilty for. He had commented yesterday that Danny had taken everything that he had ever wanted. We had plans of a family of our own once and we were so close, yet so far from having the life we had dreamt of.

"Do you write?" he asked me, passing me the hip flask.

"No, I do not write. Apart from my journals, I don't write anything."

"You still write a journal?" Henry laughed.

"Why is that funny? I write them so I can, you know, express myself, vent, let my thoughts escape." My journals are kept safe in the kids' memory boxes under piles of first baby grows and books, Danny is not sentimental like that so I know he will not find them. Having written since I was ten and having filled many notebooks, I was not willing to leave them behind in London. They had survived my move from Durham to Gateshead and back again. Henry had packed them for my move to London, they were not going to be left behind, so I had Danny break in and take them — of course he was more than willing, anything to make me happy and make the uproot more bearable.

"With your life experience I am sure you would be able to write several books now," Henry commented.

"What is the point I would never have the time; Liz can't even work a few hours in a library never mind dedicate hours to writing."

"But Liz is not real. You are Charlotte," Henry said. "This is fucked up, Lottie."

"Yes, I am aware of that."

"You fear him, don't you? You're trapped."

"Yes, I am very much trapped."

"I don't normally sit in cars with other men's wives just so you know, as lovely as this is I really do need to get back to the site, but can I see you again tomorrow?" Henry said, making me smile, I could not help it. I do not want him to leave my life again, not just yet.

"Tomorrow is Saturday, I can't come on the weekends, the kids are at home, but I can come on Monday, if you still want to see me."

"Monday is great, I can't wait."

19th September 1969

Every morning this week we have met up at ten, Henry always has a hot drink ready for me, as tempting as it is, two grown adults cannot sit drinking whiskey early in the morning every day. The chat has become easier and less morbid, he even asks me about the kids, at first I was brisk about it but then I could not help myself, they are my everything and Henry looks as though he is genuinely interested in hearing all about them.

My mornings are brightened with Henry's presence, my mood is lifted. The kids come home, and I want to sing and dance and run around with them. I feel like I am being reborn. Henry's smile, his blue eyes, everything about him makes me feel good. His company sets me up for the day. Tomorrow is the weekend and the thought of going two days without seeing him saddens me.

23rd September 1969

Henry and I met up as usual, I was thrilled to see him. All weekend I had been planning my outfit, it was relatively warm for September, so I settled on a blue halter neck swing dress with some little white boots. I kept my hair down with the ends flicked out perfectly and accessorised with a floral headband. To my delight Henry commented on my look, he said I looked lovely.

"I thought we could do something different today, I have taken the week off work so I thought I could show you my place, cook us something to eat," Henry said, dressed in casual brown tartan trousers and a beige polo neck.

"You cook?"

"I will have you know, I am a fine cook," Henry said.

"I will be the judge of that."

Henry's house was a little over half an hour away in Epsom, once we were out of Croydon, Henry obliged to my request to have the roof pulled down. As the wind gushed through my hair, I felt liberated, I could smell what freedom could taste like. Buildings became few and far between as we got closer to Henry's cottage hidden behind a small drive guarded by trees.

"This is not what I was expecting," I said as we pulled up outside the peaceful home.

"Let me guess, you imagined a bachelor pad," Henry remarked.

"Yes, that is exactly what I imagined."

"I like to get away from the hustle and bustle." Around the cottage were beautiful plants of all different varieties. Back home, my garden had been neglected, we have a small patch of grass where the kids kick a ball around sometimes but, in all honesty, it barely gets a look in. Henry's puts mine to shame.

"Did you grow these yourself?"

"I did, this place was a mess when I bought it, me and my old man built it up from scratch. Including the outside."

"They are beautiful," I commented.

"I was taught by the best, would be shameful for them not to be," Henry said, his comment relating to Mr Flint, my dear old friend who taught both me and Henry everything there was to know about planting flowers and vegetables. Henry took my hand. "Come on you."

Inside Henry's home had been updated to the max, the outside screamed cosy old cottage whilst inside it was modern and open planned. A great big brick wall held a fire in the centre and opposite sat a large yellow couch along with a brown leather chair with a foot stool. An oak kitchen was spotted at the back with a pure white bench top, needless to say mine has every stain possible from tea rings to burn marks.

"Did you make this yourself?" I asked, inspecting the handles and the finish.

"I did, and the table."

"It's gorgeous," I said, gazing at the oak table surrounded by yellow leather chairs. "Wow I love the drinks cabinet, very vintage."

"I found it in an antique shop in Cornwall."

"Cornwall? You do get about don't you."

"Got to go where the work is, I was in Cornwall for about three years. It is probably the most beautiful place I have ever been. You should go some time; the bairns would love the beaches."

"I'm sure the *bairns* will," I said finding my old lingo somewhat amusing now.

Henry popped open a bottle of white wine and set about cooking in the kitchen while I wondered around the house that belonged to Henry Hollister, I wanted to trace everything that made him who he is, for you can learn a lot about a person by their home. I sipped wine and walked barefoot on the hard wood flooring, noticing the scattered plants around the place.

"What happened to Mr Flint?" I asked curiously the thought of him eating away at my brain.

"To be honest Darling, I don't know," Henry said from behind the counter. "Last I saw of him was about seven years ago when we left Durham. I hadn't really seen much of him before that, I was in a bad place to be frank, and he was the last thing on my mind."

I nodded feeling choked. "So, we both abandoned him then?"

"I suppose we did," Henry said sadly.

I knocked back my wine and investigated Henry's music choices after a top up. He had everything from The Beatles to Dusty Springfield. I wanted to put some background music on and settled with Elvis Presley, a favourite of Nancy's.

"So is this what you do with all the ladies then, bring them back to your swanky place, cook them dinner and fill them with wine."

Henry laughed, chopping up onions and carrots something I had not ever seen before – a man cooking. Unless I have been in a restaurant, every meal I have eaten has been made by myself or another woman. "If you must know, apart from Dad's girlfriend, you're the only other lady to set foot in the place."

"Oh," I said, hiding my delight. Well, I hope I did for I

had to turn away from him as the grin was uncontrollable. "You just go to there's then?" I asked trying to sound cool.

"Something like that," he said.

"You've had many then? Girlfriends? Lovers?"

"Lovers, yes. Girlfriends, none."

"How come?" I asked, trying to keep the images of Henry's body tangled with another at bay.

"Just haven't found anyone I want to be with. I like to keep myself to myself I suppose. I find it hard to let anyone in, that is why I do not bring girls back to my house. I don't want them in my space, inviting themselves round whenever they please."

"Or when you're done with them," I added.

"Exactly." He smiled. I topped up our drinks, noticing that mine was going down much faster than Henry's. "Hold your horses," Henry said taking away the bottle. "I can't take you home to pick the kids up pissed. Lottie, you need to relax."

Placing my wine glass down on the counter, I let out a sigh, being in Henry's home had me picturing what our life could have been, I could not help but compare it all to what I was going home to later that day. Yes, I could never regret having Florence, Nancy, and Arthur. I live for my babies but being around Henry had got me thinking of what could have been, he always said that I could do and be whomever I pleased. How many babies would we have had, all sat around the table that was built by Henry's hands each evening? Would we have a dog like Henry

315

imagined family life to include, and friends round for a barbecue. Could I write while he cooked up a storm in the kitchen? The list is endless and very pointless.

"Let us put another record on." Henry fumbled around with the records while I emptied my wine glass down the drain.

The house was exceptionally clean as well, I thought, as the wine splashed into the pristine white sink. I do not think Danny even know how to use a dish cloth never mind a hoover.

"Will you dance with me?" Henry asked, *Ebb Tide* began playing out by The Righteous Brothers.

"You dance?" I asked, walking over to him, and allowing his warm arms to hold my waist in to meet his body while taking my right hand in his. As I placed my head against his shoulders and felt his head rest on mine, I felt at peace.

"I learnt that being able to dance with a girl is vital," he whispered. "You could lose her otherwise."

We swayed gently, side to side, I closed my eyes and let my feelings rush over me. I knew in my heart that in his arms was where I wanted to be, it is where I have always wanted to be, with Henry. It has always been Henry.

"I've missed you," I told him. "I've missed you so much."

"Oh, you have no idea how much I grieved you, Lottie. Not a day went by where I didn't think of you."

I pulled my arm more tightly around Henry, I wanted to take in every inch of him enough to get me through the rest of the night.

When we were young and we shared our first kiss it was such a wonderful feeling, it was my first kiss, and he was so gentle and kind. When my nana died, his kindness was sometimes too much for me. I had to lose him to realise just how much I loved him; how much he had meant to me. I knew I had needed him but had not realised just how much until it was too late, and I had feelings for Joe also. Then during our time leading up to Betty's birth we fought a lot, we were frustrated with each other and undeniably still in love. I believed he would never love me again after Joe, but it turned out he had never stopped, although our time was cut short, everything he did for me has stayed with me always. He was there on my wedding day, he was there while I gave birth, he was there through the nightmares and the lonely nights. It had been Henry who made the first move, it was Henry who kissed me before I left with Joe, it was Henry who proposed and told me that I loved him.

"I still love you, Henry."

It was time to be brave and truthful.

I had to make sure that Henry knew that my love for him was ever-present. Henry moved his hands onto either side of my face, half tucked in my hair, giving me no choice but to look right at him. He looked me up and down, his expression serious. I was not afraid; what I had been lucky enough to experience with him is something that I will carry with me for the rest of my life, or so I told myself, as another part of me waited for his response impatiently. So much so that I made another brave move (maybe it was the wine) and leaned in to kiss him. A kiss I had longed for, for many years. Henry responded to the kiss it was soft as if he were almost frightened by it. He pulled away gently and gazed at me once more, his ocean blue eyes sucking every inch of my soul.

"I've never stopped loving you."

Our lips were joint once more, this time it was not soft or gentle it was like no kiss we had ever shared before. It was passionate, it was as though we needed each other to breathe. I felt my back push into the dining table, I felt his hands feel the bare skin of my legs. He stood before me, his kisses moving to my neck sending a shiver down my spine. I wanted him, I wanted him there and then but the gentleman in Henry did not take me on his dining table instead he took my hand and guided me upstairs, where for the first time, I got to make love with Henry Hollister, and it was everything I could have imagined and more. I was not Liz the baby-making machine who must please her husband, I was Charlotte, and she gave all of herself to the man who stole her heart many moons ago.

We laid in that bed wrapped around each other's naked bodies for hours until we reluctantly had to start making a move if I was ever going to make it to school on time. I cannot stop thinking about the feel of the soft hairs on his chest, the shape of his body, the weight of it pressed against me. Nothing could wipe the smiles from our faces as we danced around each other getting dressed.

"Do you have a hairbrush?" I asked, taking in my traumatised wild hair.

"There may be a comb in that top draw," Henry replied sadly putting his top back on.

While rooting through his top draw which seemed to be a draw for pretty much anything I came across a neat pile of letters still in their envelopes, with the address written in my own handwriting.

"You kept them," I said showing Henry my find.

"Every single one," he replied, "until you stopped writing out of the blue." Henry approached me with a tender kiss on my forehead. "When you told me that I had stopped writing to you, I wanted to have a go at you, as for me it was you who stopped writing to me."

"I never stopped, when I didn't receive any more, I wrote twice as much demanding that you write back to me, I needed to know what you were thinking, what I had done wrong for such a U-turn," I said, putting away the letters, as Henry spotted the comb. Slowly he took it upon himself to drag the brush through my tatty hair.

"As did I," he continued. "It appears that a game was played on both of us, Darling. I can also bet that William was not playing it on his own."

"Or even wanted to play for that matter, as he had nothing to gain from it," I added.

"It pains me to take you back there," Henry said placing

small delicate kisses down my neck onto my shoulders. "One day I will make you mine."

Henry dropped me off two streets away from the kid's school gates. Neither of us wanted to part, with plenty of goodbye kisses, I left putting on my best cheery housewife persona only to be greeted by a tearful Nancy who was black and blue. A girl in her class had started calling her names because Nancy had chosen to play the part of Peter in the class production of Peter Pan rather than the given character of Wendy.

"I don't want to be Wendy; she isn't as important as Peter. Peter is the lead; he can fly and is in charge," my poor girl said, still tearful over tea, retelling the story to Danny who was furious. "Miss Small said I couldn't be Peter because I am a girl so made me be Wendy. Angelica then started calling me names at lunchtime with her friends, following me round everywhere so I—I hit her, Daddy. So, they all started to hit me."

"Right, you need to get this Angelica and her cronies back one by one," Danny said angrily.

"Danny!" I was appalled at his idea to resolve matters with more fighting, Nancy clearly was also, as she burst out crying.

"No child of mine is going to be seen as weak nor be used as a punch bag. I want you to get them back, stick up for yourself Nance!"

"Maybe Nancy should just stop wanting to be a boy all the

time, Daddy," Florence piped up always the one to make her opinion known.

"Shut up Flo!" Nancy shouted.

"Why is everyone shouting?" Arthur began to sniffle.

"Wait until tomorrow when I catch that Angelica's dad, I will let him know how I feel about this," Danny ranted.

"Her mum drops her off," Flo corrected.

"I'll talk to her then!"

"Please, Daddy, I just want to leave it," Nancy cried.

"Danny, listen to her. You are only going to make matters worse if you start having a go at her mother in the playground. What if she blames Nancy and she ends up getting attacked again?" I said trying to make him think logically.

"Fine! But we are going to go and speak to the head tomorrow morning. This is not going to happen again, Nance."

"Tomorrow, I can't go tomorrow," I blurted out; I love my Nancy I really do but having a row with the headteacher is something I am happy to divert for time with Henry. Danny is more than capable of sorting things out himself. "I have a hairdresser's appointment," I quickly added. Which luckily for me he bought, it is not like he would notice if I had really seen a hairdresser or not.

321

24th September 1969

The highlight of my day had to be lazing around in bed with Henry, the sheets were all tangled and the look in his eyes melted my heart. I almost ran to the car to be near him once more and could not wait to be out of town just so I could touch him again. The minute we reached the house I could not keep my hands off him. As I lay on my stomach after our breath-taking love making, Henry traced my back with his fingers, making invisible marks on my skin.

"When I thought you were dead, I carved our initials into the tree by the green," he said tentatively. "I wanted our love to be remembered forever."

"I have never stopped loving you, Henry. I'm sorry you had to go through all that pain," I said flipping over to be face to face with him.

"I'm sorry you had to go through it all as well," he said, leaning over me and taking me away somewhere dreams are made of.

I noticed that Henry had quite a collection of books, many were classic reads such as Dickens and Shakespeare. While others that filled the shelves were the likes of Harper Lee's *To kill a Mockingbird.* I have read many children's books in the last eight years as well as women's magazines and recipe books, but I could not say what the last book I read was.

"I never knew you could read," I teased as I picked up *Anna Karenina* by Leo Tolstoy.

"Now that is just plain hurtful," Henry said. "Have you read it?" he said nodding to the book.

"*Anna Karenina?* No, I am afraid I have not, it has been something I have always wanted to dive into but never have. Something about a woman in a marriage she does not wish to be in, in favour of a more handsome man she is madly in love with, it kind of triggered my liking for it," I said, placing the book back into its regimental spot on the shelf. I slowly made my way back to Henry who was perched up in bed, laid back like the king he was, his arms folded behind his head. I crawled along the bed fully naked, thrilled by the thought that when I reached him, his hands were going to be all over my body once more.

"It drives her to insanity," Henry said still talking about the book, his eyes never leaving me.

"She must have loved him a lot then," I said mounting myself on top of him. My insides screaming as I felt his touch, his kisses all over my breasts urgently.

"You should read it," he said.

"Maybe I will, but not before I have you again."

When Henry dropped me off, not only did we have the evening blues, but as it's a Friday I will not get to see him until Monday now. Danny also had the Saturday off making it more unbearable to be away from him.

"Before you go, close your eyes," Henry said gleefully.

"Why, what are you going to do?"

"Trust me."

"Okay." I closed my eyes nervously. "You're not going to put worms in my hands or put a spider in my hair, are you?"

"No, I would never do such things… anymore… now open."

As I opened my eyes, everything looked the same and no insects were placed anywhere on my body. I didn't realise at first that Henry was holding a ring, this familiar gold ring with the ruby stone sparkled in nineteen-sixty-nine just as it had back in nineteen-fourteen.

"My nan's ring!" I cried. "But how do you have it?"

"William gave it to me, he said — he said it was the only thing left of you and he thought I should have it. Your uncle couldn't bear to have it back." I couldn't blame him. Three women have owned the ruby ring, my nana, Auntie Joy, and I. To my uncle, all three of us were lost. "I have kept it with me all these years, but I think you should have it back. I know how much it meant to you just as it has for me."

"I thought I would never see it again," I said as Henry placed the ring on my finger, back where it belonged. It was like a little bit of my nana had returned to me, just as Henry had.

Chapter Twenty-Five

27th October 1969

Danny knows. He knows everything. I fear that I may never feel true happiness again. I fear I will be trapped as Liz forever and the sweet dream of being able to be Henry's has not only been short lived but has also been dampened to destruction. It is all my stupid fault; I was careless and I more than paid the price for it. Danny had the weekend off and had dumped himself in front of the TV while I fetched him bottles of beers, all the while looking after the kids and cooking. You know the usual — it would not hurt him to grab his own bottles or cut up a snack for the kids. Anyways, when passing him yet another bottle of beer, he nastily grabbed my wrist so sharply that I let go of the bottle causing it to spill onto the carpet. I yelped as he dragged my hand closer for inspection.

"Where did you get that ring?" he asked through gritted teeth.

"I can't remember, I have had it ages. Just not worn it for a while," I lied, trying to hide my fear. My heart was racing, and I just knew in my gut that it was not going to go down well.

"You're lying, where did you get that ring Liz?" Danny said, my hand still gripped so tightly that I could feel the ring dig into my skin. "TELL ME!"

"I can't remember, Danny. Please you're hurting me." I could not think of a good enough lie quick enough.

To be honest I thought he would not recognise the ring, it had been ten years and even then, I hardly thought he would remember it.

"You think I'm a fool? That is your grandma's ring, Liz, and the last time I saw it was when I handed it over to a grieving uncle who had just lost both his son and niece. So, I will ask you again, where did you get that ring?"

Pawn shop perhaps, I thought, or maybe I could say it looked like my nan's ring encouraging me to purchase it. I had to decide quickly which way to play it but in all honesty when I heard the lies come out his mouth, telling me he passed it on to my Uncle Albert who was crying for his only son, who he thought I still believed I had killed, made me feel sick to the stomach. Anger replaced fear, only for it to be rectified very quicky.

"No Danny, do you think I am a fool? I can see the panic in your face, I can see you wondering how the fuck do I have this ring, how could it be possible? What have I done to retrieve it?" With courageous strength I pulled my arm away from his grip. "Yes, your eyes do not deceive you, this is my nan's ring, the one and only and it was given to me by someone who actually gives a shit, not only do they give a shit, but they also telt me the truth. I know your dirty little secret, *husband*. I know that somewhere out there my cousin lives, he breathes, and if anything, he probably feels the weight on his shoulders that he may have been part of the reason I am *dead!*" I was livid but it felt so good to see the shock in his face, to see him realise that his time was up, his lie was out. "I feel disgusted to be your wife," I spat.

"Who told you?" he asked calmly, as though I had just told him that we had new neighbours or that our favourite takeaway restaurant was closing.

"That does not matter, what matters is that you have lied to me for ten years, Danny. You made me believe I had killed someone, my own cousin. Do you have any idea how much torture that caused me? You had me run off in the middle of the night as a criminal, leaving behind everyone I knew. Who the fuck does that? And why? Why would you do that?"

"You were miserable, you had been through so much shit. I wanted to get you out of there, I wanted you to be able to start again. When you thought you killed William, my heart overtook I saw it as an opportunity."

"Your heart? No one with a heart comes up with that idea, and so calmly. The truth is you wanted me, but you knew I did not love you. So, you saw it not as an opportunity to take me away, not to start a fresh, but as an opportunity for you to try your damned hardest to get me to fall for you. You did not like that I rejected you, you did not like that I was not interested. So, you made yourself the only person in my entire world, the only person I could rely on. It must feel great to know that the only reason I married you was because I literally felt like you were the last man on earth."

"I loved you Liz, I still love you and I'd have done anything for you to see that, to feel that. I had to get you alone, I knew then you would feel it too, away from London. Can't you see the good in all of this, we have had ten happy years, three kids." Danny tried to place his arms on my shoulders in a patronising way that I was not going to allow any longer. I shrugged him away unable to bare his calculating touch.

"No, no I can't see the good. I see this all very differently to you, clearly. I see ten years of feeling worthless, ten years of feeling like I should not have been alive, that I did not deserve each day. I have been in a constant cycle of waking up as someone I do not want to be, living the life I did not choose. You did not save me; you did what everyone else wanted to do and you chose my path for me. I did not fall in love with you, I relied on you. There is an enormous difference, but I wouldn't expect you to know what real love is anyhow."

My comment struck a nerve, Danny's lips twitched, which it does when he is annoyed, he picked up the dropped bottle of beer off the floor which had been trickling away onto the carpet and drank what could have only been the dregs before smashing the bottle against the fireplace.

"Tell me then, what is real love?" he asked in a sarcastic manner. "Enlighten me, for I believed the woman I call my wife and the mother of my kids did love me, otherwise I must be the one fooled for you've done an excellent job at making me believe so. You see Liz, everything you have from the clothes you wear and the food you eat comes from me and has done from the minute we moved here. I have never asked you to do anything but look after the kids and the home like a good wife should. I do not expect any more or any less from you. Yes, so I told some lies along the way to get what I wanted, but it worked, and I have made sure that you are happy, loved, and comfortable every day which is more than anyone in your own family did. Let us not forget that I changed my own life for you also. Is that not love?"

"You're fucking delusional, no, of course that isn't love, you don't lie to the ones you love, you don't trap them into a life they didn't want, you don't have them believe they are a murderer! You think this is love, it is selfish, and it is manipulating. You did all of this for you, and don't you dare throw your life changed too card, you walked straight into another police station, and you got the girl you wanted."

"Liz-"

"MY NAME IS NOT LIZ, IT IS CHARLOTTE!"

His calm and easy-going attitude to the whole situation was driving me crazy. There was no remorse whatsoever. He actually believed that everything he had done was for love, had been for the better. He was a psychopath.

"Be quiet for fucks sake, the kids are upstairs,"

Danny said, closing the living room door. "What is done, is done. We cannot go back; we are a family now. We have to think about the kids."

"Why can't you see what you have done Danny, you've ruined my life," I said collapsing onto the couch.

"I gave you a family that loves you, I accepted your past and still wanted all of you," he said sitting beside me.

"Would I not have got that anyway, a family of my own? Acceptance from someone who saw me and not the mistakes I had made. Was my life really in tatters to the point that I needed saving?"

"You almost killed yourself with alcohol for starters let us not forget that, then you were beside yourself when, you know, all that stuff happened leading up to that night."

"What stuff exactly?" I asked my heart racing.

"The letters, that you were exchanging with that guy from up north. You were a mess when they stopped coming."

I let a little laugh escape me and the lies kept going even still, Danny looked confused which made me laugh even harder. "What did you do to those letters? Is there a secret stash of them somewhere? Did you blackmail the postmen or perhaps you beat up William for them? Because all letters were sent both sides, they just never reached the recipients. Strange that isn't it?"

With slight hesitation Danny replied. "What's strange is

you still haven't answered my first question. Where did you get the ring?"

I thought I had it all worked out, I hoped with everything out in the open that there would be a shift, an agreement of some sort, why would I stay now I knew the truth, how could we go on knowing that he knew his secret was no longer the way that we had. In reality I knew nothing at all. "Henry."

"Henry? Your pen-pal," he mocked.

"Really? You are going to take the piss; you know he wasn't my pen-pal."

"Okay, so he was your little crush, your little fairy-tale."

"Stop it, Danny. Just stop. He was my fiancé; we were months away from getting married."

"And then what? You were going to live happily ever after," he scoffed. "You fucked his brother, Love; it was never going to be happily ever after. I did you a favour."

My hand instantly raised to give him a slap that he had asked for, only he was too quick and grabbed hold of my arm.

"I wouldn't if I were you. So, you and Henry, what exactly is going on there then? And before you start making some bullshit up, I would prefer to hear the truth straight away, if you don't mind."

"I thought you preferred lies and deceit," I said pulling my arm away from him and wrapping it around myself for comfort.

Danny laughed at my words. "Good one," he said.

"I bumped into him; he is doing some local work here. He was shocked, I was shocked, we got talking and the truth came out. It turned out William was the one who told him that I had died so that was the first lie revealed and then we put two and two together about the letters when we realised neither of us stopped writing."

"Sweet," Danny said with a grin. "Then he just gave you the ring and went off right?" I should have said yes. Why didn't I say yes? Why did I let that smug face of his get the better of me?

"You can't just walk away when you bump into someone you have missed for a decade. It might be hard for you to understand this, but you destroyed something that was good, Danny. He was not just some little girl's fantasy; he was the love of my life. We had plans and you took them from us." I could feel myself getting passionate as I spoke about Henry and me, I could feel the anger rise once more and I could not stop myself. "What Henry and I have is real love, a love that does not go away, a love that can't be hidden behind lies and ignored. Henry would never have done to me what you did. He would never have tricked me into this fake life, he let me go so many times despite not getting what he wanted but with you it's all take, take, take."

"You love him?" Danny asked laughing.

"Yes, Danny, I love him, I have always loved him. He makes me feel good, and with you I feel like I'm fucking suffocating!"

With a sharp sting the first blow to the face made its impact as Danny's hand swung round. I am not going to lie, it hurt but the anger was far greater. "How exactly does he make you feel good, eh? You been sneaking around behind my back. Is he the real reason you've been getting all tarted up?" I felt my head tilt as Danny pulled my hair back and the powerful smell of beer consumed me as he leaned in close. "What have you been up to Liz?"

"Wouldn't you like to know?" I smiled. The next blow was straight to my abdomen, it left me breathless… "Don't play games with me, have you fucked him?" he yelled, pincer gripping my jaw. "HAVE YOU?"

"YES! YES, I HAVE! And it was the best sex I have ever had."

I tried to tense my body as I knew the next blow was coming regardless of what I said, it was another to my abdomen, what came next I could never have predicted. He did not stop, the blow was repeated several times, as well as a few to my face, I think I heard my nose crack as impact was made. All the while he screamed repeatedly that I belonged to him, he reminded me that I was married to him and as his wife I was his property. "I own you; I own all of you. You can say goodbye to that tosser, I am not going to let you out of my sight. I will not have you disrespect me like this after everything I have done for you! I am your husband! Do you hear me!?"

With Danny's fist about to make its next blow the

door creaked, and my heart sank as Florence walked in clutching a doll by its hand, a face of pure innocence met with the horror of her parents' battle. I had tried my hardest to not make a sound as each impact knocked me off my feet, for the sake of the three kids playing mindlessly above us. I had not yet seen my face but with the combination of Danny's red knuckles, the amount of blood on my dress as well as the excruciating pain thumping around my body, especially from my right eye that I could no longer open, together with the look on Florence's face told me everything.

She instantly burst out crying. "No!"

Danny retreated his fist, calmly trying to comfort her before the others came down. I cannot remember much of what was said as I began to feel dizzy and could feel myself losing consciousness.

I woke up tucked into my bed, I had no idea what time it was, but it appeared to be the middle of the night, I was in my night dress, and I could feel the heaviness of Danny's body beside me. With only my left eye to guide me, I dragged myself slowly to my mirror to see the mess of my face for the first time. My right eye was purple, my nose clearly broken, still full of dried blood, the right cheek was swollen. My lip had been pierced by my own teeth; the memory played in my mind as I remembered catching it. I clenched my body not wanting to even reveal the bruises that I knew were there. He had well and truly showed me who was in control. I was his property, why would I think the outcome of revealing my relationship with Henry would have gone differently.

My heart stopped and I froze as I felt arms guide themselves around my waist from behind. They did not care to be careful over every bruise they brushed past, or the fragile skin he grabbed carelessly causing me to give a little yelp each time. He ignored my winces and instead pulled down the sleeve of my nightgown revealing a bare shoulder which he covered in kisses. Each one burning my skin.

"You will never betray me again," he whispered in between kisses as though he had just whispered words of love. Danny's hands moved down my leg and grabbed onto the hem of my gown slowly he proceeded to lift it up.

"Danny, please."

He ignored me and lifted my skirt up until my bottom half was exposed. I wanted to scream but nothing came out, I knew I would not be able to fight him, he had made sure of that when he beat me to the core. Every movement caused a wave of pain. I could hear Danny pull down his pyjama bottoms and once again I pleaded for him to stop. With a tight grip of my hair, he pushed me down, my face pressed onto my dressing table, and he took me like an animal, all the while reminding me that I was his. Last night he repeated the process.

Danny arranged for the kids to stay with Rosemary for a while, he informed her that I had fallen down the stairs and was bedridden. She was more than willing to stop with us to allow the kids to stay with me, but he of course insisted that I needed peace and quiet during my recovery. I do not know what he said to Florence, but she had not said a word when she left, leaving me worried.

I have been left home with Danny popping in from work twice a day to check on me and in his words, "ensure that I don't get any ideas of running off." He also chillingly added: "I don't think you realise just how powerful I am. I know people everywhere, changing your identity was a piece of piss. So, imagine what I could do if I learnt that you were still seeing Henry. I will have you locked up in an asylum quicker than you can blink. You would never see the kids again and I would leave you there to rot! Only I would know where you were and only my face would be allowed to go anywhere near you. So, I would think about that any time you think about running off with your fancy man. I could ruin him too while I am at it. Hollister is his surname am I right, yes, it is I can see it in your face. Runs Walter and Sons — would be a shame for such a well-built business to be pulled to the ground for, I don't know, fraud? drugs? unpaid taxes? I can make anything happen, remember that love."

29th October 1969

I write this not to remember the event and to look back fondly but to capture certain moments that I fear forgetting. I have been housebound for three days now and in that time I have not seen or heard from any of my kids. Three days may not seem a lot, but it is the longest I have ever been apart from them. I cannot wait to hold their little hands and kiss their soft cheeks. I feel like a prisoner with Danny popping back and forth to check that I am still here, even with the house locked and the keys in his possession, he is still terrified that I will find a way to escape, two hours ago I was surprised to see one of his work colleagues, Spike, let himself in.

"Hey Liz, Jesus the stairs got you good. Brought you some dinner, it's only sandwiches but Danny was on a big job so asked me to pop by."

I thought of running for it, past Spike, legging it for my freedom. I could run to Henry I thought, he would protect me and together we could grab the kids and run away. Then we could all be happy together, but then the kids would miss Danny, we would be hunted down, forever on the run, and when he finds us, he will punish us all. So, I let the thoughts disappear, thanked Spike for my dinner and remained on the sofa like an invalid. Besides, I wouldn't have been quick enough to run out in my condition. I wonder if it ever occurred to Spike why there was the need to lock me in my own house, or had he too been brainwashed by my evil husband? The sandwiches lay thrown on the floor while I lay tormented by my own thoughts and trying my best to find the most comfortable position when there was a knock on the door. I thought about ignoring it as I could not open it and I did not have the strength to move. It may be Rosemary wanting more clothes or toys for the kids I thought or perhaps a nosy mother checking up on me.

The knock grew louder and more impatient as I ignored the caller, until it eventually stopped. I slowly tried to pull myself up to turn the television on something had to be done to fill the silence and perhaps it would distract me from the pain as the painkillers Danny were giving me were not even touching the surface. He made sure I was taking them feeding me them like a child, with no remorse whatsoever may I add. The threats have stopped however the sweet talk has now begun.

"Would you like a drink my love?"
"Hold onto me and I will carry you up to bed."
"I will get you your favourite Chinese for tea on my way home, be a nice treat for us in front of the telly."

Yet every night as he lays me on the bed, he at once begins to undress me roughly and takes me at his will. All the special care given to me previously is replaced with aggressiveness and greed. I can only pray that my daughters grow up to be loved and respected by their partners, I will try everything in my power to ensure they can be independent on their own and have a great education behind them. Someone once told me that education was wealth, things are changing for women, we are powerful beings and there is so much more to our lives than being at home or following demands from first our fathers and then our husbands. I hope the world will be kinder to my daughters.

I managed to slowly lower myself onto the floor and then the plan was going to be to bum shuffle across the floor to the TV. Before I began the shuffle, I had to stop to compose myself as getting from the sofa to the floor had taken a lot of effort, I almost believe that I may even have a broken rib as even moving my arms or breathing is excruciating.

"Holy Fuck!" I jumped out my skin terrified at the sudden angry voice only to realise to my horror that in my living room, in my house, stood a very white-faced Henry. I must admit this may be the only time that I have not been pleased to see him and not because I do not want to be near him but because he just past a territory he cannot be in.

"Henry," I gasped.

"I knew it, I fucking knew it! I knew something was wrong. I am gonna kill him, I am gonna actually kill the fucker!" The Hollister fists appeared, and his face quickly transformed from a pale white to an extremely hot red. "Is he here? I will see to him now. Where is he?"

"He isn't here," I managed to say, pulling out a useless

hand to try and grab him from afar.

Henry saw my struggle and knelt to the floor before me, he took me in, examined every bruise, every cut, every swollen part of me and the beautiful man that he is cried at my pain. He put out his hands to hold me but held them back, instead holding my hands bringing them to his lips where they were covered in a flurry of kisses. His love and his kindness were just too much for me and I broke down, every deep breath hurt but nothing compared to how my heart was feeling.

"How did you know where to find me? How did you get in?" I asked.

"I started asking around when you didn't show up, I just knew there was something wrong. I saw your handbag through the letter box. I know you don't go anywhere without it, so I broke in through the back."

"Will you be able to lock it again, if Danny notices that it's open, he won't be happy?" I panicked. "I don't know what he will do."

"You're not staying here Lottie, are you crazy? My cars outside let us pack up some things, your books. We will come back for the kids later. You can all stay at my place." Henry looked so serious, and I know he meant it, which was why it hurt, even more, to have to tell him what I did not want to hear myself.

"I can't go with you, Henry. I want to, believe me, I want nothing more. I love you so much and I want to be with you, but I cannot leave. I must stay. If I leave, he will hunt us down, he has people everywhere, people that will do whatever he says because they are afraid of him or just as corrupt. We will never be free, and neither will my kids. He is powerful Henry, so much greater than us."

"We will find a way, Lottie. We have to try, there has to be a way out." I could see the desperate thoughts flash in his eyes just as they had in my own these past few days. I had thought of everything, even fleeing the country, yet Danny always found us, and I was always left in a padded cell.

"He is going to put me in an asylum Henry, he is going to take my kids away from me if I don't stay. You cannot run away with an unstable mother and the kids of a *respected man*. We will be game for everyone. I will be locked up for being a psychopath because my husband said so and you will be put away for kidnap. Then my kids will be left behind, traumatised, and brought up by a monster. I can't let that happen."

"He can't always win," Henry cried. "You don't belong to him."

"I know," I said tearfully touching his gorgeous face as I caught a tear. "I'm so sorry Henry, you have to go. He could return anytime, and I don't want him to catch you here that won't be good for either of us."

"I'm not afraid of him."

"Well, you should be, you can't come back here. You have to leave and go on as though you never knew I was still here." I tried to sound strong, I tried to sound like it was deadly important, but I kept choking on my words. "You are the most amazing person I have ever met, and you live in my greatest memories. I thank God that I got to grow up with you as my neighbour and had the privilege of being loved by you. You will always be the greatest love of my life, but you need to be someone else's now."

"Don't, don't say that," Henry said, clutching tightly to my hand. The muscley man who walked in ready to fight was now very much a frightened, clinging onto me, onto our love, and it shattered my heart to pieces to have to do it.

"Henry, we have both been through so much shit. A lot of your shit has been caused by me and I am so sorry for that but now is the time to leave me behind, move on and find someone who makes you smile, makes you laugh, makes you feel alive. You deserve so much happiness."

"You make me feel all those things. I want only you. Why can't you ever be mine?"

What made me cry far harder was the truth. Henry did once have me. I was all his, he was once there for me to see every day, he was whom I spent the long hours with, no one was against us, we were the sweet young love and I jeopardised it all, leaving the most precious human I could ever wish for behind like he had never been that important. Karma well and truly bit me in the arse, I have spent what has felt like a lifetime wanting to be that young girl again, to just be Henry's freely.

"What kind of man would I be to walk away and leave

you here with him, look what he did to you. You're barely recognisable."

"A man who loves me completely and knows it's the right thing to do, for both of us."

"I've only just got you back."

"I know, and I am so glad you found me. The past few weeks have been so magical. We never got to say goodbye to each other before but now we can."

I did not care how much it would hurt for me to lean forward and kiss Henry, it had to be done and it was worth it to feel his kiss one last time, I could taste the salt from our tears and his tender arms carefully trying to embrace me as gently as he could.

"Now go and live your best life," I whispered.

Dear Lottie

Mel Higgins

1970s

Dear Lottie

Chapter Twenty-Six

31st December 1970

Nineteen-seventy what a strange year you have been, Arthur lost his first two teeth, the girls learnt to skate, which was the highlight of their summer, we all spent a week at Butlins in Skegness for Easter, and Rosemary dislocated her hip. Danny got promoted at work which resulted with what started as a small party turning into a weekend bender, which of course was just fucking fantastic. As for me, well the most exciting thing was getting a new washing machine and sorting out our garden which now has so many flowers I think you may be able to see them bloom from space. I sometimes sit out there looking at my arrangements and smile; they were all grown by my own hands, and I know wherever he is Mr Flint would be genuinely pleased at my accomplishment.

Anyways, yes, goodbye nineteen-seventy and hello nineteen-seventy-one, please be kind! Oh, I best go before our guests begin to arrive, got to host. It may be my birthday but tonight is all about Danny Porter's party of the year.

4th January 1971

Today was a nerve-racking day, I have thought about how this day would play out so many times before but never had the guts to do it but something inside me said it had to be done, it would be wrong not to. So once the kids and Danny left for their day this morning, I made my way into London. I have to say it felt bizarre heading towards the capital and I am sure I looked out of place with my sunglasses on alongside my hat and scarf to try and hide my face from anyone who might recognise Charlotte. If Danny had found out I had returned to the city I knew I would have had a lot to answer for, so I knew I was being completely foolish, but I couldn't help feeling like there was something wrong in allowing the people that had cared for me to think I was dead, people that didn't deserve to be in the dark with such a lie. Halfway through my journey, I began to feel sick, what if Danny found out? I was dead, I thought. What would I gain from this trip? Would anyone be happy to see me? Why didn't I just send a letter first, that would have been the best way to go about it, but I held little trust in the postal service.

When the train reached its destination there was no going back, I remembered my way around London like the back of my hand and hustled my way through the busy post new year shoppers until the streets became wider, trees became more frequent, and the houses began to sprout up in size. My heart was beating so strongly that I felt I may even pass out as I approached the familiar house. The big black door stood tall, sitting at the top of the three steps, I was only three steps away from knocking on the door, three steps that is all it was, yet I hesitated, and I must have stood there for a good ten minutes unable to walk that final part of my journey and knock on the door. I even walked away and did a lap around the street before returning to the bottom of the steps and inhaled a deep breath and took the plunge for if I waited any longer, I was going to have to head back home and everything I achieved to get this far from Croydon will have all been in vain. I had to do this; I did not want to walk away without the truth being out for not just me but for my cousin. So, I threw myself up the stairs, removed my glasses and knocked on the door before I could stop myself, then I may have swallowed a tiny bit of vomit that had come up into my mouth. It did not take long before the bustle of the door being opened from the other side came, and I braced myself for the person I was going to face; would it be William, my auntie perhaps, or even my uncle.

To my delight it was none of them — the door was opened by a small boy who looked similar in age to Arthur. He was wearing a smart white polo top with navy blue trousers and his hair was jet black, and his smile, well his smile was just contagious.

"Hello there, what's your name?" I asked.

"William Junior Albert Anderson," he replied confidently.

I could see the resemblance and my heart beamed as I realised that the small boy's dad was my cousin. He is a dad I thought, William has a son. "Is your father in, William?"

"He's in the office having a meeting with Mummy, they are planning my birthday. They think I don't know but I do, they never close the door properly, so I can hear everything," William junior said in a matter-of-fact sort of tone. "Would you like to come in?" he asked.

"I would love to, thank you," I replied stepping over the threshold into the entrance hall of what was both my childhood summer days and the setting of many of my nightmares. I had mixed feelings stood there, I felt like an outsider, an alien even.

"Mother! Father!" Little William shouted abruptly. I felt a sudden panic at his calling. I suddenly felt unready to be confronted with my cousin, but it was too late to back out now as the office door opened, and there he was in the flesh with a pretty blonde beside him.

He stood frozen, looking at me as though he were working out a long multiplication sum on a blackboard.

"Charlotte?" he said inquiringly.

"Charlotte?" his wife questioned. "As in your cousin Charlotte?"

"Yes, it's me. Charlotte." I removed my woolly hat afraid it may be the reason I was not easily identified; you know forgetting the part where a few seconds ago I was a very deceased cousin. All eyes were on me in total disbelief making me feel rather uncomfortable. "I'm really sorry to invite myself round unannounced like this, I just didn't think a letter was quite enough."

"No, I don't think it would have been," William said, glaring. "Why…why don't you come into the office where we can chat."

"First, let me take your coat, Charlotte," William's wife said, removing my coat from my back with a smile just as beautiful as her sons. "I will make you a cup of tea too, you look freezing."

"Thank you, that is very kind of you."

"I'm Elsie by the way," Elsie said hanging up my coat and scarf. "I will grab some biscuits as well while I'm at it, come along Will."

William held the office door open wide for me and as I stepped in. Nana's pale-coloured walls were now a dark navy; the desk was filled with papers and picture frames and almost every wall was filled with books. It was a true office in all its glory, and it was perfect.

"Sorry, I know it is frightfully early, but would you judge me if I poured myself a whiskey?" William said, heading over to a whiskey decanter and pouring himself a small glass before I had even replied.

"Not at all, I am not one to judge cousin," I said, taking a seat into a leather chesterfield chair opposite William's desk. I held my bag close to my chest and awaited the awkward chat that was about to be held. I almost felt like I was in the headmaster's office or being called in to see Uncle Albert for making too much noise running around the house. William sat down opposite me and after a quick glance and a large sigh he put his head in his hands.

"I'm sorry if I do not seem pleased to see you, Charlotte. I am, I really am. I am just in a little bit of shock and, if anything, extremely confused. I don't understand, Charlotte, one minute we were arguing upstairs the next thing I know I'm in hospital, my father said you were missing, and no one had seen you all night. He then came back that evening to tell me you were gone, just like that," he said clicking his fingers. "What happened then? What really happened to you? Where did you go? What did you do?" he asked before necking his glass of whiskey like it was a glass of water.

So, I told him, I told him everything from our fight up until Henry leaving. I made sure nothing was missed out and William understood everything. He listened carefully, asked questions when needed and apologised repeatedly about the letters. Turns out he had been handing them to Danny who was making threats about his education and The American Eagle.

Elsie joined us with a mountain of biscuits that she ate almost by herself, hanging off every word that was coming out my mouth. There was something about Elsie that I instantly liked, she had a warm soothing energy oozing from her, and I felt as though I could tell her everything without knowing her at all. Her bright green eyes made me feel like I could trust her. She had tight blonde curls, very vintage I thought, and had the most gorgeous navy-blue trouser suit on teamed with fluffy white slippers. William had done well I thought looking at her fresh-faced beauty, he had done very well indeed. I always thought William would marry someone like his mum, but there was Elsie sat slouched on a chair catching biscuit crumbs with a cupped hand on her chest.

When I finished my story, the room fell silent, Elsie looked at William with her eyes gaping, William looked at Elsie nervously, all the while I looked at them both almost desperately.

"We have to do something William," Elsie said first.

"I agree," my cousin replied pouring another glass of whiskey. "That bastard has got away with all his dodgy schemes for far too long. He is a blackmailer, a fraudster, a wife beater, and God knows what else! He robbed you of your life."

"And Henry's also," Elsie added. "Who should we call?"

"I think maybe Edmund or perhaps even Richard. Both maybe. Listen Charlotte, I am a lawyer and what Danny does not realise is I too have friends in high places, I too have people who would drop everything to help. I too can be powerful," William said with a sneer. "I'm going to sort this out, I promise. In the meantime, lay low, we do not want him to be suspicious. Our first step is going to be getting you and the kids out of Croydon."

"You can all stay here, there is plenty of room," Elsie said. "William Junior would love having his cousins to play with."

"But what if Danny comes here?" I asked panic rising.

"To collect his wife who everyone around here thought was dead, I am going to parade you around The American

Eagle like an entertainer, Laurence and all our long-standing staff will recognise you. Danny and his uncle will shit themselves."

"The kids though, he has a right to his kids."

"That may be so, but part of me thinks the children will be the last thing on his mind, I want him out of the police force, I want him to pay, I want him punished. He will not be deemed a fit father when I am finished with him. He won't be good for anything."

"That's my man!" Elsie cheered on. "Pack lightly, Sweetie, we can get anything you can't take with you once you're all here, only bring what cannot be replaced and essentials."

"I will make some calls. Arrange some meetings for today."

"I will call the school," Elsie added.

"Can you be ready for Friday?" William asked.

"Friday? That's four days away," I asked surprised. They were planning everything so quickly that I was a little overwhelmed.

"Is that too long, we can arrange something sooner if you wish?"

"No, that's perfect, thank you, both of you. This means everything to me," I said tearing up.

Elsie squeezed my hand. "That's what family is for." Which tipped me over the edge completely. "Write your address down sweetie, I am going to call my best friend Linda, her uncle, a lovely man, is the Commissioner of the

Metropolitan Police, your husband may know people in high places but frankly you can't go any higher than that Sweetie. He will not have a leg to stand on."

"We will arrange for you to be picked up Friday morning, so make sure the kids don't go to school that day. We don't want to take any risks coming for you ourselves so I will arrange for friends of mine to get you, you will be safe with them," William informed me.

"I'm really going to leave him," I said unbelievably.

"Yes, you are,' William said.

"You're coming home!" Elsie said, scoffing another biscuit into her mouth with no care in the world for her waistline.

I feel like I got back home on autopilot. My visit to William was even better than I could have ever planned, and I only wished I had found the bottle to do it sooner. This time on Friday I will be leaving Danny for good. He will not be able to control me any longer. I will be a free woman and I will not be walking it alone; I have my family on my side. Which is something I have not been able to say for an exceptionally long time.

8th January 1971

I cannot sleep. I keep getting myself into a flurry of panic every time I picture the garden shed alone in the dark with three packed suitcases within its wooden walls waiting to be freed, just as I am. I'm laid beside a lump, which of course is Danny, his breathing is heavy, and his night is normal, he has no worries or cares in the world as he sleeps soundly. I however have all the worries and countless arguments battling in my head. Would this work? What would happen if he were allowed to take the kids from me? What would happen if he caught me leaving? What if he already knows? Perhaps he has spies that follow me day to day, who followed me to London, and he knows about the suitcases in the shed and is already a few steps ahead of me. How will the kids feel? Am I doing wrong by them, for leaving Danny? What if Florence, a daddy's girl decides that she would rather be with him than me? What if William and Elsie have changed their minds or no one they knew was willing to help after all? It is currently only two-fifteen in the morning, I have hours left before the morning properly arrives. I got up for a drink of water before examining each room, I went through taking it all in for the last time in its peaceful state.

Danny had bought the house when we found out we were expecting Florence but hadn't told me about it until our wedding night when he carried me over the threshold as a surprise. There were times in our marriage when I could tell that he was in love with me or was it just purely obsession. On the outside he looked like a hard-working husband, and I was the lucky one who got to live it up at home and raise my kids without missing a moment of their childhood. If I needed anything for the house, for the kids, or myself all I had to do was ask and my wish was his command. Before I was legally bound to him, we often fought like cat and dog, never did he raise a finger and he always returned to me full of apologies and kindness. I believed him whenever he told me he loved me, he expressed it so passionately and I loved his loyalty to me. I found comfort in him in my darkest hours, I was still a big drinker until I found out I was pregnant. That is when it all had to change, I was growing a child inside me and I had to look after us and Danny made sure I had everything I needed; he followed me like a puppy wherever I went. Before I knew it, he was down on one knee promising me the world and I agreed thinking I was not going to find any greater happiness in my life than a baby and a man who cared so much about us by my side.

After the wedding, Rosemary moved into our old flat and we moved here into our three-bedroom family home, I felt like we had the prettiest home on the street. Danny had decorators in making sure they listened to what I wanted, I was in full charge of decorating my own prison, I just had not seen it that way. Yet when Florence came along, he was besotted with her, never did he change a nappy or get up with her through the night, but he was there with a towel at bath time or sneaking into her bedroom for a good night kiss if he missed it at bedtime. He loved her so much; he grew desperate for another straight after and was thrilled when I found out I was expecting Nancy. There were no signs of evil inside him, he was just a good man who I felt sorry for whenever I looked at him, because I did not love him the same. I had settled, I needed his company, his presence, his protection but no matter how hard he loved me I could not give him the love he truly desired and I know he knew this deep down.

I was terrified through my labours and was on edge for a while after both births, I told Danny that I wanted no more, that the stress of it all was too much.

He told me what will be, will be: "You're my wife, we are meant to procreate. You are meant to bare my children. How do you suppose we prevent such things from happening, love? If you get pregnant, then you get pregnant."

That was the first time I felt a shift in our marriage, the first time I felt like what I wanted no longer mattered, if Danny wanted something he would get it and all the gifts in the world could not hide that fact. He began drinking more, staying out longer, and slowly but surely his dark side began to reveal itself. Never did the kids see it or anyone else for that matter, only me. I was his puppet, and he was in control of the strings.

Before going back to bed, I checked on the kids, all miles away in their dreams. I hoped they would like their new home; it was to be a tremendous change in their life — Croydon is all they have ever known. The big house in Mayfair was drastically different to their cosy home. I am going to pick them up from their happy lives and put them

358

into an unfamiliar world with rooms bigger than our house, strangers living with us in unusual surroundings. I can only hope that they adapt well to the transition.

This is the closest I have ever felt to a miracle, and it makes me terrified. The entire day has been overwhelming to say the least. But the Andersons had an action plan put in place.

Step One – Ensure I Was on the School Run.

I made sure the morning went as normally as possible, we all got up in the usual morning rush on top of each other as per usual. I needed Danny to suspect nothing.

"I will take the kids to school this morning," I told Danny over a plate of toast, I could not bear to touch the eggs for my stomach was doing back flips.

"Are you sure, how come?" he asked taking a sip of his coffee.

"Some of the mums are planning a surprise tea party for Bridget — a friend of Flo's mum. She is turning thirty next week, we are going to have a chat about it this morning. I hope to oversee the decorations; we all know I will be running to your mum if I'm given the responsibility of the cake," I lied partially; this was true in some respects as it had been discussed yesterday at pick up. It seems that Bridget's tea party may have to be balloon-less.

"Oh, well, I will leave you to sort that out. I don't want to take the risk of being thrown into women's talk."

He bought it. Of course, he did, my husband may be the king of lies but I was the queen of little white lies.

Before Danny left for work, he pecked each of the kids goodbye and I watched on as they all returned the gesture and Florence wrapped her arms around his neck leaving me feeling a small pang of guilt. He had never wronged the kids, they clearly loved him, my guilt instantly vanished the moment he tapped my bottom and said, "I'll see you later."

No, you won't, I thought. "Right kids, get your shoes and coats on please." A note had been delivered through the door yesterday with nothing but '*8.50am*' written on it. That gave me precisely twenty minutes to spare from Danny's departure. I held back from doing anything for a good five minutes, pretending I was looking for my gloves in case Danny would return having forgotten something.

"Mum we are going to be late," Nancy moaned. "Dad should have taken us, can't you just put your hands in your pocket this morning."

Smart arse.

At eight-thirty-five I sat the kids in the living room, the three looked confused in their smart uniforms, their school bags and packed lunch boxes on their knees awaiting information to clarify what was going on.

"Ok," I began nervously. "Today, Mummy is not going to take you to school." Nancy's eyes bulged out. "Because we are going to go somewhere else, I am going to take you on an adventure." The three of them exchanged glances, Arthur smiled at his sisters not fully understanding.

"Where are we going?" Nancy asked.

"London," I replied. "We're going to stay with Mummy's family in London."

"Proper London — where the Queen lives?" Florence asked excitedly.

"Yes, proper London."

"Can we visit the palace?" she asked, almost jumping out her seat.

"Yes, we can visit the palace. We can visit anywhere you like, there are lots of parks and museums. We will have lots of fun and you will meet your cousin, William. He is the same age as you Arthur and he is extremely excited to meet you all."

"Will Daddy be coming?" Arthur asked.

"No, Daddy won't be coming. He has a lot of work to do so it will just be us four."

"Does he know we're going on holiday?" Florence questioned.

"Oh yes," I lied. "Daddy knows all about it. We wanted to keep it all a surprise for you." I felt shameful lying to my kids, but it had to be done, we had to get out, well I did, and I was not leaving without them.

"How long are we going for?" Nancy asked.

"I'm not sure to be honest, it's a special kind of holiday, we are allowed to stay as long as we like. Why don't we just go there, have lots of fun and see what happens," I said with my cheeriest smile.

The kids proceeded to chat amongst themselves for a little while as I paced the room keeping an eye outside. I had moved our suitcases to the back gate ready to grab them quickly when it was time to leave. I did not have to wait too long before a black Chevrolet with tinted windows made a stop outside the house. Two exceptionally large men appeared from the front wearing suits. They looked particularly important and not people you would want to mess with. They were apparently William's friends, although I could not picture the two of them sat having lunch or a game of golf with my cousin. I think my cousin was being polite when he described them as his friends, they were the result of money, and money talks.

"Right kids, our taxi is here, grab your coats and let's go on our adventure!" I cheered trying to get them in the spirit of it all before they became intimidated by the two chauffeurs.

It was wrong of me to be so judgmental as the two men, also known as Larry and Roger, couldn't have been kinder. They were swift getting us all into the car with our belongings and had bought a large bag of pick and mix sweets.

"For the journey Miss if you don't mind. I have kids myself and I know they can get quite restless while travelling especially with the circumstances," Larry said, which truly melted my heart and of course delighted the kids, making it a little easier on me.

With my babies bundled in, already tucking into their blackjacks and chocolate mice, Rodger spoke to me privately, "I wanted to let you know that I left a letter for your husband in the house, Miss. It will not take him long to realise that you are all gone, and I was informed to leave a letter detailing the situation for him and letting him know that it would be a clever idea to seek a lawyer. This way your husband cannot accuse you of abduction Miss, for he knows where you are." Roger noticed the worry wave through me. "It is ok, Miss, he would be wise not to come to the Anderson house. He will not receive a warm welcome if you know what I mean," he said with a wink, leaving me to only guess what he meant.

On that note I jumped into the back of the car, and we drove away from Croydon, my residence for the last eleven years. Not only was I leaving my husband, but I was also leaving Elizabeth, now I will be able to be Charlotte once more.

Step Two – Settling in Period

When we pulled up outside the white-bricked house in Mayfair all three sugar-hyped kids gasped in awe.

"Wow!"

"It's huge!"

"Your family are rich Mum!"

The front doors eagerly opened, and we were welcomed by all three of the Anderson family members.

"We let William play hooky from school," Elsie said almost proud of her naughtiness. "He was exhilarated to not go; he couldn't wait to meet his new cousins," she said ruffling Arthur's hair.

"Come and see my room!" William Junior shouted, encouraging all three of my babies to drop all their bags on the doorstep eager to follow him inside.

"We thought it might be easier for them to have William around," my cousin William said, giving me a hug. "It's going to be strange at first, so we are going to pull some strings with the school to give him some time off."

"Thank you, both of you. I honestly don't know how to thank you," I cried.

"You just need to make yourself at home," Elsie said, linking my arm and bringing me in. Larry and Roger brought in my belongings and without a word nodded their heads and spent the day stood outside the front door.

"They are just a precaution," William said.

Whatever they were, they made me feel a little safer, especially as the day went on and I knew that Danny would have arrived home from work and found the letter telling him that I had finally found the courage to leave him. I would never have been so brave without William and Elsie's help.

When the kids were all put to bed exhausted from their four-course tea, warm soapy baths, and many games of hide and seek in the large house, I had sat myself in the *parlour* (very posh I know) with William and Elsie. I had bathed myself and was enjoying the heat from the roaring fire with a glass of wine. The girls slept in a quick makeshift renovation of what was my old bedroom and Arthur in his new very classical blue bedroom which was once Cathleen's. I could tell they had made the effort to try and transform the bedrooms as best they could with a lick of paint and a change of furniture to not stir old memories, for which I was grateful. Larry and Roger had returned to their homes and had been replaced with two new men to carry out the night shift. God only knows what the neighbours were thinking.

"Are you okay?" William asked me as I sat deep in thought staring at the embers of the flames.

"Just wondering about Henry, do you think he will be okay? Danny may think he has something to do with all of this. What if he goes after him or his business," I said, opening up about the troubled thoughts that had been nibbling away at me since this morning.

"Henry will be fine," William said. "He doesn't realise it, but he has people protecting him too, at both his house and at Walter and Sons HQ."

"You have changed William Anderson," I observed aloud, making him chuckle.

"What do you mean?" he asked with his usual cheeky grin.

"You know exactly what I mean, you used to be this pale

geeky kid who used to chase your mother around the house." Elsie let out a snort-laugh. "He honestly did, now look at you, the man of the house, getting shit done with friends in abnormal places."

"People change and if there is one thing Danny taught me, it was you need to protect your family, I can't do that if I allow people to use me for their own advantage. The only difference is I earned my loyalty through hard work."

"Amen," Elsie said lifting her glass in the air before knocking it back. "Another," she said, reaching out for the bottle of wine.

"I like you," I told her as she filled my glass.

"I like you too."

"I like you both," William joined in.

"You're alright," Elsie said pouring him a drink before giving him a peck.

After a few more glasses my head was feeling rather fuzzy; I took in my environment and told myself that this felt fantastic! The Anderson house had not felt this good since the summer of nineteen-fifty-six. I had been there a full day, however, and had failed to ask some important questions of my own for William, I had not asked them earlier due to my own selfish reasons, but sooner or later they had to be asked, I could not just go and settle onto the top floor with William's little family in the middle without asking where his parents were.

"I was wondering when you were going to ask, I thought the lack of presence from my mother would have had you ask sooner. My mother lives in Kent not far from her sister, she has lived there for about six years now since my father decided one morning that he didn't want to be with her anymore." I was both surprised and secretly quite proud of my uncle for leaving Emily, she was a real ball and chain, and I could always tell that he was never genuinely happy with her. "As you can imagine she found it tough, she struggled with the whole separation. He did not just leave her high and dry though. He bought her a cottage, let her take what she wanted, gave her money, paid all the bills, and left her a lump sum in his inheritance."

My throat went dry when I heard that my uncle left Emily money in his inheritance, it meant that he was no longer with us. It meant that I was too late to make amends with him and let him know that I was alright. Elsie kindly passed me a tissue. I had no words.

"Sorry, I should have mentioned it sooner," William said. "He died last summer; he was sick for a while."

"He spoke about you a lot near the end," Elsie gently said.

"And Joy," William added.

"You know about Joy?"

"I certainly do, your aunt sounded like a lovely lady. He left a book of poems she had written in his safe, I think you would like them."

"And there is a trunk in the attic filled with old photos and memories. You are free to take a look. From what Albert mentioned, you both seem to be remarkably similar," Elsie said.

Step Three – Breathe

Although wine has filled my body, I am still very conscious of my surroundings — due to this unbelievable day — and have found my bed beside my darling boy. It feels so strange, almost like an out of body experience. I will forever be grateful to the Andersons, but now I must close my eyes, breathe, and sleep.

Chapter Twenty-Seven

<u>16th January 1971</u>

What a week it has been. The kids have settled in well on their *holiday* together, and with either Larry or Roger alongside us I have shown them the sites of London. Seeing the great city from their perspective was wonderful, I had grown up with this as part of my world but to them it was something entirely new and magical. Our guards have become extended family members overnight. They are always professional and on guard but cannot help joining in with jokes or the occasional ice cream. We all feel at total ease with our gentle giants, especially Arthur who sneaks his little hands in theirs as we walk. William had stuck to his word and has been in constant meetings with different people he knows to help with my case against Danny.

Yesterday evening he told me that he may have found a loophole regarding my marriage. "On your marriage certificate, it states that Elizabeth Reid married Daniel Porter, not Charlotte Ridley. Elizabeth Reid is nothing but a fake name. It may be that you are in fact not legally married at all."

I have not heard a more beautiful sentence in all my life! Not even married at all. I wish I could see Danny's face when the news reaches him.

Ever since we strolled into the hotel, causing gasps and smashed glasses (from my dear Laurence) I have had beautiful messages of support, and a bundle of laughs from Laurence who has become a frequent visitor along with his charming partner, Eugene. The kids love him, and I think the feeling is mutual.

William had made quite the entrance at the hotel: "Yes your eyes do not deceive you, you are looking at the one and only Charlotte Ridley, granddaughter of the legend that is Florence Anderson." Before revealing everything to the shocked staff and guests. Laurence came over to me like a shot spinning me around and smothering my face in sweet kisses. He recalled the night as very suspicious and had always felt hurt that Danny had moved away without a word.

Danny had made no efforts to physically come to the house but one of our night guards had received a letter from an unknown man. It read:

Liz,

I write this with a heavy heart. I understand why you left for I have wronged you, but I miss you and the kids terribly. The empty rooms of our house and the empty space in our bed is overbearing. We are a family; how can you walk away from ten years of marriage? How can you say that you feel nothing towards me? I lied to you about William and that was wrong of me, I sincerely apologise for that from the bottom of my heart but please, Liz, forgive me and come home. I promise I will be a better husband. I promise I will be more attentive; you could even get a job if that is what you really want.

I feel ashamed for every time I have hurt you, I love you more than anything in the world, my life has no purpose without you. I knew from the moment I met you that I wanted to be yours. I have been told I may have to serve a sentence for my wrongdoings. Please, love, put this right if not for me then for our kids. How can I look them in the eye from behind bars? Together we can make this all right.

Tell the kids I love them please,
Your loving husband Danny xxxx

"Thank you," William said taking the letter swiftly out of my grip once I had read it out loud, "evidence," was all he said, placing it in a red envelope.

The kids have asked about Danny a few times, mainly at bedtime when the fun of the day has expired. They are beginning to question when we are going home and are starting to miss school. I have yet to tell them that we are not returning.

Today, however, is not about Danny at all, for after much persuasion from Elsie and nagging from William I am currently sat in the car with Elsie on my way to Epsom to see Henry. I am hoping we arrive there before I pass out. After much thought and discussion, everyone believes I have to tell Henry in person what has happened and to let him know that I need him, that I love every bone in his body and can completely and freely belong to him at last. We have waited for this for so many years and to be honest when I told him to go and live his life without me, I never expected to ever be able to see him again and, in my heart, hoped he would not really and that I would always belong there somewhere. I am incredibly grateful to Elsie for not only driving me there but for curling my hair and letting me borrow her pretty white headscarf which she has tied in a bow as a headband. It goes well with my camel flares and my white blouse.

As we drive closer, I can barely write for my hand is shaking. Henry has no idea that I am on my way, which I know is going to be a huge shock for him nor do I know, come to think of it, if he will be there.

17th January 1971

Elsie dropped me off outside Henry's cottage, noticing that his car was not there she offered to stay with me but honestly, the nerves were bursting out of me and despite the frosty weather I needed to just get out and be on my own, to try and compose myself, it was around teatime so I hoped he wouldn't be long. The plan was for Elsie to return to London and if all did not go well, I would get a hotel for the night somewhere. With a blanket from the boot wrapped around me I waited for Henry to return, the night arrived quickly, and heavy snow began falling around me causing me to back up against the door with the blanket over my head to stop me from getting too cold and wet, but I was freezing; I was beginning to get numb and prayed that Henry would return soon. Panic rose that he wouldn't come at all. Perhaps he had gone away somewhere, or he decided to stay at work due to the weather. I remember beginning to feel foolish, foolish for just turning up out of the blue, foolish for wearing a thin mac, and foolish for potentially freezing to death. I waited for what felt like hours, as the snow thickened and came down faster until I began to get sleepy.

I could hear wood crackling and felt the heat brought to me from the woolly blanket wrapped tightly around my body. As I slowly opened my eyes it took me some time to take in my surroundings. The only light came from the fire and a small lamp glowing in the corner. I took it all in slowly, the yellow sofa I lay on, the brick wall, and the small leather chair filled with a man, whom from what I could gather, did not look too impressed. He looked worn out, his tie was hanging off, his buttons loose halfway down his shirt and in his hand, he held not a glass but a bottle of whiskey.

Henry stared at me in a way that almost made me feel uncomfortable. I said nothing as our eyes met and all the feelings of foolishness I felt earlier filled me again. I know in my heart that Henry and I have something special, but we have parted and been hurt so many times that I fear one day he will turn around and detest me.

"What are you doing here, Lottie? Shouldn't you be at home?" Henry said, leaning forward in his chair giving me a better look at him. "Isn't this a dangerous move to be here?"

The room was silent apart from the fire burning, waiting for my reply, the words escaped me croakily. "I just wanted to see you. I have…I have left Danny. I found a way out." I felt nervous, the news I was giving him was great news, but his reaction didn't look too swell. He sighed at my words and then took a big gulp of his drink. "Would you have preferred me to have stayed with him?" I asked baffled and somewhat annoyed by his reaction.

"No, of course not," he said leaning back into his chair. "But why now? What has changed for you to finally be free of that bastard when you couldn't leave him before?"

"I have power on my side now, I visited William and he is helping me. He is a lawyer and has people in top places that can help us, I have bodyguards, even the head of the met police is fighting my corner. I never had that before, love alone wasn't powerful enough," I said, believing I caught his face soften a little. "We needed something bigger than him and now I have. It even turns out that I may not even be married to him at all," I said not able to hide my glee.

"Because of Liz," he guessed correctly.

I nodded, giving him a small smile. He was as gorgeous as ever even if he was frowning and in a strange mood. Just being in his presence made me feel like I could fight the world and that everything would be ok from now on He reminded me of home but only the good parts, he reminded me of my childhood, and he reminded me of how his torch was the light that gave my soul moments of peace in dark times.

"William ensured that you were protected also, if Danny were to try anything with Walter and Sons or you for that matter."

"Thanks," Henry sulked. "Fuck!" he whispered but I heard him. "You're free now, Lottie. Free to do whatever you want, be whoever you want."

I hoped this realisation would soon be followed with his declaration of love for me, a signal that told me that I would not leave without him. I wanted him to tell me that this was our time at last, but he said nothing and took another drink. It was then that I noticed many boxes stacked up around the room. "Are you moving?" I asked, suddenly alarmed.

"What?" Henry asked, looking as though he had only just realised the boxes himself. "No, I'm not."

It was then that I had concluded that his face was not angry or annoyed, he was greatly upset. I don't know why I hadn't noticed it earlier. "Henry, what is it? Why are you so troubled? Have I caused you distress?"

"No, it's not you Lottie. It's just the timing of all this.

Darling, I'm…tomorrow…I'm getting married." I heard him say behind the beating of my now rapid heart. Of course, he was getting married, why would the universe allow me to be with him now, after all this time?

I pulled the blanket he had placed on me earlier tighter around myself hoping the soft material could protect me from the blow and from the embarrassment I felt for just arriving unexpectedly on his doorstep hoping to reconcile. "Oh, well congratulations," I managed to say.

"Don't Lottie, please."

"I mean it Henry," I lied. "So, what's her name?"

"Lottie," he said shaking his head, obviously not interested in sharing his new love with me. I stared him out until he gave in with a sigh. "Grace, her name is Grace." The very name of her sent a bolt of jealousy through me. "We met in Ireland; I was carrying out some work over there on her dad's estate. We ran into each other in the local bar. It was a few months after I last saw you and to be honest, she was a distraction from everything."

"Well, I am glad you found someone. I really am, I wanted you to find love and to be happy. You deserve it, Henry."

"I don't love her, Lottie. I love you. I always have and I always will." I would have lied if these words did not make me happy. "I am only marrying her because it is the right thing to do — she is expecting a baby."

The words cut me like a knife. Marriage is one thing, they can be miserable, and they can end, a baby however, well that's just different. I couldn't take much more, the boxes surrounding me were most likely to be filled with Henry's new wife's belongings and things for their new baby. The room began to feel rather stuffy, I swiftly kicked off the blanket and stretched my legs.

"Wow, Henry, you've got a lot to look forward to, do you have a phone by any chance so I can call Elsie — William's wife — she can come and pick me up and you can get some sleep? I've kept you up far too late already."

Henry placed his whiskey on the floor before standing before me and holding my hands in his at once. "Lottie, I didn't want any of this to happen. My choices were to hang out with Grace or get slashed in the bar. Then before I knew it, she was telling me she was in the family way, and I felt obliged to do the right thing but please do not for one second picture me driving off into the sunset with my new family because every day I wish she were you. It's a kick in the dick that you are now free, and it is I who am not."

I wiped away a tear that had trickled down my cheek, one of many that I have shed for Henry. "Do you have a phone?" I whispered.

"Yes," he whispered back leaning his head onto mine. "But please don't go. Stay with me tonight and I will take you home in the morning. Besides, it's much too dangerous for anyone to be driving in this weather at night. Please stay."

As I felt his fingers find their way into my hair and felt

the softest little kisses on my head, I agreed to stay, an invitation that was more than inviting. Henry's mood picked up with my acceptance and he poured us both a drink. It had to be the late hours of the night, together we sat under the blanket on the couch and chatted for hours, he wanted to know everything about my great escape from Danny and I painfully asked more questions about his relationship with Grace. I can only hope that the bride-to-be realises just how lucky she is. I truly hope she loves him as much as I do. After a rather lot to drink and lighter conversations, we stuffed our faces with cheese, crackers, and crisps, making a pig of ourselves.

"Dance with me," Henry said pulling me up before I even said yes. "I want us to dance but to no music."

I giggled. "Okay."

He pulled me in close in front of the roaring fire, the heat warming my legs. "I don't want to get lost in the music; I want to get lost in you. I want to get lost in your smell, your touch. I want to get lost in the sound of your footsteps and how beautiful you are."

We glided together closely holding onto each other with no other sound than our feet on the wooden floor and the beating of Henry's heart I could hear against his chest. I too could feel myself getting lost in him. The feel of his arms tightly around my waist. The smell of his cologne. I also knew everything would disappear the next day, only for them to still live in my memories, just as they had from the very first time I left Henry behind.

Maybe it was karma who thought it would be funny to now have him be the one leaving me behind.

I felt the tiny peck of a kiss placed on my shoulder, stopping my thoughts in their track, followed by another one this time on my neck sending a shiver down my spine. Sweetly a third kiss was placed on my cheek.

"Please forgive me for what I am about to do."

Before I could ask further questions about his need for forgiveness he kissed me again, this time on the lips. All it took was the feel of one kiss to have my body begging for more, Henry must have felt the same as we both lunged into another kiss only this time we didn't stop. I forgot everything in the heated moment, all I knew was Henry Hollister's hands were all over my body tugging away at my shirt for access to my skin and I was burning for it as his lips dared to part from mine for longer than a second.

In the midst of passion and the pulling apart of the remaining buttons of his shirt, an uninvited word popped into my head — Grace. I do not have an image of this woman or any care for that matter but what I did know was I empathised with her for the position she was in. Henry had said she was just nineteen, young and unmarried was a scary place to be even when the father was by your side. Somewhere, she was laying asleep in bed most likely after battling the excited nerves as she thought of the big day ahead of her which would not only make her a wife but would also protect her from scrutiny and perhaps her parents from shame. I reluctantly pulled Henry away.

"Henry, we have to stop. This isn't right."

"I'm sorry," he gasped. "I just…"

"I know," I said.

Henry rubbed my face gently before calling it a night. There weren't many hours of the night left before dawn would break and he had a long day, and I had my first one knowing dreams of me and Henry had to stop. I had to take my first steps without the hope that one day we would be allowed to just love each other. I know we make each other whole, there is something strong and invisible that pulls us together time after time, but now that must be cut loose.

I tossed and turned with these thoughts in my mind as I tried to sleep in Henry's bed. He was below me on the sofa downstairs, while I lay in his bedroom with memories of stolen time. I thought back to our moment of madness earlier, with our hearts acting before our heads, wanting only each other desperately. Should I have pulled Henry away? Or should I have let him take over my guilt?

I made the bold decision to tiptoe back downstairs, not to jump on Henry and continue from earlier, but only to be near him while I could. I thought if this was to be our last encounter then I didn't want to be far away from him. Like me, Henry was wide awake, so I quietly approached the couch and without a word snuggled in beside him fitting perfectly in his arms as he covered me in half of the blanket.

"I love you," he whispered.

"I love you too." And with that, we slept.

"So, this is the famous London house," Henry said as he pulled up outside William's house, speaking for the first time in a little over an hour, minus for a few directions.

There was a time when we both held on to the thought that one day Henry would be picking me up from the house to start our life together, not dropping me off on his wedding day to another. How strange life turns out sometimes, some things really are not in your control and no wishing and hoping can change it. You just have to live your life the best you can.

"You weren't kidding about the security, were you?" he said eyeing up Larry and Roger who stood on either side of the front door. "It all frightens me, Lottie, I know I am not getting married for the right reasons. The baby is the one and only one, is that enough? Does that justify it all. I should be wearing this suit waiting at the altar for you, I want you to be my wife, Lottie."

"I want that too," I sobbed, tears gushing now as I apologised, making such a mess of my face. "I'm sorry Henry, this is all my fault. I should never have gone to that stupid dance, I'm sorry I ran away, and I am sorry I didn't just leave London and make my way back to you. I should have told you that I wasn't dead, and I should have fought Danny sooner. Now I've lost you forever, I will forever be sorry."

"Hush now," he said wiping my tears as his own escaped. "You must not blame yourself. You are the most perfect thing, and it was me who let you down. I should have gone to the dance, you had begged me, and I was stubborn. I didn't fight for you when you got involved with my brother, I just let you go. I should have gone with my gut feeling and just picked you up from here as soon as I had enough money, and I most definitely should never have left you with that bastard. It worries me that maybe Joe would have fought a lot harder. He left to protect you while I left you with everyone that was hurting you."

"I have never looked at it in that way, to me you have always been the saviour of my story."

Henry desperately suggested that he wouldn't marry Grace. He thought perhaps if he gave her enough money and support that it would be enough to keep her happy and he could be with me instead. My heart wanted to scream yes. I would love nothing more, of course. It is all I wanted, yet he was two hours away from his big day, Grace would most likely be in her dress already or getting her hair and make-up done. I don't have it in me to hurt any more people for my own gain. I told Henry perhaps he will learn to love Grace; she was the mother of his child after all and together they were going to embark on a wonderful journey. He didn't look convinced.

"If I cannot be yours then I hope you find someone who

loves you just as I do. Someone who will worship the ground you walk on Lottie Ridley. Anyone who treats you any less is not worthy of you."

I nodded in agreement thinking another partner was the very last thing on my mind right now. The only man who holds my heart is marrying another, my husband is abusive and looking at a prison sentence, and the father of my oldest child whom I have not held since her birth is potentially still running from town to town maybe even country to country. I think it would be wise to concentrate on me and my kids and how I can support us all alone. "I should go," I said.

Neither of us moved at first. Time was ticking and it was all going to end sooner rather than later, so I leaned in, and I kissed him goodbye, I kissed him for every morning of the rest of his life and for every night he will lay to sleep. I kissed him to thank him for the joy he brought me, and I kissed him to leave a reminder of me with him. Then I swiftly left because it was just too God damn hard to prolong the pain of our parting any longer. He didn't call me back; he didn't send me off with sweet words and nor did I. I just walked up the three steps to the front door avoiding Larry and Roger's gazes and collapsed into William's arms, who was waiting in the entrance hall ready to catch me when my body gave way.

1st February 1971

Today is to be my last entry, my cousin has sold The American Eagle, it felt strange watching the papers be signed but it felt right. William told me I don't belong in London, and I know he is right. I don't believe he enjoys it very much either, hence the increasing talk of moving to Australia where Elsie's brother has emigrated and giving up on the hotel. She is as beautiful as ever and I am sure the new owners will give her a new zest for life, none of us could do it the way my nana did.

Things are going to get better now; they can't get any worse. At least now I am free, free to make my own choices and write my own path. Once everything is settled, and Danny can hopefully be put behind me, I think I would like to move somewhere far away, Cornwall perhaps. The kids would love it there with its sandy beaches and warm summers. It's just me and them now and the world is our oyster. I've written so much over the years; it was Nana who bought me my first journal for my tenth birthday. I never really got into it until we visited her house back in the summer of fifty-two.

How life and this house have changed since then. I've decided to put my writing into good use elsewhere now, it was William who suggested I think about my writing again — he even had some old notebooks of mine from my time here after I had my sweet baby Betty. The majority of the pages were empty, but I was touched that he had kept them after all this time. He believes in me, as did my nana and Henry, and even Joe did too. Perhaps I owe it to them and myself to try again.

Well, this is me signing off now, it's time to swap the journals for the blank pages of the unknown future.

Oh, one more thing, Larry has just brought a package in for me. I recognised the handwriting at once. Hidden under the brown paper was a black hardback copy of *Anna Karenina* by Leo Tolstoy and the first page has a carefully written message, reading:

My Dear Lottie,

May your life be filled with happiness, love, and no regrets. Do not reach for the clouds, reach for the stars.

Forever yours, H xxx

Epilogue

<u>2020</u>

The gentle breeze tickled the man's face as he stood leaning heavily on his cane. His roughened black leather jacket protecting him from goosebumps gathering on his skin. Beside him stood his daughter who had said nothing since their arrival at the cemetery. Her olive skin was hidden under layers as she carefully placed a bouquet of flowers amongst many others in all the colours of the rainbow. He asked his daughter to read the messages attached to them, he thought some names would be recognisable but only a few rang a bell.

Rest in peace Charlotte from everyone at Penzance Library
x

May you shine as bright as the brightest star, love
you always Mum. Love Nancy, and Dennis XXXX

Gonna miss you Nan, say hi to Grandad for me, see
you one day. Noah xx

Thank you for being my inspiration, I hope you and Dad
are sitting in your favourite chairs or are laying in the

Mel Higgins

sun, young again in the allotment. Sarah, Ollie, and Matilda xxxxx

The book club won't be the same without you lovely, Margret and the gang x

We may have lost you, but your voice will always be heard through your stories, Meg, and Jimmy xx

You have always been one of the bravest women I have known, you are my best friend, and I am going to miss you every single day Mum, love Florence, and Stuart xxxxx

Love you Mum, thank you for always being our rock, Arthur. Xxxx

At the end of the rainbow, we will all meet again, lots of love William and Elsie xxx

"We were too late," the man stuttered, gazing at the black inscription written on the marble headstone.

Charlotte Florence Hollister
Wife, Mum, and Grandma
1941 – 2020

"She'll know we're here," the woman softly said, linking

her arm to her dad's. He had wanted to make the trip as soon as he heard the news of the woman's passing. They had avoided seeing her when she lived, so the feeling of betrayal was strong in her thoughts, but she couldn't let her old man down, knowing what it meant to him.

"At least she isn't alone." Above her name was another, Charlotte's companion in death.

Henry John Hollister
Husband, Dad, and Grandad
1941 – 2018

"He always was the one who took better care of her. Took me a long time to admit it but he was the right man for her. Could you write the message on the card for the flowers for me Sweetheart, I didn't want it to get wet in that shower."

His daughter pulled out the white floral card that her dad had carefully hidden in her coat pocket protecting it from the rain when they left the florists, now with the sun creeping behind a dark moving cloud making a clearing of pure blue she prepared to write it with a new pen her dad bought from the airport, especially for this purpose.

"What shall I write?"

"Write: Charlotte we are sorry we didn't come sooner; the right time just never came. We watched you from afar and cheered every success. We hope one day we will all be able to meet and forgive the years between us that have passed. Fly high angel. Love always, Joe and Betty xxx"

To Be Continued...

Mel Higgins

Acknowledgement

Writing Dear Lottie has been a journey.

The idea for this novel began in 2012 and it was so different to how this final version of the story evolved into but the core was always the same. I remember laying in the dark while staying at my mams, my daughter asleep between us as I whispered my idea to her in the night. We sat up for hours as she listened eagerly and told me I had to write it. In wasn't until 2020 that I told myself to get on with it, it was never going to write its self and the characters and the plot had all evolved just as I had by then. Ever since my mam has cheered me on every step of the way. So thank you mam for telling me to do this and encouraging me along the long path from idea to published book.

I would also like to thank my husband and my girls for putting up with me while I've sat in the office for hours, listening to the same playlist on repeat (and I also would like to add an apology to my lovely husband for putting up with me while I have stressed over things – quite a lot). I love you all dearly and your excitement for me has only made me want to write this even more.

To my editors Jessica Runyard and Sophie Tate,

thank you for all the hours spent fixing my mistakes. You were both the first people I ever let read Dear Lottie and I remember feeling so anxious but both of you have giving me such positive feedback and advice along the way making me believe that this could be a success.

I have to thank Bespoke Book Covers for the beautiful cover design, they listened to my ideas and produced a book cover that I am so proud of, thank you!

Lastly I have to give a little shout out to Sian and Beth, while I wrote Dear Lottie I barely told a soul that I was writing a novel and for some reason felt rather shy and nervous mentioning it. While working with these lovely ladies I let the cat out the bag and their interest and support has encouraged me to just be open about it and share the news that I – yes I, have written my own novel.

It's been long, it's been exciting and it's been emotional but I did it and now I get to share Dear Lottie with some wonderful readers.

Thank you everyone for making this dream happen.

Follow @Melswritingjourney on Instagram for all upcoming updates and exciting news for Love Lottie the sequel to Dear Lottie.

If you enjoyed Dear Lottie, please share your review on Amazon, Goodreads, or Instagram. Thank you.

Printed in Great Britain
by Amazon